THE PROCURATOR FISCAL

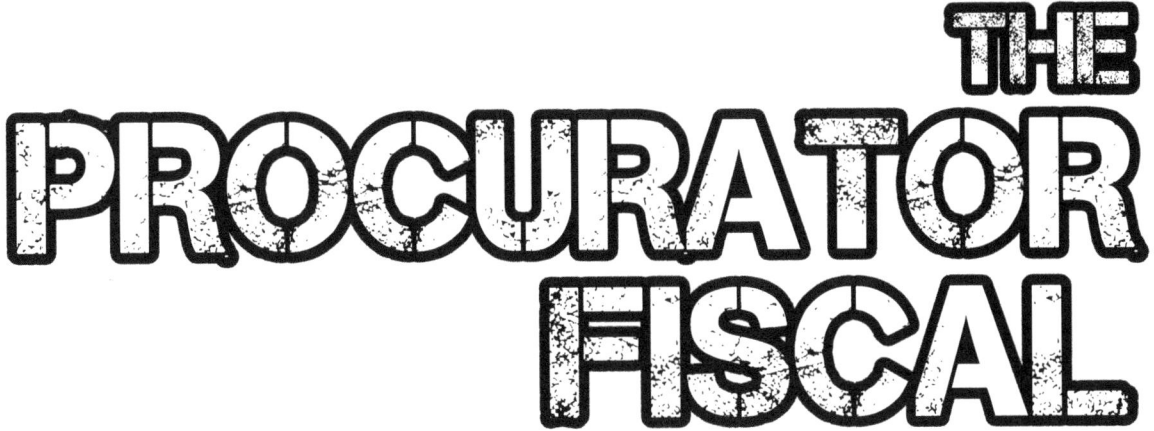

THE PROCURATOR FISCAL

Episodes 1-3

Viktoria King

urlink
PRINT & MEDIA

The Procurator Fiscal

1603 Capitol Ave., Suite 310 Cheyenne, Wyoming USA 82001
1-888-980-6523 | admin@urlinkpublishing.com

URLink Print and Media is committed to excellence in the publishing industry.

Published in the United States of America

ISBN 978-1-64367-400-1 (Paperback)
ISBN 978-1-64367-399-8 (Digital)

Fiction
03.05.19

Episode 1

Bodies in the Barrels Case

Chapter 1

Lieb sat tucked into the corner of the doctor's surgery keeping aside from the general melee of waiting patients; he wasn't sick and he wasn't fearful of catching whatever had brought these people through the doors of the clinic this morning; if he was honest with himself, he'd admit he was somewhat embarrassed by his predicament and was wishing himself anywhere else but right here right now.

But, he knew Rose' impending stay with her sister in Aberdeen would kick-start a discussion and he needed to 'be prepared': Roses' sister Heather had just delivered her first child, a daughter, Felicity. Lieb knew this would eventuate in discussing when the time was right for him and Rose to procreate.

Lieb loved Rose; although their first encounters were less than ideal. Rose's role supporting families with children in need had had included the unfortunate death of two of her charges; twin five-year-old boys who'd run away together instead of starting another new school. Sleeping on a train track the boys had been hit and killed by a train before they were found. Lieb as Procurator Fiscal had been called to the scene to help ascertain if the deaths were accidental or something else. Whilst working with Rose, initially on the details of the investigation and then in a supporting role to Rose who was called to account for the boys' absence from the family home, Lieb had found Rose left a mark on him and he often found himself throughout his day thinking about her.

So, when he found her beside her stopped car outside Arbroath he took full advantage of the situation. Lieb had been sailing off the Arbroath north headland and was on his way home; Rose had been returning from a morning hiking the Special Protection Area of the Barry Buddon Training Area watching the Birds of Prey when her vehicle had stopped. Lieb waited with her until Roadside Assistance had the vehicle operational again, by which time romance was triggered and further plans were made.

He let his mind wander, hoping to calm his anxiety, but he once again drifted back to that morning when he was fifteen years old; the one that had started it all.

He'd awoken after a particularly intense dream; not exactly a nightmare but fast paced and threatening in the way dreams can be when they want to invoke fear without substance. And he had awoken feverish and drenched in sweat.

Lieb threw back the covers and swung his legs over the bed. The pain that hit him was a freight train, the kind he'd watched shunt through the railway yard when he was on holidays in Inverness at his

Nanna's. He stifled a squeal; at 15 he wouldn't have it said he screamed like a girl. But the effort cost him his breath as he exhaled with explosive force.

Whilst waiting for the pain to lessen, Lieb took stock: yes, he had a headache and he felt he had spent the previous day in hard labour with all of his muscles achy & sore, but the source of his intense pain was his testicles. "what the...?" he muttered.

Gingerly he rose from the bed intent on making it to the privacy of the bathroom. He may have been alone presently but his young cousin was staying and that meant Lieb currently had a room buddy; Jonathon could return at any moment.

Managing to reach vertical Lieb took his first steps but his testicles, which had now grown to the size of grapefruit, swung back and slapped against his thighs. Another rapid intake of air suppressed the impending squeal and tears flooded his eyes. Stranded in the middle of the room with the bathroom a massive twenty paces further on, Lieb leant forward and tried another step with his massive testicles swinging freely.

And that's where his mother found him.

Lieb came back from his reverie with the doctor calling his name. This wasn't Lieb's family physician; he'd used his own medical credentials to line up a specialist with whom to share this embarrassing circumstance. Lieb was already painfully aware that the diagnosis of testicular mumps at 15 years of age had most likely left him sterile, and so a stranger was a preferred candidate to confirm such news. Problem was, he could think of no-one but himself to tell Rose.

And so the consultation had followed the script Lieb had imagined in his head for many years: 'yes Lieb the tests confirm Azoospermia.' 'remember there are new options available now, depending on the actual mechanics of the problem' 'a few more tests can determine if it's just a blockage or if your sperm isn't maturing properly.' 'and there are ways you can still have a biological child, you just need some interventions to be successful'.

Lieb thanked Dr Goodman for his assistance and aimed for the door; he couldn't get out of there fast enough.

The April sun was weak as Lieb headed for the car but the light wind kept the clouds at bay and so sitting in the driver's seat the sun strengthened and he basked in the warmth. It didn't matter how many scenario's he spun in his head; telling Rose was going to take timing and that could prove nigh on impossible. Lieb remembered all the plans he'd rehearsed when he'd bought the engagement ring; and then how that homicidal fiend had interrupted and frustrated every plan until Lieb had eventually left the ring in Rose's coffee cup. Dashing through the Perthshire countryside next to Senior Inspector Marcus Campbell in an attempt to get to another body dump before the fickle weather wiped out vital evidence, Lieb had phoned Rose and chatted through her morning routine until he heard her reach for her favourite coffee cup and gasp; then he'd asked her to marry him.

That time she'd been most supportive; understanding his role as the Fiscal (or Coroner) for Perthshire, Angus & Dundee could mean unpredictable work schedules. Would she be as supportive this time he wondered, upon hearing he couldn't father children?

Chapter 2

Dundee is the fourth largest city in Scotland and the University houses the Department of Forensic Medicine. Directly funded by the Scottish Crown Office, the University provides forensic autopsy and toxicology services to procurators fiscal in Tayside, Fife and Central regions.

As in many European Countries, criminal law in Scotland is administered by a Public Prosecutor. The prime holder of this office is the Lord Advocate, who with the Solicitor General and Advocates Depute (collectively known as Crown council), prosecutes on behalf of the Crown for the High Court of the Judiciary. These officials preside at Edinburgh but sit on a regular Circuit of the major Scottish towns. In each 'Sheriffdom' the Lord Advocate appoints a Procurator Fiscal: Lieb was the Procurator Fiscal, for the Tayside, Fife and Central regions.

The range of cases the Fiscals are mandated to investigate includes road traffic fatalities, suicides, accidents at home and at work, homicides and sudden natural deaths, as well as in-hospital deaths under anaesthesia and other unexpected hospital deaths.

Lieb parked his car in the privileged parking spot and walked back through the lane to purchase a cafe latte from the OTI coffee shop before walking through the campus grounds to his office. The cases in the mortuary that morning had been cleared before he'd left for his appointment, and his afternoon was allocated to look through and sign reports, review some suggestions on changes to the forensic medicine curriculum and vet a number of applications for placement by overseas students: hence the coffee. And the four afternoon hours passed without significance, except it kept Lieb's mind occupied on matters other than his health report and his impending discussion with Rose.

Heading north out of Dundee Lieb chose the A930 north toward home; it was definitely a longer route but he had the time and the long expanses of the North Sea he viewed on the way always calmed him. He'd had a fairly easy day at the 'office'; it was the rest of it that had created his angst.

And as if in recognition of his gnawing anxiety, the sea offered Lieb his greatest delight: travelling along Ferry Rd Lieb spied a two-masted yacht. A yawl he noted, not a ketch which made sense as the North Sea winds could be real demons and any smart sailor in these parts would know a ketch would be too hard to handle. This was a beauty, royal blue hull with white trim and smart white sails, both full and skipping northward; probably heading home to Arbroath harbour he thought. Lieb pulled in near the

Tayview Caravan Park and watched the yacht until it rounded the point and was gone from sight. Maybe with Rose away this weekend he may get a sail in himself.

Thinking again of Rose and the ten upcoming days without her, Lieb called into the market in Barry and selected items for a special dinner, including champagne and a gift box of dark chocolate coated orange slices in preference to flowers: there was little point in buying Rose flowers this evening, for tomorrow morning she was heading north to Aberdeen to stay with her sister Heather following the birth of her first child. Lieb knew it was Heather's delivery that had prompted Rose's mentioning's of their baby-making.

Arriving home Lieb put the groceries in the kitchen and set the table: fresh candles in the candelabra that his best man had presented as their wedding gift, the glass table mats that had etched a selection of Scottish birds of prey, flatware and their favourite red wine goblets. At Roses' seating Lieb also placed the box of chocolates.

In the kitchen he made garlic butter, sliced the French loaf and prepared garlic toast for heating. He opened the mushroom butter sauce, placing it atop the stove on a simmer setting, and then put water on to boil for the pasta. Whilst he was preparing a tomato & onion side salad he heard Rose arrive: full of excitement she called a hello from the front door as she climbed out of her coat and boots. Then her head appeared at the kitchen doorway with a large grin and dancing eyes. "Hello there". "Hello yourself" Lieb replied.

"This looks good, what're cooking?"

"Just something simple so dinner doesn't take up all our evening".

"Can I help with something?"

"How about choosing a bottle of wine?"

Rose returned to the dining room, opened the wine cabinet and selected an Australian shiraz. Raising her voice a little so they could continue a conversation between the rooms she asked about his day and Lieb responded such that the next few minutes a warm and comfortable banter passed between them.

Appearing again at the kitchen door where Lieb was heaping fresh pasta into bowls, Rose took up the two salad plates and headed for the table. Over her shoulder she tossed the comment "so, are we up for making our baby tonight?"

Lieb flinched, took a deep breath and responded "I thought we'd had this conversation and agreed with what we saw at work each day we didn't think children were a good idea? They'd either be social horrors terrorising the local society, like you see each day, or they'd be the victim of some monstrous horror and end up on my autopsy table. I vote to keep on practicing."

Lieb brought their meals to the table and kissed Rose, one of those short but deeply meaningful types that put aside any further conversation.

Rose chose to not break the established conventions, smiled and turned the conversation by making a fuss over the chocolate treat left for her. And Lieb responded in kind, visiting once again Rose's travel plans, examining her chosen route and timings and exacting a promise she'd drive safe, keep the doors locked and stay hands free.

Rose giggled like a schoolgirl, teasing Lieb on his white-knight approach and reminding him she was travelling familiar roads, in good weather and that the travel time was only two hours. Lieb defended his concerns as he cleared away the dishes into the kitchen and returned with chocolate mousse and coffee. The settled down on the sofa in front of the fire and began a slow roast of their passion, each mindful of the absence before them.

As the mousse offered playful suggestions and the coffee remained largely undrunk they allowed their passions to consume them and at some point found their way to bed; curled up within each other until morning broke and disturbed them.

Lieb started the coffee and put croissants into the oven whilst Rose showered, then Lieb claimed the shower and Rose finished the breakfast.

Lieb had hoped breakfast would be undertaken at a slow pace; a chance to savour each other's company and reaffirm their place with each other before the world called them back to the dance. But Rose's exhilaration for the theme of her trip escalated once she fired up and so Lieb was somewhat thankful for the call that cut their breakfast short; before the baby talk had a chance to rear its head.

He looked sufficiently dismayed when the phone rang but Rose shooed him to answer, buoyed in her present mood. The call was everything Lieb had come to expect from such calls: a body discovered in a well at an old churchyard. Lieb took the information and said he would be on his way immediately. It was expected he'd say this, but he was prepared to delay for thirty minutes to ensure Rose was safely away. Rose was unconcerned however: "go. I planned to fuss around here for a while anyway".

"Will you ring me when you get to Heather's?"

"I'll text. You'll be busy all day with whatever this case presents. And anyway, I need to shop for a few things on the way and I'm sure there will be lots of talking and cuddling when I arrive. And there is the phone reception issue at Sis's. But at some point, I'll text, so off you go and stop worrying. You know where I'll be and you can be assured that in ten days I'll be right here."

Lieb pulled Rose into his arms and held her tight. They'd been married for four years and their passion for each other was as strong as always; maybe his little secret was fuelling his reluctance to let her go. Maybe he should ring his deputy to take this one and get Rose to delay for a day so they could work this issue through?

Rose squirmed in his embrace enough to consummate the embrace with a kiss: deep and meaningful and full of later promises. She then pulled away and laughed at him; a light chuckle that lit up her eyes and softened her features.

"It's just ten days. Unless the baby lets me get no sleep and I need to come home sooner. Now go."

"OK. Give my regards to Heather and Mike. Oh, and baby Felicity."

Lieb kissed her again; this time just that quick promise kiss that married couples share. The kiss that promises all is okay and there is more to come; the bridging kiss that keeps the momentum of love continuing until next time.

And he gathered up his outside layers, put on his boots and picked up his keys and hurried into another day of horror and mayhem.

Chapter 3

Lieb and Rose had moved into a small cottage on a half acre of land in the north of the hamlet of Barry shortly before they were married. A short year before that, Lieb had been promoted to the role of Procurator Fiscal and had been living in a one-bedroom apartment in Dundee.

Similarly, Rose was living and working in Dundee at the time: as a Care Manager working with the Mental Health Officer Service. Rose had taken on a challenging portfolio within the Multi-Agency Assessment Team supporting children in need of care. Oftentimes it was parents, families and Carer's who needed Rose's intervention as her charge was the perpetrator of hostilities, not the victim; and a significant barrier to helping families was changing everyone else's understanding of this dynamic: 'they're only a child' mentalities often allowed difficult children the leniency they needed to manipulate those around them. And this left Rose's families emotionally exhausted and increasingly isolated.

Like Lieb, Rose was on the end of a phone and if a family was in crisis because their child needed intervention, or because they were to be discharged from inpatient care the families thought too soon, Rose's phone would ring.

And so, they had looked for their ideal retreat, somewhere they could breathe and relax; somewhere away from work and away from the damaged families they at times encountered on the street in Dundee.

Barry was such a place: a small village at the mouth of the River Tay and Mill Rd Barry was just off the A92 which provided excellent all year access into Dundee. The cottage was adjacent to Barry Burn, a minor river which rose in the eastern portion of the Sidlaw Hills and flowed past Newbigging, through Barry and the western part of Carnoustie, before taking a meandering course through Carnoustie Golf Links.

It had been the miller's home for generations. The mill (Barry Mill) was a working Category A listed watermill; a three-floor building, containing a meal floor (basement), a milling floor and a top (or "bin floor"). There had been several mills at the site since at least 1539, and was commercially operational until 1984; it was then restored and operated by the National Trust for Scotland as an educational tourist attraction.

Their cottage was set back from the Mill and separated now by a hedgerow so visitors to the Mill could only catch a glimpse of their home as they entered the mill carpark. There was nothing of monetary value at the mill but its historical importance ensured there was a security presence. This was a bonus providing Lieb especially peace of mind when he was away long hours when a case was underway.

Lieb was underway at 07:15 that morning, about ninety minutes earlier than he had planned. It was cold, that crisp early morning air that promises much, and without rain. But a heavy fog still hung over the hills that the promising sun hadn't managed to burn off.

The A92 south to Dundee was still quiet traffic-wise with only those with business to tend to, motoring this early. Lieb didn't have long on the A92 however when he took the right turn, sign-posted for the Monikie Reservoir, onto the B-road for Newbigging.

Newbigging was a village just two miles north-east of Dundee.

The oldest buildings in the village (exceeding 200 years), were the village church and the old church manse. The church had been bought by artist and had been converted into a studio with room to hold art classes. The old manse, which was superseded by the new manse behind the church (neither of which are used as the church manse anymore), was given the dwelling name of "Davidsons Cottage".

The village also contained a redundant church and a shop which was now closed. Lieb remembered the shop had been voted the best village shop in Scotland in 1997 due to a selection of hot pastries that would stop many a passing motorist.

It was to this church and shop Lieb was now headed. DI Marcus Campbell was expecting him.

Marcus and Lieb had been working partners for six years and had become firm friends: Marc had been his best man at his wedding to Rose. He was a proclaimed bachelor; long and loud, especially after a second pint. But Lieb, at quiet times, thought Marc proclaimed too loud, as a measure to calm his distress at not having discovered a loving partner. Still at 38 there was still time.

As he suspected, Lieb had no trouble identifying where he needed to be. The large police presence and Marc's standout frame made it easy. He pulled over, not needing to flash his ID; he was well known amongst the extended crime team.

Marc walked over as Lieb climbed out of his Pathfinder and collected his scene bag which contained the mobile objects of his profession.

"Did Rose get away OK?"

"She was still in a robe when I left, drinking coffee."

Marcus identified a tenseness to Lieb voice and asked, "are you nervous about her getting biologically agitated cuddling that new niece of hers?" The gentle chuckle in Marcus' voice wasn't lost on Lieb.

"Something like that" he responded. "Give me something else to think about; tell me what we've got."

Marcus led Lieb around the back of the old church and beyond, walking a disused path to a second gathering of police standing a couple of hundred metres further on. Their destination turned out to be an old well. Peering over the crumbling wall Lieb spied a large drum; pale blue paint still predominant, along with a large WB insignia on the side, and the rim was welded shut.

Trembling throughout like a low harmonic hum, Lieb looked at Marcus: Marcus was watching his face for his reaction.

"Another one? Could it really be another one?

"It certainly looks that way." Marcus replied.

"How did this one come to light"?

"Would you believe a Canadian researching his Scottish roots? Of course, he wasn't concerned about the drum in the old well; it just came up in conversation at the pub when he was asked what he was doing so far off the tourist route. Said he was researching his family tree and when he hadn't found the grave he was hoping to in the new church graveyard, he decided to check out this one."

"The barkeep asked something vague about his discoveries at the old church; 'you know, just being social and all', and was dumbstruck when he mentioned the blue drum in the old well."

"And why did the barkeep think to call it in? That bodies in the drums case we worked got lots of coverage at the time, but that was over four years ago."

"Someone decided to do an anniversary documentary and that was on the tv only a few weeks back. Seems the barkeep had it on at the bar and it had generated lots of discussion amongst his patrons; especially a comment by the reporter, wondering if we found them all?"

"Maybe we didn't?" Lieb responded.

"Well the crime lab team are through taking photos and I've got the lads and lassies do a grid search out from the well down to that back laneway which seems the most likely access." Marcus explained. "Also, I've put a call into a crane company in Dundee and talked though our problem of extraction. They've got some ideas and are on their way over. Biggest problems we seem to have is lifting the drum out without damaging it or compromising any contents or trace on the outside of the drum. Oh, and the state of the well itself; doesn't seem to stable to me."

Lieb peered over the edge again and his focus was again drawn to the insignia painted on the barrel side. It was distinctive; it had been six years and there had been many other cases since, but Lieb was reasonably certain it was the same as previous ones. Of course, it may not contain a human body; then again it may contain something more valuable; clues to the killers' identity.

A low rumble alerted Marcus and Lieb to the arrival of the crane and the specialist contractor with a solution for extraction. The crane was rigged into the design of a flatbed truck; the kind used for delivering packed goods pallets. The engine rumbled silent and the driver / contractor climbed from behind the wheel and approached them.

"Howdy." He announced as he walked up to Marcus. Marcus and Lieb shared a questioning look. The man, Roger according to the name on his coveralls, barked a laugh at their reaction. "I felt I should get into character seeing I'm needed to rope a barrel. Which one of you would like to show me where it is?"

Marcus introduced himself and then Lieb and explained their roles. He then indicated off to his left and the three men wandered over to the edge of the well.

"We really need to preserve the integrity of the drum, inside and out." explained Lieb. "It could hold vital evidence in a murder investigation."

"Well, I believe I can hang a loop over it, down below that ridge there (Roger indicated an area about a third the way down) and cinch it tight. I'll then raise it straight up and swing it round onto the flatbed of the truck. Biggest chance of failure I can see is the bottom falling off."

"Well the lid is soldered shut, so let's just hope the bottom is too." countered Marcus.

Roger returned to his truck, fired the engine into life and manoeuvred it alongside the well. He lowered four metal feet from the truck until the truck was lifted off the ground and sitting on a secure platform. He then climbed from the cab again and secured a hoop, topped with three heavy duty chains and a hook, onto the hook of the crane. Roger then walked to Marcus and handed him a rope, "Can you hold that for me whilst I manoeuvre the crane?" he asked.

Using a large hand-held controller Roger then he swung the crane jib over the well. Once the loop had stopped swaying he commenced slowly lowering the loop over the drum. Marcus assisted; using the rope to provide horizontal guidance the two worked in tandem to get the loop in place.

Roger then flicked a switch on his controller and a new machine sound filled the air. Roger walked as close to the well as was safe and, peering over the edge, he continued holding the switch that operated the cinching tension until the sound deepened and alerted him to a secure hold.

"OK. Now for the edgy bit." Roger said. "Let's lift it".

Lieb and Marcus looked at each other and involuntarily held their breath. Slowly, slowly Roger raised the drum. When he was sure it had cleared the well he stopped and let the drum hang there. "Shall we inspect the bottom and determine how secure it is?" he suggested.

The three men peered at the underside of the drum. Roger spoke "That rust looks like surface rust; are you OK for me to continue?"

Marcus and Lieb nodded consent and Roger used his controller to swing the crane jib and its cargo until it was positioned onto the flatbed of the truck. Whilst Roger secured the drum and the attached chain rig, Marcus and Lieb considered what more they could get from the site.

"I think we should get this well covered and secured" Lieb stated.

"I can't really afford to leave a man out here twenty-four-seven, unless you're adamant that there is more in the well that will need to be reclaimed".

"Really hard to call: we aren't even certain this has anything to do with the other cases. It sure would be hard to explain if we finally had some hard evidence and we'd let the scene get compromised though" Lieb countered.

"How about this? We let the locals know it was simply a dangerous hazard, what with the crumbling well and all, and we've secured the site until we can arrange to have it appropriately dealt with" Marcus suggested. "I could have fencing and signage erected and get the local neighbourhood watch to maintain regular observations."

"We could also spread the word about a potential toxic spill, that should keep the locals away?" Lieb added.

"Sounds good to me. I'll make those arrangements."

"Senior Inspector – over here". Marcus looked to where a constable was calling him.

"Looks like I've got plenty to do here still; how about I meet you at your lab when I'm finished?"

"Sure" replied Lieb. "I'll supervise the barrel unloading and get the team examining it for any trace evidence. Then I'll find someone to break the weld on the lid and hopefully you'll be back for the unveiling?"

"Sounds like a plan. I'll give you an ETA once I see what they've found" said Marcus indicating his team of constables. "And I'll organise those other items. See you in an hour or so hopefully."

Lieb walked over to Roger and discussed delivery to the coronial lab. During that conversation Lieb rang the office and spoke with Darren. Darren was a more senior member of his team; 68 or thereabouts. He'd been an entrenched fixture when Lieb had taken office and Lieb quickly found him to be an invaluable asset.

There wasn't any aspect of the office machine Darren was unfamiliar with: from where to find technicians who could repair equipment, and suppliers of unusual tools or requirements, through to specialist personnel who could advise on elements of unusual evidence. It seemed Darren had acquired a vast knowledge database over his twenty-eight years on the job and his only request was he remained useful. Lieb took every opportunity to assure Darren he was a valued member of the team.

Lieb called him now and explained the incoming delivery and what Roger would need available to help with off-loading. Darren assured Lieb it would all be ready when the truck and its contents arrived.

Lieb raised an arm in a wave as he stood at his car door. Marcus acknowledged and Lieb climbed behind the wheel and started the engine. He'd been fortunate that his position came with an allowance for a vehicle and that the bureaucrat understood the terrain Lieb was likely to encounter on a regular basis, so there had been sufficient for Lieb to secure a Nissan Pathfinder from SDM motors. It provided him with all his needs on the job and allowed him to move his yacht when annual leave offered an opportunity to sail in harbours other than Arbroath.

When Roger signalled he was ready to proceed, Lieb led the way out of the church grounds, through the village Newbigging and onward to Dundee.

Marcus watched them leave and walked past the old well and down to the laneway at the rear to turn his attention to the discovery Constable Addams had found. The ground alongside the laneway was unpaved and it showed significant disturbance where it was apparent the barrel had been placed and moved: distinct rim marks were visible along with scuffed shoe marks.

It was obvious the laneway was rarely used: whilst the barrel and shoe marks were softened by weather, no other activity had disturbed the scene. However, the weathering had destroyed enough detail to ensure opportunity for evidence gathering was impossible. Constable Addams had already taken plenty of scene photos.

Assured Senior Inspector Campbell had taken in all there was to see, Constable Addams spoke up, using the friendly moniker senior members of Marcus' team used for him "The more important find is over here SIM" and Jon Addams walked back towards the well.

Senior Inspector Marcus – SIM followed Jon Addams, listening to the deductive diatribe Jon was using to explain his understanding of the clues he'd uncovered.

"So, considering the deep marks at the kerbside and the occasional wheel grooves found along the path, it's apparent the barrel was heavy and it was moved using a two-wheeled trolley. It would also appear the perpetrator was unrushed and unconcerned about discovery because here he stopped for a smoke." Jon stopped at a small scrubby bush alongside the path, a variety of willow that was probably planted along the path to reduce the bogginess of the soil, and pointed to a patch of ground about a metre away. There were remnants of headstones stacked together and nestled amongst them at the base was a cigarette butt.

Marcus looked enquiringly at Jon who looked back with a twinkle in his eye. "I know it's a long shot, but remembering the butts we collected at the other sites I thought this may be a clue that linked the cases?"

"Well I like your theory Jon, but we never got anything useful off those other butts remember; the perp used a cigarette holder" Marcus responded.

"OK but what about this then?" and Jon gently lifted the bush's foliage to show a shoeprint. Pushed into the soft soil as the smoker had leaned forward to flick the butt away, protected from the elements by the thick scrubby bush, two-thirds of the shoeprint from the toe to the start of the heel was clearly evident.

Marcus whistled softly and a grin broke across his face as a flicker of optimism took root. "You really are ready for that promotion" he stated. "Well, let's not stand around. Lots of photos, a good plaster cast and that butt please. I'm off to open a barrel."

Chapter 4

Hands were all over her, intimate yet rough and uncaring. Her terror increased exponentially as they taped her wrists and stuffed cloth into her mouth, gagging her. She kicked and fought but there were too many, and they whooped and cackled like it was all part of a game. Except for one, he giggled: a maniacal sound that had her skin crawling and if it could detach itself she was sure it would crawl away and leave her further exposed.

There was a short ride in a van and all but the driver seemed to delight in her terror and struggles as if they were foreplay. At their destination, she saw little of where she'd been brought as they were parked close to a door and they dragged her through it and into a kitchen area.

Continuing the fight with all the strength she could muster she only once landed a blow that made a difference; they dropped her to the floor and she felt her chin slam onto the tiled floor.

From there they dragged her, lifted her and hung her taped arms onto a metal hook hanging over a commercial cooker and its adjacent stainless benches. Her hips slammed into the cooker edge, her toes were just able to make the floor. The position had her slung like a long piece of meat, stretched from the hips up over the centre of the cooker and the lower half draped to the floor.

Already her shoulders burned from the strain and her hips exuded exquisite pain as it was ground into the metal edge of the cooker. And then the ultimate indignity as they ripped her clothes from her.

One of her attackers, she could not think of them as men, stood behind her grinding her buttocks and rolling her nipples between his coarse fingers. He leaned in and licked her neck, pulled the gag from her mouth and began roughly tugging her nipples out and squeezing.

Whilst she whimpered and squirmed, begging him to stop, his accomplices grabbed and secured her ankles such that she was spreadeagled and without any means of support; there was no way to ease her weight from her shoulders or hips. The tears started.

The attacker molesting her nipples let the right one be, concentrating on just the left. He stretched it until she felt the attaching breast tissue tear. Then more pain as he clamped something heavy onto it; and she screamed.

Foreplay finished her attacker bit into the soft tissue of her shoulder and slammed his penis into her and her mind exploded. As he pounded into her like a storm wave attacking the foreshore the heavy weight swung and clanged: a toll bell rocking and rolling with his rhythm; biting and tearing at her nipple.

She prayed for unconsciousness; ran screaming through her mind looking for an open door, a corner, anywhere she could hide. But they were all locked. And just when she thought she had found some darkness a new pain ripped though her: emanating from a point on her arm it burned through her blood vessels like acid and exploded in her mind like fireworks. And her cover was exposed and all the torment came back into sharp focus.

And it continued unrelenting; her attackers trading places in a tag-team effort to tear her apart.

One two three four
Make the brass bell toll
Five six seven eight
Rock & roll the chiming weight
Nine ten eleven & twelve
Take a pill, rock the bell
Tearing the nipple til it fell.
Thirteen fourteen fifteen sixteen
Take a pill, start again

She tried to hide in the rhythm. Her screams had echoed off the walls until she could no longer make noise, so no-one could hear her, no-one was going to make it stop.

Fluid was running down her legs, she'd started to hope it was blood and she would soon die of blood loss. But no, the torment continued. Her attackers whooped and shouted encouragement to the mounted one; examining the tearing nipple and betting on how many more swings would rip it from its attachment.

They were having a party and she was their entertainment.

Suddenly there was a climax of sorts. The biting attacker was mounted and in his thrall her nipple ripped and the bell tumbled onto the cooker top with a resounding crash. After a crescendo of pain, the attacker dismounted and she found a spark of hope flair.

They scooped up the fallen bell and paraded it like a trophy, tossing it between them and recounted how many swings it had taken to succeed in their goal.

The party escalated behind her and they left her be. She allowed hope to spark. The pains that enveloped her were substantial; her shoulders were aflame, the blood vessels of her arms burned, the ground pelvic bones were shooting daggers though her back and down her legs and her genital region was pulsing as if hot pokers were inserted deep. And her nipple, well she wondered if they reattached them.

She rested her head on her arm, trying to ease the knot in her neck muscles. Then an attacker was behind her and she, just for moment, thought they were releasing her.

But know, the nipple ritual started again and she found enough spit to beg them for no more. One of them appeared above her, standing on the cooker and looking down with an enormous erection, a maniacal look in his eyes and a syringe in his hand. He was the cackler and he reached down and shoved the needle into the blood vessel of her arm.

The terror started again but this time the first entry was anal; slamming and tearing into her rear canal and deep, deep into her pelvis. She vomited but with no food in her stomach and her upright position all it did was ad to her torment, as acidic stomach juices slid into her oesophagus and burned.

Time was lost to her; she was unaware of how often the attackers entered her or how long the second bell tore at her right nipple. Every time she hoped her body would give out for her they drove more drug into her veins and her consciousness flared again, ensuring her continued participation until they were concluded.

And there was a new pain, a furnace of agony in her belly. She supposed they had torn through her intestinal walls and a septic soup was infecting her internally. She wasn't going to survive this she realised; but when would it finally stop?

Chapter 5

Local Government reorganisation in 1975 created a new Tayside Region by the amalgamation of the previous three unitary authorities of Perth and Kinross Council, Dundee City Council and Angus Council. Police forces that previously existed within these areas were amalgamated into the newly formed Tayside Police who assumed responsibility for the provision of policing services for the newly created Tayside Region.

The Crime Intelligence Division was formed through the amalgamation of Headquarters Crime Division and the Force Intelligence and Information Division. It is located at Force Headquarters, Dundee and the Divisional Commander is Detective Chief Superintendent Jack Abercrombie. He is supported by his deputies Detective Superintendent Declan Macdonald who is responsible for Operations and Policy, Major Crime Support, Public Protection, Criminal Justice and Custody and Detective Superintendent Elise Scott who is responsible for the Force Intelligence Bureau, Intelligence Development Unit, Special Branch and Information Services.

Senior Inspector Marcus Campbell's role is within Major Crime Support; the members of this team act frontline in response to all major incidents.

The bodies in the drums case, portfolio actually, were Marcus' first serial murder as Lead investigator, and it was during this series of murders he first worked with Lieb Canavan who was new in post as the Procurator Fiscal.

This series of murders had taken up a lot of the manpower and energy of the Tayside Police and the Procurator Fiscals offices in the 2005 and 2006 years. In all, four bodies were discovered, one male and three females, throughout the Tayside and Perthshire counties.

The first body was discovered in Crieff, just west of Perth. It was opened by a storeman at the plastics workshop when he was undertaking a stock-take during the property handover. The new owner wanted to ensure all the chattels that were included in the purchase were accounted for: he was counting on what her did find.

Investigations showed it was the twenty-year-old daughter of a prominent Perth businessman. She had been killed by multiple stabbings and had died elsewhere, then placed in the barrel. The lid had been welded shut and the barrel left in an old storeroom along with similar barrels which held liquid priming stock for new plastic mixes.

The second body had been found at Newburgh, a town on the southern shores of the Firth of Tay. A large antiques dealer had ordered a dozen barrels to store incomplete collections of antique pottery in. The barrels had been left late one evening and when the store manager checked them the next morning there were thirteen. He'd initially thought the additional barrel was a likely a mistake by a delivery driver who couldn't count, so he quietly accepted the boon. He became suspicious when one drum was significantly heavier than the rest. And when it was opened: well it shortened the life of the gentle natured man whose life had been unearthing antique pottery.

Investigations showed this was a fifteen-year-old lad; a runaway from Essex in southeast England. His postmortem findings were similar to that of the body in the Crieff barrel.

Body number three was located in Bankfoot, a small parish of only 760 peoples. Whilst it's located in the heart of Perthshire, Bankfoot is only five minutes from the A9, a major road from Stirling to the north and on the National Cycle Network route 77; which had provided easy and nondescript access for the perpetrator to leave a barrel.

And this time it was left amongst barrels loaded for collection from the local distillery. The barrels the distillery used were distinctly different but they had been loaded onto a flatbed truck and secured under a tarpaulin for travel. However a major vehicle accident on the A9 had closed the road so it had been decided to hold the transport til the following morning.

The driver, a long-time employee of the trucking company affiliated with the distillery, proved his value that morning when he rechecked his load before driving off. He discovered his securing knot had been tampered with so he uncovered the load, and thus unearthed the ringer.

Investigations showed this was the body of a twenty-two-year-old pharmacy assistant from Stirling: and again the post mortem findings were similar to the Crieff and Newburgh bodies.

Body four was found at Methven, 8km west of Perth amidst the rolling farmland of lowland Perthshire. Students from Glenalmond College were testing a prototype hydro power unit in the River Almond, and found the barrel tucked into foliage near the river's edge. Concerned for environmental contamination they called the local police who secured the barrel and called in SI Marcus Campbell and the Fiscal Lieb Canavan when they recognised the barrel met the descriptive alert they had been issued with.

Investigations showed victim number four was a twenty-year-old nursing student from Perth.

And despite having four bodies with similar injuries, similar disposal and close geographic areas, exhaustive investigations failed to link the four people and never yielded any potential suspects. After twenty months and significant resources being brought to bear, no further barrels were found and no prominent lines of enquiry remained so the investigation was passed to the Tayside Police's Major Crime Review team. Senior Inspector Grace Scott was now the Lead on the case and Marcus collected her before attending the autopsy at the Fiscal's office.

Grace was a stunning redhead, long-legged and well proportioned; the younger sister of Elise Scott the Detective Superintendent responsible for the Force Intelligence Bureau, and Marcus was staggered when she flagged him down outside police headquarters. He'd rung ahead, hands-free of course, to alert her to the find. She agreed, was eager actually, to grab the case file and accompany him for the autopsy. Marcus however, had never actually met SI Grace Scott and was so unprepared to be flagged down by such a goddess. He quickly tidied the front passenger seat, throwing used food wrappers and drink containers onto the back seat and mumbling apologetically as she waited to climb in.

Grace chuckled amusedly; a deep throaty sound that reminded Marcus of spring streams flooded with snowmelt. He decided immediately he liked it; he liked her. He tossed her his best smile but she was reading a synopsis of the latest information on the case. An hour ago, standing in the old church yard with Lieb, Marcus had wished this was a false lead; that this case was for him, over. Now Marcus found himself hoping it could start all over again: twenty months in regular contact with Grace was worth all the sleepless nights and unfruitful man hours.

Marcus turned his car left at Court House Square, drove to the Port Roundabout and then into the university campus; parking in the reserved bays. The Department of Forensic Medicine was located in the Fleming Gymnasium building on the Main Campus. Entry was via Small's Wynd (meaning a narrow path), opposite the OTI coffee shop, and Marcus led Grace through the maze of paths and passed building entrances to the staff entry for the forensic medicine department.

As they signed the visitors book Marcus introduced Grace to Fiona, the receptionist, and asked where they could find Lieb. Fiona replied he was still in the loading dock.

As Marcus lead the way he introduced Grace to the layout and discussed the protocols they should follow when they were in the building.

"Well it's nice to know you're aware of them even if you forget to abide by them on a regular basis." Marcus turned to find Marianne Donald, Lieb Executive Assistant had come out of a room behind them.

"Hi Marianne, are you trying to make me look bad?"

"I don't need to Marc, you do that all by yourself" Marianne replied with amusement obvious by her large grin and twinkling eyes.

"Marianne, may I introduce Senior Inspector Grace Scott from the Major Crime Review team."

Marianne and Grace exchanged pleasantries and then Marcus intervened "Lieb will start without us if we don't hurry." And then Marcus led Grace toward the back of the building where they could hear instructions being barked.

Entering the loading area via an open-door Marcus and Grace found Lieb standing to the side watching Roger unload their cargo under the watchful eyes and clear instructions from Darren. Lieb saw them enter and walked over; Marcus made the introductions.

"Darren has this in hand; how about we go to my office and catch up on the case details until the barrel joins us?" Lieb suggested. And the three of them moved back into the body of the building and on to Lieb's office.

Chapter 6

The main autopsy suite was state-of-the-art with key card and video-monitored access: it contained a total of four autopsy stations in an open space, divided in half symmetrically by a central island to which the autopsy stations were attached; and a separate suite for contaminated cases, photographic center, two adjustable height grossing stations, formalin specimen storage, supply room, clean area/office, and a locker room with shower.

Opposite each autopsy station was a workstation providing an area for clean papers and computer access. The layout allowed for maximal efficiency of space and a large skylight provided ample natural light for examinations. The entire room used surfaces that were impervious to water and biological penetration making it easy to clean and maintain.

Lieb, Marcus and Grace sat in the office drinking coffee and reviewing the previous case-notes and adding in the information from this morning.

"What about the distinctive barrels" asked Grace?

"We tracked them down to a chemical waste transport company, the 'WB' was for 'Waste Business', who were contracted to collect and disposed of a company's chemical & hazardous waste." Marcus explained.

"And there weren't missing any?" asked Grace.

"No" responded Marcus somewhat annoyed; it was, after all included in the file notes.

"I was only thinking aloud Marcus" responded Grace and flashed him that dazzling smile. Marcus dropped his angst like a hot potato.

"And I was also wondering, if maybe they had sold extra stock?"

"Well", said Marcus willing to let Grace 'think aloud' "not that they thought to mention. We did check their inventory along, with the actual stock, and found no discrepancies; along with their staff who all checked out, except"....

"Except what?" both Grace and Lieb asked inquiringly.

"The company went bust about the same time as our investigation was underway; for failing an Environment Protection Agency investigation."

"What was the EPA's finding?" asked Grace.

"Well, from memory, one regulation requires the EPA to carry out periodic inspections of the registers, and a second requires the company to keep a register for three years, and they hadn't."

"So, if they failed an EPA register inspection, maybe the other books were bogus too?" suggested Grace.

"That's certainly a good place to start" agreed Marcus.

"Well let's see if this new barrel needs to be added to the pile, shall we?" offered Lieb; and he led them into the suite for contaminated cases.

Autopsy Report – LC2012_024

Initial Observation: in response to the four previous cases of human remains found inside distinctive blue barrels (LC2005_16, LC2005_23, LC2006_09 & LC2006_27) this barrel is being opened in the autopsy suite of the Procurator Fiscal's office Dundee.

On examination, the container is a 205 Litre Open Top Steel Drum with clamp lid which has been welded shut using a backhand method; meaning the torch is positioned so that the wire is feeding opposite to the direction of arc travel. Filler metal is being fed into the weld metal previously deposited. And the penetration is deep.

Review of documentation of the previous barrels shows the barrels have been welded by someone with the same high ability in welding techniques. It would be reasonable to conclude they had been welded by the same person.

Before opening the barrel, it has been placed on plastic sheeting in case of content spillage.

Previous barrel openings were difficult, as cutting through welds is much harder than cutting through metal. So, using techniques learnt at the first barrel openings, a small blowtorch was used to cut through the barrel under the rim and avoid the welds.

Once the lid had been removed the interior contents were visually examined. It was apparent a body was within the barrel. Two ten-centimetre holes were cut low in the barrel and the contents allowed to drain into receptacles. These have been sent to trace.

The body was then carefully extracted and submitted to autopsy.

Autopsy Report

Name: Felicity Boyd

Age: 27

Gender: female

Race: Caucasian

Date if Death: estimated at 2008

Date of Autopsy: August 2012

Procurator Fiscal: Lieb Canavan

Witness to Autopsy: Senior Inspector Marcus Campbell and Senior Inspector Grace Scott; both from Tayside Police.

Body Identification: the body was identified as Felicity Boyd on the basis of physical parameters of height, age and gender as determined from skeletal reconstruction and are consistent with antemortem passport and drivers licence data found with the body.

External description: the body was extracted from a 205 litres metal container. There is advanced post-mortem decomposition with extensive skin slippage and gaseous distension of tissues. The head hair is short, black and straight. The thorax and abdomen are of the usual configuration and the genitalia are those of a normal adult female.

Evidence of Injury: there are eight punctures of the tissues of the thoracic and abdominal organs from a sharp pointed stabbing weapon which has a flat blade with cutting edges on both sides, 3cm wide double-bevelled at a sharp degree. Seven defence cutting wounds are found on both hands and forearms. In addition, the left upper arm has a patterned contusion and a misshapen humerus angle confirmed as a comminuted fracture on xray. No other obvious injury is noted externally.

X-ray findings: total body x-rays reveal no metallic fragments of any kind. Apart from the left humerus shaft fracture, no other fractures are noted.

Body cavities: the thoracic and abdominal organs are located in their usual positions and are markedly friable by decomposition and containment. The membranes lining the pleural and peritoneal cavities are smooth. There is a deep puncture wound of the intercostal muscle, transecting the diaphragm.

Internal Description

Cardiovascular System: the heart is normal in shape and size. There are three puncture wounds to the pectoralis muscles, one of which continues into the myocardium. The vessels are normally distributed. The cardiac chambers are of normal size; the myocardium is of normal thickness without evidence of myocardial infarction, old or recent.

Pulmonary System: the trachea, right lung and bronchi have no apparent lesions. The left lung has significant disruption that communicates with the pectoralis muscle puncture wounds.

Gastrointestinal tract: the mucosa of the oesophagus shows no lesions. The stomach is empty. The duodenum, small and large intestines are normal.

Liver: the liver and gallbladder organs are normally located and show no lesions.

Pancreas: the organ is normally located and shows no lesion.

Kidneys: the kidneys are normally located; the left show no lesions; the right has significant disruption that communicates with an abdominal puncture wound. The ureters and bladder are normally located and free from lesions.

Reproductive System: the uterus and ovaries are free of obvious lesions.

Spleen: the spleen is normal in size and position and free of lesions.

Adrenal Glands: the adrenals are normally situated.

Neck Organs: the thyroid is normal. A puncture wound is seen in the strap muscles. There are no fractures or haemorrhages of the bony or cartilaginous structures of the neck.

Brain: the brain is grey-green and liquefied. Few normal structures remain intact. There are no skull fractures appreciated.

Specimens for Toxicology: brain, kidney, muscle, liver, lung and spleen samples have been submitted for analysis. In addition, scrapings from under the fingernails and the teeth ave been taken and submitted.

Microscopic Description: sections of the lung, heart, aorta, liver, spleen, stomach, kidneys, uterus and ovaries show no pathologic diagnoses other than marked postmortem decomposition with gaseous distension of tissues and loss of nuclear detail.

Comment: the condition of the body, specifically marked decomposition, made examination difficult. However, a thorough and complete examination was possible.

Examination of the body fluids found within the container that housed the body supports the opinion the person was deceased when contained. The reduced volume of blood contained within the body, along with the documented organ damage from the eight puncture wounds, supports the defensible cause of death as exsanguinations.

Lieb concluded the autopsy and allowed a lab technician to commence the scrub down.

"Thank You" Lieb said to the technician as he removed his coveralls, autopsy mask & shield and gloves.

Marcus and Grace followed him back into the office.

"Well we have work to do" Lieb commented as they looked at each other.

"I'll alert Detective Superintendent Declan Macdonald, so he knows the case is again active. I'll also alert Detective Superintendent Elise Scott and ask her if I can stay with the case – if that's OK with you Marcus?" Grace enquired.

Perfect Marcus thought. "I couldn't agree more" he said, "a fresh pair of eyes and an additional pair of hands may be just what we need to crack this case open."

"I'll brief Crown Counsel and then follow through the barrel contents and trace and give you a call if there's anything" Lieb added.

"And I'll take the delightful task of tracking down Felicity's family and giving them the news. And then start on trying to trace her last days – four years ago!" Marcus lamented.

"Let's all stay in touch and keep everyone up to speed; Marcus will you take point?" Grace enquired.

"Absolutely. Well let's hustle, shall we?" and Marcus led Grace from Lieb's room.

Chapter 7

Marcus and Grace left the office and hurried back to the car. As Marcus drove the short distance back to Tayside Police HQ the two of them shared small talk rather than use the time to rehash the case: neither of them seemed to want to waste time getting to know each other.

"So, you've known Lieb long?" Grace enquired

"This case actually. It was my first serial homicide as Lead Investigator and Lieb was new in post. This case, cases as it turned out, meant we spent a lot of time together." Marcus responded.

"And do the partners in your lives get along well too?" Grace punted

Marcus chuckled, appreciating Grace's interview skills. "Lieb has a wonderful partner, Rose; I was best-man at their wedding."

"And yourself?"

"There's no-one special in my life, unless you consider two Bengal cats?"

"Bengals?" Grace enquired. And as they walked through police HQ to their respective offices, Marcus regaled Grace with the stories of Ophelia and Fuzzbutt, his mother and daughter Bengal cats.

When they reached the top of the first-floor stairs they stopped. "I'll start with my boss and then speak with yours; maybe you'll be ready to join me for that second briefing?" Grace enquired.

"Great idea. I'll track down the whereabouts of Felicity's next-of-kin and meet you at the Detective Super's office. We can than agree next moves and kick on." Marcus completed their thought-path.

Grace nodded her agreement, blessing Marcus with her indomitable smile and turned to climb the stairs to the next floor. "See you in fifteen minutes then" she tossed back over her shoulder.

Marcus strode toward his desk, stopping at Constable Addams' desk and asked, "anything further at the scene?"

"No SIM. We got the cigarette butt and shoeprint cast to trace and I was just trying to identify the shoe make and size."

"Great work, keep on it." Marcus knew the value of positive reinforcement and how regimented communication channels could result in wasted manpower and lost opportunities.

As he tossed himself into his chair and fired up his computer Constable Addams enquired "Is this another body in a barrel for the case?" Other members of the team, and other police officers and detectives nearby turned expectantly.

Marcus sighed. What Marcus, Lieb and Grace had not yet discussed this morning was how the media would respond to such news. Marcus raised his voice so everyone could clearly hear his response.

"Yes, it seems most likely we have found another connected victim. May I remind everyone of their Data Protection responsibilities? Even the Super hasn't been briefed: if I hear one word of this until it's been cleared for general conversation, I will have you report for a performance review. Is that clear?"

There was a mumble of consent throughout the squad room and people returned to their tasks.

Marcus fired up the Drivers Licence database and extracted the information on Felicity Boyd. He then examined the Missing Persons data base and cross-referenced the information, writing all the relevant information into his notebook. Looking up he spied Grace crossing the floor toward the Super's office, so he got up and joined her.

"A word of advice if I may; be decisive." Marcus spoke quietly into Grace's ear as he pushed in front of her and took the lead. Grace was uncertain of his meaning, and before she could enquire further, Marcus tapped on Detective Superintendent Declan Macdonald's door and opened it in response to the 'enter' he heard.

"Mac, we have something major to brief you on" Marcus spoke as he entered into the Super's office. Declan Macdonald leaned back in his chair expectantly and then rose when he spied Grace entering behind Marcus.

"Mac, this is Senior Inspector Grace Scott from Crime Review; she's been Leading on the bodies in the barrel case that went cold".

'Mac' and Grace shook hands and they all seated themselves.

"So, by your appearance together do I take it that there's been a development?" Mac enquired.

"Yes sir, another body." And Marcus went on to brief the Detective Superintendent of those new developments and the findings from the autopsy they had just come from.

"And what's your role now Inspector Scott? Are you handing the case back to Inspector Campbell? Mac enquired.

With Mac's sudden use of the formal title's Grace seemed unsure how to proceed, and she looked at Marcus for guidance. However, Marcus kept his eyes firmly on the desk in front of the Superintendent.

Grace considered her options and then let instinct guide her: Marcus had said to be decisive so she composed her face to show the pause she had taken was to give due consideration to the next actions.

"Well sir, it seems we need to take control of the situation and then ramp up the investigation as if it had never been made a cold case. There's already a lot of people who could escalate this find through the media because of their peripheral involvement, and if the public think we'd let this case slip and allowed another murder to occur, it won't win us any favours.

I think, we should have you call a press conference and introduce this recent find as a new development, and then let us give the new evidence a priority and see if we can break this case." Grace finished her speech with an expectant look deep into the Superintendent's eyes.

"We, Inspector Scott?

"I am currently the Lead on this case in my division sir: I am fully up-to-date with all the details. And I believe that current knowledge is a vital resource in bringing this case to a conclusion with a conviction."

"And Detective Superintendent Elise Scott; what does she have to say about this?" Mac enquired.

"She said it's your call sir."

"OK then, welcome to the team Grace, my name is Mac."

"Mac then flipped a switch on his phone and asked his assistant Deborah to call Vincent in media and ask him to come to the office. Mac, Marcus and Grace then discussed details for the media until Vincent arrived.

An hour later, Detective Superintendent Declan Macdonald stood on the steps of Tayside Police, behind a bank of microphones and in front of a rabble of reporters and cameramen. Marcus and Grace stood to his left.

Vincent introduced Detective Superintendent Declan Macdonald, explaining he had a breaking news statement, and that once he had delivered it he would take questions. Mac stepped to the microphones and said,

"Members of the public, our **ongoing** (spoken with emphasis) investigation into what the media call the body-in-the-barrel case, has found further evidence and leads that we hope will finally draw this contemptible episode to a conclusion; a conclusion with a conviction. Unfortunately, this ongoing investigation has unearthed another body. It has confirmed our belief we had not discovered all there was to tell in this sorry saga. Now we will continue to work diligently and with increased vigour to draw this investigation to an end. Are there any questions?"

There were questions; they were spat from the attending reporters with such an intensity Grace had difficulty separating one question from the other. But SI Mac handled the screech with practiced aplomb.

"I'm sorry, no we have not confirmed the identity of the last victim."

"No this isn't a recent killing, just a recent find."

"Yes, there are additional items of evidence, which freshen previous information."

"Yes, Senior Inspector Marcus Campbell will be continuing to Lead the investigation, along with the fresh eyes of Senior Inspector Grace Scott from the Major Crime Review team."

"Thank you, members of the media, for coming today. As always, when I have more, you will have more." And Mac turned and strode through the door with Marcus, Grace and Vincent in tow.

Once inside he turned and watched the media disperse; the focus of a media storm abrewing.

"OK, Marcus and Grace, keep this momentum going. Firstly, confirm the ID and alert the family and then take steps to follow up every lead. Grace, I want Marcus to lead this as a new case; I want you to keep bringing the threads back to the older information. Let's tighten this net and catch this mongrel."

Mac then spoke to Vincent: "watch the media: I don't want them getting off-track over the length of time the case has taken. Keep them focussed on new developments; get them feeling involved; part of the team that's on the case."

Vincent Marcus and Grace muttered words of acknowledgement and then hurried off to their assignments.

Chapter 8

Lieb watched Marcus and Grace depart then walked down to the laboratory to follow-up on trace and other investigations from this new barrel case to ensure everyone knew the priorities and their assignments.

The term forensic investigation refers to the use of science or technology in the investigation and establishment of facts or evidence to be used in criminal justice or other proceedings. Forensic investigation is a rather broad field with many different subdivisions. And hence the laboratory section of the Procurator Fiscal office involved many different sections, manned by specialist staff for each field.

As he entered the lab area he received an email on his *e*tablet from forensic odontology which confirmed the victim's identity.

"Got something here Lieb" Daniel called as he Lieb entered the Physical Evidence lab.

"I've been working on the plaster cast of the footprint taken from the churchyard." Daniel continued. "So far I've not identified the make of the shoe, I've got the computer running a comparison through the database, but I have learnt something." Daniel handed the plaster cast to Lieb and pointed to a small round impression on the outer edge. "This is an imprint of a die for casting plastic; the logo identifies it as the plastic workshop in Crieff where the first victim was found."

"Excellent work Daniel. This gives us a strong link between case number one and this case. Let me know if you get anything from the database search." Lieb moved on into the DNA lab.

"Hi Lieb, no luck on the DNA from the cigarette butt" Colleen reported when Lieb arrived at her work station. "It's been too long in the weather. I am however, using new techniques to see if there is more than one DNA sample in the body fluid soup" Lieb moved on.

There was some intense discussion going on in the fingerprint lab: Lieb stopped at the door to pick up the threads of conversation. When Byron and Abbey saw Lieb they stopped and then included him in the conversation. "Byron's asked one of his dumb questions again" said Abbey wrinkling her nose: "and it's got us discussing extraction techniques."

"Like we discovered on the other four barrels" Abbey continued, "the prints on this barrel are smudged and of little value, however – oh it's your bright spark Byron, you explain."

Byron was a new graduate who was spending time with all of the forensic experts a post-grad grounding program Lieb had introduced. This allowed the newbie to identify if they developed a passion for one particular service, and gave the experts a chance to identify exceptional traits. Hopefully this would more quickly advance a new grad and also keep them in the field for much longer.

Byron presented as a geek and typecasting would put him behind a computer somewhere or in Lieb's opinion, in the chemical lab. However, he was proving to have an eye for detail and an intelligence for lateral thinking Lieb could foresee taking him into the field. Only time would tell. For now, he was working in the prints department, and Abbey was enjoying the challenges Byron's 'what if' questions were supplying.

"Well "Byron explained, "what if the lid was on the barrel initially and had to be removed so the body could be interred?" "There should be prints on the underside of the clamp" Abbey finished for him. "Of course, we didn't think of that initially so the other barrels may have been compromised, but this time we went straight to cutting the lid off below the welds so the clamps are still in place." Abbey concluded.

"Excellent" Lieb responded. "Can you print all four clamps for comparison please." And Lieb moved on to let them work.

In the Chem. Department, he found Stanley checking results and instructing next steps to his team. "Hi Stanley, anything to report?" Lieb enquired.

"We've given a sample of the soup to Colleen to see if she can find multiple DNA samples. Who knows if that will provide anything. There's also some larger objects found in the drum I passed on to Daniel's team. One interesting find so far, vinegar." Stanley said the word vinegar as if it was a full statement and left Lieb to ask for more. Stanley could be a little too focussed at times.

"There's not enough to suggest the body was pickled, but I'd conjecture the barrel held vinegar previously. And it hadn't been washed out. We've just agreed the results of the mass spec; vinegar with chilli, garlic and fennel in equal portions. And seeing the barrel held 205 litres we think it's a commercial product so I've just set Anne to search the internet for possibilities."

"Great work" Lieb supplied. And Lieb left the teams to continue with their activities and walked back to his office to phone and brief the Crown Counsel.

On the way, he checked his phone. There was a text from Rose 'arrived safely. Lot's to do. See you in 10 days. Love Rose. Ps landline phone out of order.'

OK Lieb thought. If I want to sail this weekend I have three days to clear this case. He closed his office door and added notes to his report template. He'd kept up-to-date with the ICT revolution and was using a computer tablet that allowed him to make entries into an ongoing case, and thanks to a clever program, allowed him to create an executive report which summarised the investigation findings and activities as he made entries. Lieb used this summary when he spoke with Suzanne and James.

Suzanne Hamilton was the Solicitor General, and James Bruce was the Lord Advocate, the Ministerial Head of the Crown Office and Procurator Fiscal Office's. Lieb, as the District Procurator Fiscal for Perthshire, Angus & Dundee was accountable to James. As a team, Lieb and the detectives from Tayside Police investigated a major incident; Lieb and his teams in the lab identified and collated the evidence; Lieb wrote a comprehensive report and then Suzanne and her team undertook appropriate prosecution.

Suzanne was already aware there had been another development in the case: when the three of them spoke on the video conference she reported what Detective Superintendent Declan Macdonald has just reported on tv.

"What can you add Lieb?" asked James.

"We have confirmed the modus operandi between this and the previous four, barrel cases. We can also identify the victim as Felicity Boyd and Tayside detectives are leading with notification and the victim's movements before her demise.

We have a shoeprint from the scene with an indentation that links this incident with Crieff. And we have a number of other findings which may provide leads." Lieb concluded.

"Mac has spoken of finding a conclusion and obtaining a conviction via the media this afternoon." James spoke with a weariness of experience; he had faced the media criticism on not concluding this case on previous occasions.

"I'll keep you both apprised of any developments." Lieb assured them.

After they finished the video call, Lieb put a call into Marcus. He and Grace were in a vehicle when the call connected and Grace took the call and put it on speaker so they could all hear the conversation. Lieb updated them on the lab findings and ongoing lines of enquiry

"Thanks, Lieb. We'll call in on the way back from notifying Felicity Boyd's parents and we'll discuss the next line of enquiry together." Marcus concluded the conversation and Lieb started reviewing two other case reports that had been put on his desk.

In the print lab Abbey explained to Byron the print options they had "Most experts consider magnetic powder to be a little bit more sensitive for lifting and that it tends to work better on the harder surfaces. I've found it will not work well, however, on any surface that is wet or even slightly magnetised."

"But the superglue cabinet is too small to use for the barrel" mused Byron, "Unless we can remove the clamps?"

"Great idea, let's get some tools and look at our options." agreed Abbey. And after some careful examination, they determined the clamps were completed by using 3 metals pins to hold the hook of the clamp to its fixed foundation. Byron held a fine screwdriver to each pin head whilst Abbey gently hammered out the pins.

They laid each clamp hook onto a tray and placed it in the fume cabinet. They locked the door and set the timer for five minutes. The timer rang off the five minutes and Abbey vented the cabinet and removed the tray containing the four clamps. Good prints were visible on all four.

"OK Byron, let's dust and snag these babies and get the database searching" Abbey instructed. "Then we should try for prints on the other drums. I'll arrange their return from evidence storage."

As the lab teams hustled Marcus and Grace arrived at the door of Felicity's parents; a B&B on a pleasant cobbled street near the University of Dundee. What ensued was that devastating unpleasantness that no police officer liked to partake in. Everyone likes to write about 'getting closure' and loving parents always know, even if they won't admit it, that a missing family member must be dead when there is no reasonable assumption they would remove themselves from society without explanation; but the delivery of confirmation is still such a blow as to be unconscionable.

Grace sat in the large kitchen at the family meal table with Mrs Boyd, Marcus stood quietly by watching them and Mr Boyd fretted and paced, unable to find a space in which to settle. Grace suggested she help Mrs Boyd – Anne, make a cup of tea and Marcus suggested Mr Boyd – Angus, ring other family or friends that could come and be with them: Angus agreed and moved to the phone.

Ten minutes later a teapot and tray of cups was placed on the table. Neil Grainger had arrived along with Prue, Felicity's older sister. Neil had helped Angus close the business front door and redirect the phone to the Information Bureau which would alert the staff there the B&B was not taking guests.

They were all seated around the table holding cups of tea and looking expectantly at Grace and Marcus' each showing their personal grief on their faces, in their movements and deep in their eyes. Marcus, remaining focussed, paid close attention to these reactions: for a detective, these raw emotions provided vital information. He continued to quietly observe as Grace gave the particulars they needed.

When it was time to turn the information flow around, for Grace and Marcus to learn what they could of Felicity's life and movements at the time of her disappearance, it was her big sister Prue who spoke up.

Felicity, she explained had been a business manager in the biotechnology sector in Dundee. Internationally renowned, with both academic and private sectors continuously showcasing cutting-edge research and groundbreaking product development, the biotechnology sector was highly competitive. Felicity had excelled in university and been quickly snapped up by a local company.

Felicity had been on her return from Aberdeen where she had delivered a business proposal to a supply company. She had been reported missing by her executive manager when she had failed to make a report at the staff meeting the following morning: her car had been found in the parking lot of a rest stop on the A90.

Grace wrote all this information down whilst Prue left the table to visit the study and find the contact information for Felicity's executive manager. Grace then got the parents talking; what Felicity was like, who her friends were, what she did in her spare time. Angus particularly took the opportunity to talk and the information he gave Marcus and Grace allowed them to see a more three-dimensional image of the body they had met that day in the morgue.

"She was always busy" Angus explained. "She loved her job and that kept her late some nights, but she always found time to call during the week. And Sundays she'd come for morning tea. We couldn't leave the B&B much, but we sat around this table and had tea and scones: for an hour, most Sunday's she was all ours." Angus took a shuddering breath and stopped.

Neil took up the story of Felicity's life as Prue returned to the table and sipped at her tea. "Thursday nights was dance night with Prue and some friends. They rarely missed a Thursday."

"What about boyfriends?" Grace asked. Prue shook her head and then quietly responded "Not for a while. Sissy had career expectations and the couple of guys she met with were 'friends with benefits'. She said career development was a priority for all of them. They're the two names on your list with the asterisks': I guessed you'd want them. The other names were close friends." Prue concluded passing over a sheet torn from a lined A5 notepad.

Marcus and Grace thanked the family members and left them with their grief. Marcus climbed behind the wheel of his vehicle and drove the short distance to the university to meet with Lieb: Grace called the office and asked Addams to follow up on the names they'd collected. It was getting on for 16:00 so Grace told Addams not to worry phoning this evening unless it was something extraordinary; tomorrow morning would suffice.

Marcus parked his car, stopped to purchase a round of coffee and pastries, and then walked with Grace through the maze of buildings until they reached the Department of Forensic Medicine. They signed in and worked their way back to Lieb's office.

"I come bearing sustenance" Marcus announced as they marched into Lieb's office.

"Wow, food and coffee – excellent" exclaimed Lieb climbing out from behind his desk. The three of them sat around the small conference table and no-one started talking until them had consumed a goodly portion of their pastry and swallowed down some cafe latte.

"OK" said Lieb taking the lead. "Here's the results we've gathered so far. Odontology confirmed the identity of Felicity Boyd. An impression found in the plaster cast of the shoeprint has been confirmed as being a plastic die used in the workshop at Crieff." Lieb showed Marcus and Grace a picture of the plaster cast on his etablet and then emailed it to their devices.

"There was no DNA from the cigarette butt – too degraded, but they did isolate tqo DNA samples from the bodily soup taken from the barrel. There's no match on the database, but we can determine we're looking for a man. And," Lieb flashed a grin, "when you apprehend him, we have his fingerprints as well, thanks to some bloody marvellous detective work in our prints department."

Lieb was presented with congratulatory comments from Marcus and Grace and then went on to add "and we managed to find the same prints on the other barrels."

"The other major development; the chem. lab identified the barrels had contained vinegar with a particular combination of ingredients. I've just emailed that to your devices as well" Lieb concluded.

Marcus then briefed Lieb on their afternoon with the Boyd family.

"Tomorrow we'll interview Felicity's manager and 'friends with benefits'. I'll get Addams working on the barrel angle, combining the inventory search with the vinegar one. Maybe he'll get lucky heh?"

"OK it's 17:30 now and I need to get back and brief Mac before I can call it a night" Marcus said. "We'll let you know what tomorrow morning brings." And with that Marcus and Grace departed.

Lieb checked with Marianne as she was leaving and she had no new cases on the Board needing Lieb's attention. Lieb then did a walk-through of the labs to ensure the work was 'routine' and the on-call team for a major incident was assured. At his desk Lieb checked through the incoming worksheet for the evening and was satisfied nothing required his attention. He made a check of his personal email and text to see if Rose had sent anything further, but that showed she hadn't so he switched his office lighting down to the night setting and headed out for an evening alone.

"Hmmm, I wonder how long this can last?" he asked himself?

Chapter 9

Lieb woke from an unsettled sleep to the bark of his phone; it was 03:30.

"Lieb Canavan" he said in response to the voice on the other end of his connection.

"Sir, sorry for the hour." Lieb never did understand the apology; it was his job after all. "This is a particularly awful one" the voice continued to explain.

"Text me the address and I'll be there" Lieb responded.

The text beeped an incoming which gave an address in Arbroath; Robert Street. Lieb dressed warm and made himself a coffee to go using the new capsule coffee machine Rose had given him for Xmas. Lieb enjoyed the smell of the brewed coffee and for a moment forgot Rose wasn't curled up asleep in their bed. 'I wonder if she's awake too' he pondered to himself as he headed out the front door.

The trip to Arbroath was less than twenty minutes and he arrived at 04:08. A Senior Inspector Adam McAdam was standing outside awaiting his arrival; not far to Adam's left a couple of forlorn constables huddled, avoiding eye contact and speech.

'Ominous' Lieb muttered to himself as he climbed out his vehicle and grabbed his kit bag.

"Adam?" Lieb opened askantly. "Really bad one heh?"

Adam looked at Lieb and Lieb flinched at his haunted eyes. Adam was a season SI and Lieb had found his stoic character a boon in troubled times. The last time they had worked together was three weeks ago on a vehicle mess where five young adults had danced with a tree and lost.

Adam handed Lieb his phone which displayed a photo of a sweet little blue yacht. Lieb looked at the picture and then expectantly at Adam. "Do you recognise the tattoo Lieb?"

"No, should I?"

"If you did you could ask someone else to take this case. And that may have been be a blessing." Adam replied. "This is tattooed onto the young ladies left breast: and it's likely our best chance at ID." Lieb raised his shoulders and bobbed his head asking for more: There was little point in pushing DI McAdam, he was obviously struggling to cope with whatever awaited Lieb inside.

"They've left the young woman strung up and the rats have taken her face. "Leon from your team has been in and taken your photos for you; I'd like the team to process the scene after you're happy to cut her down and we can cover her up, if you're OK with that?"

This was highly irregular but not unheard of. When a heavy haulage vehicle had hit a bus of preschoolers last year Lieb quickly realised the trauma to the responders would be monumental. He and three of his hand-picked team documented and extracted the five kiddies before the responders and crime scene crews returned to go about their business. Lieb had learnt to control the pain as best he could.

"Of course." Lieb moved toward the open doorway from which the stark scene lighting was emanating. Adam moved along behind him and Lieb nodded his appreciation.

What confronted Lieb inside the building was both visual and olfactory. He was trained to focus on and record what he saw, not feel it; and that helped somewhat.

And what he saw was very confronting.

They were in a commercial kitchen which appeared to have not been used for its intentions for a while. Laid out across the centre of the room was a bank of cooking and food preparation benches. Beyond the bench and in shadows was an area set aside for packing and storage. This wasn't an eatery in the usual sense: food could be prepared here, but not served.

Toward the left side of the bank of cooking appliances was a young woman who had been strung up by her wrists, which had been taped together. The woman was naked and physical trauma was easily apparent. Lieb moved to her side and examined the trauma to her face. Her head hung down, chin resting on her chest and the resultant congestion of fluids left her face engorged: this the rats had found particularly delectable, and all that was left was the bony structure and scraps of flesh they had not managed to enjoy before they were disturbed.

Lieb looked up and over to the door where Leon was standing waiting. "Did you get plenty of shots from all angles?"

"Yes Sir."

"Both the body and the scene?"

"Yes sir."

"OK. Adam could you help Leon bring in the gurney?"

Adam nodded and left with Leon, returning a short time later. Placing the gurney near to the body, Leon waited for Lieb's instruction.

"Adam, if I lift her from the hips, could you unhitch the arms? Leon, once she's unhitched she's likely to slump forward; please control her movement by manipulating the shoulders so she's lifted back into your hands. I'll then pick up her legs and we'll lift her onto the gurney. OK?"

The three men got into position and less than a minute later the woman's body was on the gurney and encased in a protective body-bag.

"Leon, are you alright?" Leon nodded and lifted his head so Lieb could look into his eyes and see he was coping. "I'll meet you back at the lab shortly; I need to get some more details from SI McAdams."

"Sure Lieb. Should I unload?"

"Yes please, but only the gurney. I'll unpack myself" Lieb responded.

Barnie appeared then at the back of the van and tipped Lieb a salute. Lieb thought she must have been kept back by Adam; now she was taking up the mantle of Leon's partner which relieved Lieb to know he was accompanied for the journey into Dundee.

As Barnie and Leon went about the business of loading their cargo into the van, Lieb turned to Adam for a more comprehensive briefing.

Adam read from his notepad: "Night security officer noticed the door unlocked at 01:20 and called it in. He was instructed to maintain observation only and wait for police backup; apparently there have been some issues with a couple of vagrants who aren't afraid to protect what they feel are theirs. Police patrol arrived at 01:42 and checked the scene. When they entered they only had torches, and what they saw distressed them somewhat. One call led to another and at 02:24 I got called and asked to attend. I arrived at 03:18 and after getting little information from the first responders, I had them call you and arrange the lighting."

"Well rigor mortis is still limited so I put the death at around 10 to 12 hours ago." Lieb stated matter-of-factorialy. "And I'm not going to hazard a guess at what took this young woman's life until I complete an autopsy, so don't ask." Adam nodded.

"I'll see you at autopsy?" Lieb enquired.

"It's a little early to get ID started, so yes Doc. I'll arrange the team here and follow you down" Adam answered.

Lieb climbed into his vehicle and kicked the engine into life. Before he set out he checked his blue-tooth was activated so he could talk hands-free whilst he drove. He thought again about Rose and wondered if the baby had her up: she was always understanding if he rang her from such a scene; not to discuss the details of what he'd encountered, but normal things that helped him detach and cope with this job.

But it wasn't Rose he rang: if they had the baby asleep he would not get a kind reception waking her, Lieb rang the responder phone and Leon answered.

"Yes Lieb?" Lieb could still here the pain behind his words. He was hoping a different focus may be helpful.

"I was just wondering your ETA?"

"We're still about fifteen minutes out. I rang night security to alert them" Leon answered.

"I'm about ten minutes behind you. Leave room for me in the delivery bay and it will save time for my getting around helping you. Was that Barnie I saw at the vehicle?"

"Yes Lieb; she's been my shift partner for over a year now." Leon didn't sound peeved: he knew what Lieb's intentions were and he did appreciate it.

"Say Hi for me then."

Leon muttered something and rang off. Fifteen minutes later Lieb pulled into the delivery bay to find the lights on and Leon and Barnie unloading their client. It was nudging 06:00.

Chapter 10

Autopsy Report – A037

AFIP168172

Name: unknown

Age: approximately late twenties to forty

Gender: female

Race: Caucasian

Date if Death: August 2012

Date of Autopsy: August 2012

Procruator Fiscal: Lieb Canavan

Witness to Autopsy: Senior Inspector Adam McAdam

Senior Inspector Adam McAdam arrived at the forensic offices autopsy room at 07:03. Lieb looked up from his examination and stopped recording the observations he had been dictating.

"Anything more before I start?" Lieb enquired.

"Just to let you know I have the team looking into the tattoo: it may take a while."

"Methinks so will this." Lieb finished.

Lieb had covered the young woman's face with a soft thin cloth which had a dual effect: it not only covered the gory mess, which was proving to be very distracting, but the cloth softly lay across the bony features giving her the resemblance of a face.

Lieb started the recording device and went back over the external features, giving himself an opportunity of thoroughness and providing Adam the same insight.

Body Identification: "the body is yet to be identified: facial features are destroyed. Physical parameters of height, age and gender were determined from skeletal reconstruction.

A distinctive tattoo of a blue yacht on her left breast is being pursued as a Lead."

External description: “the body was found in a hung position; wrists taped, stretched from the hips up over the centre of a cooker and the lower half draped to the floor. Her head had dropped to her chest resulting in engorgement of the facial soft tissues and tongue: the facial tissue and tongue has been eaten by rats’ post-mortem.

The head hair is thick, short, red-brown and straight.”

Adam interrupted Lieb and asked, “what did they use to strangle her?”

“Her own head. When you see a congested face like this with petechiae, then it is more likely they were killed by strangulation rather than hanging. With strangulation, it is difficult to get complete closure of the arteries, so that some blood still flows up into the victim’s brain. However, it is easy to get complete closure of the jugular vein, so that the blood cannot escape from the brain and face. This causes the congestion. And the mere weight of your head is frequently enough to cause closure of the jugular vein and carotid artery, which will kill you in 4 minutes.”

“Also, see this Non-v-shaped furrow around the neck? This is where the victim just leaned against a ligature. In this case, the strap muscles of her neck.”

Lieb continued to dictate. “Apart from facial congestion, Rigor mortis is restricted to the upper body, putting the time of death at mid-afternoon yesterday.”

“The external skin of both upper arms shows distinct linear markings covered in a sticky substance which has been sent to trace, along with duct tape found on the floor at the scene. When both arms are raised above the victims head they line up: it is reasonable to postulate the victims head was taped upright to ensure she didn’t strangle until the perpetrator(s) wanted her to.”

Adam groaned softly.

Evidence of Injury:

“Further examination of the arms showed injection sites in both arms: blood has been sent for toxicology.”

“Both shoulders show extreme laxity. Incisions into each joint show all 4 muscles (the supraspinatus, infraspinatus, teres minor, and subscapularis) have significant tearing, along with full disruption of the rotator cuff tendons.”

“Is all that damage from the hanging? Adam asked softly. Lieb nodded. “It’s a wonder her arms managed to stay connected” Adam added and again, Lieb just nodded.

“The thorax and abdomen are of the usual configuration and the genitalia are those of a normal adult female.”

“However, the nipples of both breasts are absent. Examination of the structures of both breasts shows extensive discontinuity of the Intralobular connective tissue. In addition, the areola of both nipples is macerated. The remaining nipple areola has been excised and sent to the pathology lab for further examination.”

“The skin of the lower abdomen, measuring 24cm wide and 16cm high, shows central necrosis, surrounded by zones of stasis and of hyperaemia; indicative of contact burns.”

“Burns? From what?” Adam asked.

“I would suggest you check the cooker” Lieb answered. “With her positioned draped over the cooker and the constant repetitive striking of her hip, she’s most likely nudged the cooker on just enough for a slow burn" Lieb suggested. This time it was Adam who nodded and wrote himself a note to follow this up.

Lieb continued "Below the burn area, in a linear trajectory crossing the pelvis and reaching two-thirds of the length of both upper thighs, is a complex contusion. This correlates with the body placement touching the metallic surface / cooker she was hung against."

"So that's bruising and not burning? Adam enquired. Lieb nodded and continued.

"Incision of the contusion, bruising" he said raising his eyes to ensure Adam was still with him "over the upper thighs shows hematoma maturation, inflammation, necrosis of damaged myofibrils, and phagocytosis of the necrotic debris. In addition, both femur and illium bones show comminuted fracturing. Both lateral femoral cutaneous nerves are avulsed, the Great Saphenous veins and external iliac arteries are contused and thrombotic."

"So, let me make sure I have this straight" Adam said. "She has very deep bruising across her pelvis with fracturing of her pelvis and both upper thighs?"

"Yes" was all Lieb said.

"This must have taken ages to occur?" Adam's voice spoke with a voice imploring Lieb to say it was not so, but Lieb just nodded again.

Adam groaned softly - again.

"The lower legs are unremarkable."

"The skin from the digits of both feet show extensive abrasions."

"Turning the body over, the upper back shows signs of biting around the nape of the neck and across the shoulders."

"The lower thorax and lumbar regions show signs of cigarette burns (X 3) and blunt force trauma with extensive bruising of the buttocks."

"Examination of the external genitalia..." Lieb stopped the tape and looked at Adam.."is brutal." Lieb commenced taping again.

"Examination of the external genitalia and colposcopy examination with digital image capture shows an injury pattern consistent with rape. There are extensive lacerations to the external and internal organs and anus and rectum."

"X-ray findings: total body x-rays reveal no metallic fragments of any kind. Fractures of the nasal bones are noted."

"Alright, let's see what's inside, shall we?" Lieb spoke to Adam, but continued without waiting for his consent.

<u>Internal Description</u>

"Body cavities: the thoracic and abdominal organs are located in their usual positions.

The right and left pleural cavity contains 10 ml of clear fluid with no adhesions. The pericardial sac is yellow, glistening without adhesions or fibrosis and contains 30 ml of a straw-coloured fluid. The peritoneal cavity shows diffuse peritonitis of the sigmoid mesentery."

"So, all normal and healthy" Lieb said to Adam.

Cardiovascular System: "The heart has a normal size, shape and a weight of 400 grams. The pericardium is intact. The epicardial fat is diffusely firm. Upon opening, the heart was grossly normal."

"There is minimal atherosclerosis with no measurable plaques along the full length of the ascending and descending aorta."

Pulmonary System: "The right lung weighed 630 grams, the left weighed 710 grams. The lung parenchyma is pink without evidence of congestion or haemorrhage."

"So, again, all normal and healthy" Lieb said to Adam.

Gastrointestinal tract: "The oesophagus and stomach are normal in appearance without evidence of ulcers or varices. The stomach contains no evidence of any pills or other non-food stuff material. The pancreas shows a normal lobular cut surface. The duodenum, ileum, jejunum and colon are all grossly normal. The liver weighs 2850 grams and the cut surface reveals a normal liver with no fibrosis present grossly. The gallbladder is in place with a probe patent bile duct through to the ampulla of Vater. "

"So, that's all normal and healthy" Lieb said to Adam, however, "The anus and rectum are macerated. The anal sphincter retains no muscular vigour. The rectum shows full thickness tearing."

Spleen: "The spleen is normal weighing 140 grams, the cut surface reveals a normal appearing white and red pulp. No abnormally large lymph nodes were noted."

Kidneys: "The right kidney weighs 200 grams, the left weighs 210 grams. The left kidney contains a 1.0 x 1.0 x 1.0 simple cyst containing a clear fluid. The cut surface reveals a normal appearing cortex and medulla with intact calyces."

Adrenal Glands: "The adrenal glands are in the normal position and weigh 8.0 grams on the right and 11.6 grams on the left. The cut surface of the adrenal glands reveals a normal appearing cortex and medulla. The thyroid gland weighs 12.4 grams and is grossly normal."

"That's, all normal and healthy" said Lieb.

Reproductive System: "Both ovaries show normal pathophysiology. The uterus is retroverted and shows evidence of early pregnancy. On dissection, the amniotic fluid is turbid and congealed: a sample has been sent to pathology for confirmation (of boiling?). The uterine decidua is thick, and there is the presence of a foetus (4-5mm) and a placenta."

"Is that right? Adam again implored, hoping her was hearing it wrong "she was pregnant?

Lieb cringed inwardly; it seemed as if the winds of fate had a theme for him of late.

Lieb lifted his head and looked into the haunted eyes of SI Adam McAdam.

He spoke into the recorder "Specimens for Toxicology: blood, areola, uterine contents, colposcopy samples and tape & residue from the upper arms have been submitted for analysis." and switched off his recording device,

Adam continued to speak, saying "Someone must be missing this young woman. And I'm going to have to tell them she's died. I just hope whoever did this resists arrest and gets shot and killed. For the family to have to hear this during a trial....Gads!"

"Let me finish up here and I'll join you in my office to debrief" Lieb spoke, softly, gently.

Adam stirred and gave the Jane Doe with the blue yacht tattoo a last look; then quietly left to find a quiet corner in Lieb's office.

Lieb closed the y-cut made in the chest and Leon arrived: together the two worked quietly and without word. They wrapped the body and placed in on shelf in storage awaiting a name and the claim f a loved one.

Leon then started the clean-down process and Lieb visited the restrooms to wash and freshen up. He then joined Adam in his office.

"Finding identity from the tattoo is going to take time" Adam spoke as Lieb entered. "And there's not much to go for finding the perp. Perps?" Adam asked Lieb.

"With that much damage, perps plural is most likely." Lieb agreed. "I'll get the labs to give us a preliminary on the colposcopy samples so we at least have an idea os how many. Then we'll try for DNA."

"Before you go let's brief the Crown Counsel?" Lieb put in a conference call and soon Lieb, Adam, Suzanne and James were having a conversation.

As Lieb briefed Suzanne and James they sat silently letting him finish.

"Adam, please let's keep a lid on this media-wise. It seems the family is in for a rough ride without first knowing about it from a Dome line while collecting morning coffee" Suzanne instructed.

James just asked for regular updates. And the phone conversation concluded, for now.

"Would she have known she was pregnant?" Adam asked Lieb.

"Four to five centimetres is about five weeks. Even a woman who is irregular would most likely be aware, even if she wasn't planning it."

"I suppose you could get all the pharmacists to supply a list of pregnancy test kits sold over the last month and cross-reference them with missing persons?" Lieb suggested, trying to offer encouragement.

"It might be just as fruitful as trying to locate a tattooist who specialises in marine designs?"

"Let's touch base with any news, or 14:00 whichever comes first?" Lieb requested.

"You got it Doc." Lieb really didn't like the moniker, but he let it slide for now: Adam left the office to start his search for a missing woman's identity and the monsters who'd dealt her a truly horrendous final episode.

Chapter 11

Marcus and Grace stopped for coffee and lunch. They had spent the morning visiting Felicity Boyd's boss and friends, including those 'with benefits'. No-one had shed any light on a possible motive for anyone to harm Felicity.

"Well, it's no wonder this case ended up on my desk" Grace spoke.

"It was like this with all the cases; no-one drew flags. We spoke with dozens of people for each victim without luck. The profiler's felt they were all victims of opportunity, but we couldn't put anyone in those places at those times" Marcus added. "Let's go back and see if John Addam's has had any luck with his searches?"

Grace gave Marcus a ten-pound note and Marcus paid for lunch: it was an unspoken rule amongst members of the force that they always paid their way. It saved conflict or innuendo developing.

They found John at his desk quite animated.

"What does a good Scottish lad have with his fish n chips?"

"Pickled onions if you're my Dad" Grace replied.

"Exactly" John went on excitedly. "And the most famous brand?"

"Granaidh" Marcus answered, "But that's not been around for ages."

"But that was the composition of the vinegar used to pickle Grannies onions." John explained.

"So, do you have an address for the factory?" Marcus enquired.

"Argh, no – but" John said before Marcus could object "I have located a former supplier." John tore a sheet from his notepad and handed it to Marcus.

"Excellent" Grace said and turned from John's desk to leave with Marcus. She'd taken a couple of steps and stopped and turned back. "John, could you look further into the company and see if the owner's still around?" "Thank you" she added and graced John with one of disarming smiles. Then she hurried off to catch up with Marcus.

The address they had was north-west of Perth; the A85 road to Crieff. In all a forty-five-minute journey.

"This feels promising" Grace commented as they started out. With the first victim from Perth and found in Crieff: we may be onto something?"

"Well, we could hope so heh?" Marcus felt it was wrong to wish the time he had Grace captive in his vehicle could end anytime soon, so he didn't give his thoughts voice.

"Tell me about your cats" Grace suddenly asked.

"Really?" Marcus responded.

"We have a while to travel and we've discussed the case through and through. I'd find something else will give my brain a chance to freshen so I can focus when we arrive" Grace explained.

"OK" Marcus started. "They're Bengals, a relatively new breed whereby they crossed a domestic cat with the Asian Leopard cat and came up with miniature leopards. They're not your usual housecat; they're very independent and inquisitive; always climbing and exploring. Fuzzbutt"

"Fuzzbutt?" Grace interrupted treating Marcus to one of her throaty chuckles.

"Yes, Fuzzbutt. She was born dead; one of two kittens to her mother's third litter. The delivery went poorly so the vet did an emergency c-section."

"C-section, on a cat?" Grace interrupted again.

"Yes" Marcus answered prickling at the constant interruption, so Grace raised her hand and mimed zipping her lips. Marcus continued: "After they saved Ophelia's life the vet managed to resuscitate Fuzzbutt. But she was poorly and small and they didn't think she'd live, so the breeder gave her a pet name. But she did live and continued to thrive. They needed to sell Ophelia because she was no longer a breeder and Fuzzbutt came with her as a pair."

"So, mother and daughter?" Grace felt it was the right time to ask.

"Yep. And like I was saying, Fuzzbutt loves to climb into shopping bags and to be carried around in boxes; but don't pick her up. They hate to be picked up. Very independent but so entertaining. You should come meet them sometime." Marcus gave himself a gold-star for slipping that in so nonchalantly.

"I'd like that" Grace responded as they drove across the South Street bridge and took the north ring-road around Perth and exited at the Dunkeld Road and then into the A85 Crieff Road.

They found their destination just before the A9 interchange.

Climbing out of their vehicle Marcus approached a small building with an office sign displayed. Behind it was a large parking lot with numerous transport vehicle of varying sizes and configuration.

As Marcus entered the office a young lass looked up from the computer she was entering data into, flashed Marcus a cheery smile and asked how she could help.

Marcus showed his police ID and responding to his warm welcome, addressed the lass by the name displayed on her nametag. "Rosslyn I need to speak with a manager please."

"That will be Mike, let me buzz him." Rosslyn picked up a mobile phone and sent a quick text message; after a brief moment, a response came back and Rosslyn informed Marcus Mike was on his way.

"Thank you, Rosslyn. Tell me, do people rent the vehicles?" Marcus asked.

"At times, yes. But mostly they want a driver as well."

Marcus heard Grace start a conversation so he left the office to join her. Grace introduced him as he arrived.

"How can I help you?" Mike enquired.

Marcus took the lead and asked "Mike, do you recall deliveries you made for Granaidh?"

"Arrggh, that was a while back. Some years at least. The old lady died and the son let the business go I believe."

"You wouldn't happen to have a name or address for them?"

"All our account records are computerised so there should be something. I learnt the hard way about not having evidence of attempts to get outstanding accounts paid. Come in and I'll get Rosslyn to search the archives."

Ten minutes later Marcus and Grace were standing outside; Grace putting a call in to John Addams, asking if he could use the information to locate the son. Unfortunately, all Mike had was a post office address.

Whilst she was on the phone Marcus asked Mike "what sort of barrels did you deliver do you remember?" Mike looked at the sheet of paper Grace was holding and replied "205 litre blue ones. They were reconditioned chemical drums but the old lady said they were passed for her to hold pickling vinegar in them."

Marcus heart paused: could they have cracked the case? Grace had hung up the phone just as Mike made his statement; now she looked at Marcus, wondering how he would take her news.

Just then Rosslyn put her head out the door and asked Mike a question regarding a service booking. "I've got to get on – is there anything more?"

"Thanks, no for now" Marcus answered. "We'll call back if there's anything more."

Marcus and Grace climbed into the vehicle and turned to each other to discuss where they were at and what the next step was.

"Got a name for the son, and a date of death" Grace explained. "Arthur Ronald Neill, died November 2009 aged thirty-three. Cause of death? Lung cancer."

"Last known address?"

"Old Gallows Road, Tibbermore. There's a problem" Grace added.

"Oh?"

"The property is in dispute. Seems a nephew of an elderly cousin feels he's entitled to the property and whatever else is there. But a girlfriend is claiming she was a common-law wife. Two years later the property remains in dispute. We're not going to be able to search it without a warrant."

"Let me ring Mac." Marcus made the call and briefed Mac on the situation. "It's 16:30 now, I won't be able to get you a warrant until tomorrow morning. Stay in Perth and I'll organise a warrant for you first thing" Mac instructed. "Oh and good work – both of you" Mac rang off.

Marcus filled Grace in on the conversation and turned the vehicle back into Perth. They found the Mecure Hotel and checked in – two rooms. Grace found Marcus on the phone to Lieb after she had checked out her room and freshened up.

"Sounds like a positively awful case" Marcus was saying. "And here I was feeling gee'd up because we have such a strong lead. Gads, we may have even cracked this case. I'll let you know tomorrow what we find."

Marcus rang off and asked Grace if she was up for a walk before dinner.

"I have a favourite restaurant here; they make these amazing goat's cheese spring rolls."

"I'm game" Grace responded.

They wandered down to the High Street, turned left and walked to the river. After forty minutes, they turned back into the town centre and wandered through smaller side streets until they arrived at a cozy French cafe. Then after a marvellous meal Marcus lead them back to the hotel. It wasn't late but the message they picked up from reception was the judge would arrange their warrant before he started the following morning. They were to meet him in his rooms at 08:00. So Grace and Marcus wished each other 'sweet dreams' and closed their doors at 22:00.

At breakfast, the next morning the tension was palpable. Marcus and Grace both ate heartily knowing it was going to be a long day with little chance of finding food during it. Over breakfast Grace read from an internet download she had found "*Tibbermore, a parish, in the county of Perth, 4½ miles (W.) from Perth; containing, with the villages of Hillyland and Ruthvenfield, 1651 inhabitants. The parish, which is bounded on the east by the Tay, and on the north by the river Almond and the rivulet called the Pow, is about six miles and a half in length, varying from one mile to three miles in breadth; and comprises an area of about 5900 acres, of which 250 are woodland and plantations, 180 heath and peat-moss, and the remainder arable land in high cultivation.*

There were formerly several villages; but they have mostly disappeared, and the only villages worthy of notice at present are the buildings in connexion with the bleaching and calico-printing works at Huntingtower-field and Ruthven-field.

Facility of communication is afforded by good roads, of which the turnpike-road to Crieff passes through Tibbermore for nearly three miles: the parish roads are kept in excellent order."

They used the express checkout and were standing at the judge's door at 07:50.

And at 08:15 they were on their way to Tibbermore. On the drive Grace spoke with the representatives of both parties involved in the dispute of the Neill estate; only to be told that neither party was intending to be present. They were unobstructed.

Marcus drove west on the A85 until Grace found a small sign indicating the road in to Tibbermore. From there they identified Old Gallows Road and drove until they located the narrow track that led to a small property set back from the road.

Pulling up at the house Marcus and Grace took stock of the desolation of the property. No-one had been here for a very long time. Grace grabbed a camera and Marcus took out his notebook and together they documented all they saw; including the isolation of the property. It took fifteen minutes before they walked around the back and saw it. Parked under a tree was a metallic blue Volvo 4X4 with Perth plates.

"John, can you run some plates for me?" Grace asked over the phone. "It's victim number one's car" Grace told Marcus.

"Get the team out here." Grace relayed the message to Constable Addams. "What about Lieb?"

"I'll ring him" which Marcus did.

Once they were assured the team was on its way, Marcus and Grace continued their documentation by photo and pen.

"Inside or out?" Grace asked.

"Let's keep working out here, and then we'll start inside." Marcus directed.

"Onto the workshop then" Grace said. And they walked over to where they could see a door standing ajar.

And there is was. A blue barrel! They were still documenting the findings of the large workshop when they heard the sound of vehicles approaching. Marcus walked out to meet Constable Addams.

"Well timed John."

"Was it him?"

"We'll have to wait for all the evidence to make sure he wasn't just an accomplice; but yes, it's most likely. There's even another barrel." Marcus shared.

"So, after you get the vehicle on its way, can you get another vehicle down here to take the barrel for Lieb?"

For the next two hours, the team worked tirelessly: taking samples, organising the barrel for transport and even spreading themselves around the parish to speak with people who knew the Neill's and could give statements.

Chapter 12

SI Adam McAdam called into the Procurator Fiscal's office for an update meeting with Lieb. Marianne met him at the front desk and showed him through to the biochem lab where Lieb was waiting for him.

"Hi Adam, I thought it would be helpful if you could hear firsthand the explanation of the drug we've identified in our blue yacht tattoo victim. So let me introduce you to Stanley; he's the clever one who's worked out this Lead and he's the one you should direct all questions too." Lieb made a gesture to Stanley to take the conversation.

"We found a stimulant in the tox screen" he started. "Now when a person uses a stimulant or 'upper,' the drug stimulates the user's central nervous system and by doing so, causes the brain to produce a higher level of dopamine, which is what produces the sense of euphoria and well-being that is commonly known as the 'high.' The chemical signature of this stimulant is marketed as Modafinil which enables the user to stay awake and alert for 40 hours or more."

"But we didn't find results consistent with a typical stimulant usage. Yes, the dopamine levels were exceptionally high like we'd see in a high dose short acting upper but there was something more, benzamidenafil which was sold and recalled as a natural herbal supplement for the enhancement of sexual function."

Seeing the 'so what' look from both in his audience, Stanley continued "Together they would have produced a perfect storm whereby the victim could not find unconsciousness for escape as well as the pathophysiology to enable sexual intercourse to be maintained – for hours."

Adam just stared, stunned as the information seeped into the very marrow of his bones and burned terrible images into his permanent memory. He looked at Stanley, then at Lieb but he couldn't find voice to ask a question: did he really want to know more?

Lieb looked as shattered as Adam felt. Stanley broke the strained silence and quietly said "I have a potential lead for you." They broke the gaze they had locked onto each other and as one they looked at Stanley. It was as if Adam and Lieb were mentally sparring for the right to have the only life-preserver and then Stanley offered a second one and the chance they might both survive; they held their breath and waited.

"The military is interested in modafinil as a drug to maintain combat alertness" Stanley offered. And, benzamidenafil was marketed as Stamina-Rx and since its recall, can only be procured from Asia and a dubious herbal pharmacy."

Adam clapped Stanley on the upper arm and said to the two of them "This is our little secret OK?" Both men nodded in agreement.

As Lieb led Adam from the chem. Lab toward his office, he told him about the other results. "We didn't get much useful info from the DNA results. They used a chlorine based wash internally before they left. What sperm wasn't destroyed by the body's septic response was wiped out by the wash; and then of course the abdominal heat."

"Did the foetus boil?" SI McAdam asked.

"Yes, so DNA will have a go but that takes time and the sample has been compromised."

They arrive in Lieb's office and Lieb closed the door: this was unusual but necessary. All Lieb's staff knew his open-door policy; if the door was open anyone may enter regardless of who was inside. However, if the door was closed, it was a clear signal 'not to be disturbed'. Lieb and Adam did not want this conversation overheard.

"Any news on the tattoo?" Lieb asked.

"Still tracking it down. You'd never believe how many tattooists there are in Scotland alone."

"Does Stanley's information help with a lead?" Lieb enquired.

"Absolutely. But I'll need to let Mac know so he can open channels to the military in case we need to question members of the forces."

"I'll do the same with the Crown Couple."

Adam nodded and climbed out of the chair; he looked at Lieb and asked "Are you referring your key staff for counselling after this case?"

"Stanley has a scientific mind and isn't privy to the autopsy file so he should be OK. Leon who you met at the scene won't know of Stanley's information, but I will send him for an assessment in case he needs some follow-up" Lieb replied.

"And what about you?" Adam asked.

"Like yourself, catching these monsters before they think to strike again will keep my demons at bay for a while. But I am smart enough to know that the nightmares only stay away once you've given them voice in the clean light of day and learnt to lock them away. But there'll be time for that after."

Adam nodded in agreement and walked through the office door. Lieb escorted him to the reception desk where he found Marianne speaking with Fiona.

"Marianne, if you're heading out for lunch, can you bring me back a coffee and subway please"

"Sure Lieb" she replied.

Back in his office Lieb spoke with Suzanne and James and briefed them on the case findings. He then busied himself until Marianne brought him his lunch and he ate it for no reason other than he had eaten little in the last twenty four hours and he needed to keep working efficiently through this caseload or someone else would need to take over.

The blue yacht tattoo case did not need another victim.

At some point the phone rang "Hi Lieb, busy?" It was Marcus.

"Not anything special presently; my other case is still waiting identification and the labs aren't proving helpful."

"Have you spoken with Rose?"

"I was just doing that when you rang. I found her phone charger by the bed last night so her mobile's probably flat. I just tried the landline but it was awful. Heather said Rose wasn't there and then other stuff I couldn't make out. Rose had said there was trouble with the line."

"We've hit pay dirt here. Are you able to join us?"

"Where are you?" Lieb enquired.

"Tibbermore, just west of Perth. You need to bring the team." Lieb noted the excitement in Marcus' voice and smiled to himself. He remembered how despondent Marc had got when the case had gone cold previously.

"OK" replied Lieb. "Text me the address and we'll leave immediately. Do I need a body extraction team?"

"No just all the techies please."

Lieb placed the 'attendance call' to Marianne who collated the requirements and placed the call to staff through the pager system. Members from each specialty worked on a field roster and carried a pager that alerted them to a call-out and gave them the address. They always kept the field kits ready and there were a number of vehicles they used; the page showed them who was called and between them they worked out the vehicle assignments and arrived as required. It worked well and Lieb never had a need to ask where an expert was once they were on site.

As he walked himself to his vehicle, Lieb stuck his head through Marianne's door and thanked her for lunch and the page-out. "It's Perth, so I don't guess I'll be back before you leave. Have a great evening." Marianne responded by gifting him with one of her smiles: Lieb was sure the world was a better place for having Marianne in it.

Once he was mobile he placed a courtesy call to Adam "Marcus has a conclusion in the body in barrels case, so I'm heading to Perth. I'm on my phone if you need anything." And Lieb signed off.

Chapter 13

Marcus and Grace continued their methodical and comprehensive review of the property. They had a back-porch area to examine and document, calling instructions to the team taking samples and bagging & collating evidence.

The two teams worked harmoniously together; each respecting the other's expertise and each knowing their colleagues from the other office wanted the same outcome as they did.

This was a big case; a career spotlight. No-one wanted to screw it up for themselves; no-one wanted to be the source that let a conviction fail.

After the back porch had yielded up some unlikely items for a young adult male but likely for a female, and most likely discarded personal items from female victims, the pace remained methodical and thorough.

Once inside from the back porch, the next room was the kitchen. Here all knives were inspected, tested and bagged but nothing else raised red flags. Photos and notes taken they moved into the living area.

Here they found the remains of the disorganised life of a single uncaring man; and a man in poor health to boot. And here they found a hunting knife, one which was 3cm wide, with double-sided bevelled cutting edges. And it tested positive for blood.

Lieb nodded affirmatively at Marcus.

Across from the living room and at the front of the house was a large bedroom that looked at if it hadn't been entered for a decade.

"Mrs Neill's room?" Grace postulated. Marcus nodded but entered anyway. He wasn't about to miss anything or provide any doubt because he hadn't been thorough. This room was photographed and documented as well as the other rooms and outside.

The next rooms down the hallway, and in between the two bedrooms, were the bathroom and toilet. These both looked like the living room and showed the evidence of his poor health and uncaring nature. Again, the rooms were photographed, inspected and documented.

The final room was another bedroom, evidenced as Arthur Ronald Neill's room by the old framed cross-stitch hanging on the wall above the bed. Like the mother's bedroom there was little evidence of the Neill lad being a mass murderer. There were some old clothes about and some may have had blood washed off them, by Neill had been poorly with lung cancer, so there was a possible explanation.

And then Marcus hit gold; sitting on the bedside table was a notebook. When Marcus picked it up and flipped to the first page his heart stopped momentarily, then started flapping around in his chest like a fish out of water.

Marcus sat heavily onto the bed and a cloud of dust rose around him. Grace looked over, concerned. "Are you OK?" she asked.

Marcus took a deep shuddering breath and raised a hand toward Grace trying to indicate she could stop worrying. Instead Grace called out to Lieb who was still in the bathroom examining the medications they had found.

Lieb appeared at the door "What's the problem?" he asked as Grace indicated toward Marcus.

Marcus coughed and raised his hand again in a stop sign. "I'm OK, but listen to this" and Marcus began to read.

5 August 2005 *It's all building up again. Just like when Pa killed my baby sister. The doctor had me write everything down then and it helped me gain control. Maybe it will work again – gotta try. It's all going to hell in a hand basket. So the girl's gone? good riddance. But did she have to sneak out whilst I was laying Mama in her grave?*
And now they done run over me dog. Towser didn't deserve that!
It's wrong WRONG WRONG!

28 August 05 *I feel awful! Been doing lots of drinking & smoking. Feel I have the right. Diary says it's been a 3 day bender.*

31 Aug 05 *Feel better now. The drink stopped helping so I took a walk, initially for just some smokes but I walked all the way to the farm shop. There was this girl. She was asking the storekeep for the directions to Madderty. When I got outside she was sitting in her car swearing about the phone reception. Acting all self righteous because she was important and the phone should work*
It all became so clear. I climbed into the passenger seat behind her, held a knife to her throat and told her to drive. She cried the whole time, sort of a moaning sobbing sort of noise. Real pathetic. That's what it was all about, my whole life. A pathetic baby sister who whined all the time so Pa lost concentration on the road and smashed into that tree. He never made it to my rugby match.
Then Mama, always begging me to do for her, comfort her cos she'd lost so much. That cloying bitch who said she loved me, wanted to care for me and then snuck off at the first opportunity.
And that snivelling bitch who killed my dog Towser.
Enough was enough!

We drove into Westmuir Wood. We followed the Ranger's road a ways and then turned off down a track I had found, that ended near this tiny loch. I used to bring my girl here for some quiet time in nature.

I used the knife to make her get out of the car. Her sobbing became a begging whine but I threatened her with the knife and she moved wherever I wanted. All I had to do was push the knife at her and she moved.

Suddenly she was backed against a tree and I pushed the knife again. It went into her and kept going. What a rush I got. Then she was screaming. I pulled the knife out but she kept screaming and fell to the ground. So I hit her with the knife over and over again until she shut up and lay still.

There was blood everywhere. I rubbed it between my fingers. It was warm and thick and smelly and didn't feel as thrilling as when the knife went in. I pushed the knife into her belly again but it didn't feel the same so I stopped.

She was bleeding everywhere, making a mess of my special spot of nature so I opened her car boot and picked her up and dumped her in there. Then I went to the loch and used an old takeaway drink container to ferry water to the spot she spoiled until I'd washed it clean. The little midge insects liked the smell and taste of her blood and were all over me so I sat at the edge of the loch and washed it all off.

Then I drove her care home. Tibbermore where I live is such a small village no-one noticed when I drove through it and up the lane to our small farmhouse. I parked the car out back under the oak tree. No-one can see it from the road and no-one comes visiting so that'll be OK.

1 Sept 05 *I woke feeling alive. I had the most amazing memory of yesterday and went to check the backyard. Sure enough the car was still there and yep, she was still in the boot.*

2 Sept 05 *In the village this morning to collect my mail and some smokes. A Copper called in to put a poster up in the window of a missing girl. She's not missing to me. I know where she is.*

3 Sept 05 *Been thinking about the girl. Guess it's not a good idea to have her at my place. It would be good if I could enjoy that rush all over again and there's no room for 2 in that boot.*

I have a disposal plan. There's those barrels out in the shed Mama kept vinegar in for pickling her onions. I could use one of those.

4 Sept 05 *Perfect end to a long day. I spent all yesterday emptying the barrel out and filling it with her. Then I remembered how a body fills up with gas. Her body exploding may pop the lid so I went back and welded it shut. Did some of my finest work right then.*

Then I loaded the barrel onto the back of the utility and covered it with a tarpaulin.

I drove until it started getting dark. I was at Crieff by then and saw a sold sign on a warehouse so I left them a little bonus.

And to top the day off, there's a young fella on the side of the road thumbing. He was most eager to get to Perth so I drove him all the way. Little shit stole my cigarettes when I stopped for petrol. So he felt my knife too, right into the chest. He was making this gagging noise so I stopped by the side of the road and hauled him out of the cab and into the utility tray. Then I drove home and cleaned my car.

6 Sept 05 *That young lad is attracting flies so I've put him into a barrel too.*
Was going to put him with the girl but decided to not been seen in the area.

16 Dec 05 *Saw a flyer in the post office for the Hogmany Parade in Newburgh. Seemed like an ideal place to leave a barrel.*
As it turned out other people had the same idea. When I got there I saw twelve other barrels left in the rear courtyard of this antiques dealer. So I put mine with them.
Then I had fish n chips for dinner but they weren't so good cos I stopped just out of Perth and threw up.
Got an early Xmas present though. A young lass saw me being sick and came to offer her help. Said she knew about drugs and health and things. Well she offered to drive me to the hospital.
How can someone turn down a gift like that. As soon as we left the petrol station I used my knife to convince her to keep driving.
It was dark by the time we got to my special wood so I kept her in the headlights of the car.
It felt even better then I remembered. I slid the knife into her belly and just held it there.
She didn't scream like the first one. She just looked at the knife and then at me and started to shake.
I pulled the knife out and pushed it into her belly again in a different place. Man it was so amazing and I was so excited.
Then she spoiled it and started to scream. Well cough and scream at the same time. Strange noise but too loud and it spoiled the moment.
So I pulled the knife out and stuck her with again and again until she stopped.
Then I put her into the tray of the utility and drove home.

19 Dec 05 *She's welded into her barrel. I need somewhere to leave her but later. I'm not feeling so good. I think that fish n chips is still poisoning me.*

16 Apr 06 *It's Easter Saturday.*
Police have been doing door to door searches cos they found the barrel at Crieff. Don't suppose it's a good idea to have that barrel in my shed. Time for a drive.
Headed up the A9 cos there's an old railway yard at Byres Wood.

Stopped for lunch at Bankfoot and when I drove passed the old distillery there's a flatbed truck loaded and ready to go. Only took me a couple of minutes to add mine to the load. Ha I even used his own trolley to load the barrel up the ramp. Left the truck just like i found it; he'll never know there's a ringer

5 May 06 — *Been in the hospital. Got smashed up coming back along the A9 after leaving the barrel on the distillery truck.*
Got a concussion, some broken ribs and a diagnosis I wasn't expecting. Lung cancer.
Gonna sue that lousy bitch who smashed me into the guardrail cos I reckon it was the broken ribs that caused the cancer.

12 June 06 — *Been getting radiotherapy to shrink the cancer. Seems to be working.*
And leaving the hospital I just happened upon a young nursie who's going to make me feel a whole lot better.
Visited the special nature spot and wow what a thrill.
I'd been looking at the anatomy books whilst I was in getting treatment and I figured out how to get the most from my time.
First a quick stab to the throat so she couldn't scream and spoil it.
Then the first thrust into the left lower quadrant. The knife went in smooth and deep. She groaned and slid to her knees.
As the pleasure slowed I put my hand on her head and pinned it against the tree and then pulled out the knife and then thrust it into the right side of her belly. Oh heaven, such joy. Her blood was dripping off her throat and onto my hand as it held the knife and I could feel her life ending so I pulled out and thrust one more time.
She collapsed from her knees o the ground and dragged my knife out before I was finished. How dare she!!
I struck her around the chest and neck lots until I was exhausted and coughing.
Damn. She's started my cancer again.

25 Dec 06 — *I made Xmas. Ho Ho to me!*

8 April 07 — *What a glorious Easter.*
I've been to stay with my cousin in Forfar. I think she felt sorry for me. It's just Agnes and three cats but it was nice to have someone make my tea for me for a change.
She got a call from her sister whose husband had taken ill and she need Agnes to stay over for a few days. I promised to stay on and mind the cats. She was going to be back Sunday.
Saturday night I drove out of town to eat at a small restaurant on the A90. It was quiet / not many people in that night.
And as I was leaving there was a woman inflating the tyres of her car.
It had been so long since I had felt that rush but I have been poorly so it wasn't as easy. Still I had a new zapper device that should help.

I pulled into the bay alongside her and walked around my car as if I was waiting for the airhose. Whilst she was knelt down on the ground I zapped her. It worked so well. I simply opened my passenger door and shoved her in.

Then I drove home. The cats would be OK until Agnes arrived tomorrow.

I kept her tied up and gagged in the car until first light and then I drove to my spot. She gave me some trouble then.

I dragged her out of the car and cut her ties free. She fought me and I cut her about the hands and arms pretty bad as she kept trying to grab the knife.

Finally she stopped fighting me and backed away. But my faithful tree was waiting so I got a good stab into the belly. Then she was on the ground and screaming so I stabbed her in the neck but she wouldn't let me at her stomach and she grabbed the knife again so I just finished her of.

April 30 07 *She's in her barrel and in the well at the church at Newbigging.*

She was not so much fun. She fought too much and spoiled it!

Sep 2 07 *Been in for more cancer treatment.*

They say my time in short. Really want to go out on a high.

Sep 30 07 *She just walked up to my house. Said she was looking for a place to hide cos her fella was mean.*

I showed her the shed. She turned to say something and I slid the knife into her belly. It was wonderful.

When I pulled it out and picked a second spot she started to scream and fight me. There was lots of blood. It was just like the last time. She was waving her arms to strike me and blood was flying everywhere. I stabbed at her throat and chest until she stopped hitting me. As I saw her loose the fight I slipped the knife back into her belly wound again and thrust a couple of times until she was dead.

1 Nov 07 *I woke in the shed on top of her.*

My chest and head hurts.

I emptied another barrel of vinegar onto her so her blood washed away and she reeked like a drunk.

I felt too weak to lift her so I lay the empty barrel beside her and pushed her into it. Then I used the winch to lift her upright and I welded the barrel shut.

I'm too tired and I don't feel well. She can stay there for now.

By the time Marcus had finished reading there was a silent audience crowded at the door.

Marcus stood up and took control. "John, call the vehicle impound yard and get them to have the team work on the boot for signs the victim had been bleeding inside. Can one from each team pair up and investigate Westmuir Wood. Jack, can you take Paul and check out the farm shop and then join the pair at Westmuir Wood. And then John, can you organise two constables from HQ to investigate the other scenes and see what they can learn."

"OK teams, we may not have anyone to arrest over this, but we can bring closure and comfort to the families. Let's not drop our standards now."

As Marcus watch the members of the team go about their final jobs he stopped to say to Grace and Lieb "well this one's over except for the paperwork. How often does it end like this heh?"

Chapter 14

Lieb Marcus and Grace stopped in Perth for Indian before making their way home.

Over a meal of tandoori and shiraz they chatted and celebrated and made plans for doing it again soon.

Marcus lived in Barnhill, 9 km north of Dundee and Tayside Police Department. He had a secured a detached house converted from a former mill building at the end of a quiet street. There was a large communal garden which gave the feeling of countryside without being isolated. In addition, was a small garden and outdoor living area off from the conservatory which he had successfully covered in birdcage fencing, so Ophelia and Fuzzbutt could be allowed out into the garden without being able to wander off.

Grace lived in Dundee proper: in a top floor 2 bedroom flat located in the well sought Lochee area of town. The property was within a secure entry tenement block which gave her the security her job made her feel she needed, and had the luxuries of double glazing and electric heating, so when she needed 'me time' she didn't need to go out to find it.

Marcus pulled up outside her flat and she invited him for a coffee; it was an offer he didn't refuse. Upstairs she gave him a quick introduction to the floorplan which ended in the kitchen. She set coffee going in the machine and he hovered close. Pretending not to notice Marcus' interest, Grace chatted as she headed for the bedroom "I need to shower before I can relax."

Marcus followed and stood in the door way, leaning comfortably on the door frame, watching her strip off her uniform, pin her hair atop her head, drop her bra and then slip out of her panties. Marcus liked what he saw and Grace took pleasure in his long lingering look.

Then Grace turned and walked through to the bathroom and started the shower. She had barely managed to soap her body when a naked Marcus joined her in the shower.

He stepped up behind her and used his strong hands to massage her neck and shoulder muscles, then he ran the massage over her buttocks and reached around to carrying the massage over her upper thighs and up across her breasts. Grace groaned and leaned into him. Marcus rolled her nipples in his fingers, gently tugging them as he started nibbling on her neck. Grace reached behind her and ran her hands over Marcus' thighs, sliding her hands up so her thumbs could lightly stroke his testicles. Now it was Marcus' turn to moan.

He reached down and grabbed Grace inside her upper thighs and let his thumbs tease Grace's fanny so that her response was to widen her stance and allow him more access. Marcus bent at the knees and lifted Grace onto his erection. They danced in the confines of the shower, Grace gyrating her hips and Marcus controlling her actions so they could both take delight in the moment.

Panting, Grace asked him to take her to the bed; he thought he would explode if he had to uncouple but he succeeded and when she turned he wasted no time in hooking his hands under her buttocks and lifting her back onto his erection.

He carried her to the bed this way and continued their lovemaking without interruption. Their passion was insatiable with a number of uncouplings and position changes until both of them were spent.

They lay together afterwards, comfortable in their nudity and closeness, and talked, both of them most appreciative of their passionate compatibility. The conversation came around to more mundane items and Grace asked "would you like to stay tonight?"

"And have more of this – most definitely, however.."

"You have another girl waiting?"

"Two actually. Ophelia and Fuzzbutt will be wanting food and play themselves. Besides, I'll need a clean uniform for tomorrow; Mac's bound to have a press conference and we'll be expected to appear."

"So that coffee would be good" Marcus concluded and grinned at her.

Grace climbed from the bed, slipped on a robe and went to pour coffee whilst Marcus got dressed.

Whilst Grace and Marcus showered together, Lieb showered alone. He checked for a message from Rose when he got home but there wasn't one: Hmm he wondered. But he was tired and trying hard not to ruminate on the case info he'd heard today, especially the bit about the drug cocktail and what that meant. He managed to sleep but it was fitful at times so the morning delivered him from bad dreams but left him feeling sluggish and restless.

Lieb received a phone call from Marcus as he drove into the office "Can we meet? I've got coffee and pastries?" Marc enquired. Lieb could clearly hear the tone in his voice and asked him what it was about. Marcus was excited and reluctant all rolled together, like a child who'd discovered mum and dad's hiding spot for their Xmas gifts.

And by the time Lieb walked into the reception area, Marcus was already waiting. Lieb grinned at him and shook his head; it looked like mum had bought him a new bike.

When they got to his desk Marcus started talking; it was fast and his encounter with Grace gushed out of him like pressurised water from a broken pipe. Lieb let his friend expend his news and stop to breathe.

"So, it was a good day yesterday heh?"

"Amazing, it was amazing." Marcus stopped when Leon stepped into the office to give Lieb a briefing on what had occurred overnight. "Looks like we have work my friend. Let's take this up later shall we?"

Lieb and Marcus stood, Marcus to head downtown to see Mac, and Lieb to visit the labs and prioritise the morning's work.

Not ten minutes later Marianne text Lieb and said he 'needed to meet Adam in his office – closed door.'

Intrigued, Lieb walked back to his office and saw Adam looking even worse than when they'd spoken yesterday. Then Lieb saw Marcus and he looked like Adam..."what the???" he asked himself out loud.

Adam ushered Lieb into the office and closed the door. Looking back into the corridor Lieb could see Marianne hovering and turning people away; giving them some privacy. Lieb looked enquiringly at Adam, then Lieb.

"Lieb, there's been a break in the blue yacht tattoo case" Adam started but his voice broke and he stuttered to a halt. Adam looked at Marcus beseechingly and Marcus audibly groaned. "Lieb" Marcus said, all the earlier joyousness absent "It was Rose."

"Sorry?" Lieb asked.

"It was Rose" Marcus repeated.

"But it can't be, she was.." and the enormity of the realisation made Lieb choke. His reality broke and his senses reeled. He felt Marcus grab him by the shoulders and push him into a seat.

Then there was noise, people moving about, coming and going, a sharp pain and nothingness.

When Lieb awoke he thought about the dreams; they had seemed so real and were obviously emotionally charged because he felt sluggish and dull. He tried to sit up and swing his legs over the bed, but Marcus stopped him.

"What" he croaked so Marcus handed him a glass of water. He was amazed to see his hands shaking, so violently much of the water splashed over him. He drank what was left and looked at Marcus and tried to gather his thoughts but his information processing remained dulled.

Marcus' face showed signs of great strain and lack of sleep. Along with the other emotions on Marcus' face Lieb clearly saw concern. Marcus started talking "You've had a great shock; we've all had a great shock, but it's obviously worse for you. You're in hospital, you've been sedated, you, you need to rest."

Marcus' words came out in short sharp sentences, a staccato of information about how they had confirmed it was Rose, how they had informed Heather, how Mac had given the case a familial priority which was usually issued for a cop killing and which meant priority and whatever resources needed to be brought to bear.

Lieb listened and absorbed the information and when Marcus stopped for a breath, a slow shuddering inhalation, Lieb said "Take me home."

Marcus started to protest but Lieb stood up from the bed and looked at him with steely cold eyes, so Marcus found his clothes.

Lieb dressed into his clothes and into a suit of armour that blocked all efforts of emotions to either penetrate or escape.

That was Thursday: They buried Rose in Aberdeen the following Tuesday, near her sister. On the days in between Lieb wouldn't answer the phone except the first one from Adam who rang to say the investigations were ongoing but the progress was slow.

When Heather despaired at his resistance to answer the phone, she texted the funeral arrangements.

And Marcus tried everything he could think of; he even spent a night in his vehicle at Lieb's front door, but Lieb didn't respond.

And so, on that Tuesday morning, at the graveside, they hesitated to make eye contact, except for Marcus who stood in front of him as he exited his vehicle. Lieb stopped and looked deep into Marcus' eyes, a cold penetrating gaze that didn't flinch – but Marcus' did. "Lieb I know this has rocked you to your very core, but you don't have to suffer this alone" Marcus tried.

Lieb just stood there.

"I'm missing something aren't I?" Marcus enquired. Lieb just stood there, but for just a fraction of a moment his anguish flared in his eyes; a sudden dilation of his pupils. Marcus was a damn good copper and a really good friend; he saw it.

"Tell me. Let me in and I'll help carry the burden" Marcus implored. And for the first time in a week Lieb spoke.

"One day." And then Lieb walked to the waiting party and stood apart at the side of Rose's grave. As the ceremony dragged on, Lieb examined the faces of the people arrayed in front of him. Whenever anyone looked up under the scrutiny of his gaze he let his eyes bore into the soul of that person, searching. He felt he was standing at a precipice more than at his wife's gravesite and he wondered if he could ever avoid falling.

After the ceremony, the mourners gravitated to Heather to comfort her and hope for consolation of their own. Anyone who intended to speak with Lieb had no opportunity as he hurried back to his vehicle and drove away.

And whilst they gathered at Heather's home to share their grief and find comfort, Lieb arrived at Arbroath harbour and took his yacht out.

The ebb had already set in so he got underway as fast as he could, sorting out and hoisting the sails once clear of the shore. In the light wind, he was six knots over the ground so Lieb allowed the boat to wander. Bell Rock Lighthouse charged towards him; its` fresh white paint gleaming in the bright midday sunlight. Passing just inside it at, he hauled the sheets for the fastest sailing of the day. So distracted was Lieb, he wandered a little too close inshore and suddenly realised the marker buoy was way out to port. He hardened the sheets further and realised that the wind was rising fast. In fact the wind seemed to funnel off the land with sheets of spray coming back to the cockpit. Wisps of cloud gathered over the shore he lost the sun for an hour or so.

A long swell was coming in from the southwest and wave crests were galloping toward him like white horses. The wind shrieked through the halyard and for a time Lieb shrieked back, howling his pain into the elements.

The squall subsided as suddenly as it had arose and Lieb's emotions lay spent on the floor along with the salt spray. A long inshore tack brought him to the backdoor of Arbroath; a few more tacks and he was in line with the buoy at the western end of the channel.

Back home he showered and dressed warmly but little seemed to ease the chill in his marrow. Once again, he ignored the phone calls but he did respond to a text from Marcus 'I'm here when you want me' to which Lieb simply replied 'thank you'. This was not of Marcus' doing and Lieb realised there may come a point where he would need a friend.

The next morning Lieb was in his office at 06:30: and he closed the door. He checked messages and deleted all the well wishes without playing more than the first few words; when he discerned the tone and content he hit delete.

He checked the case sheets and sent text messages asking for detailed updates to many staff members: by 07:20 he had cleared out his email inbox, requested twenty-three updates from seven staff on eleven cases, read and signed three reports for the Crown Couple, approved two applications for leave and rejected five.

The door opened and James appeared. Lieb stood when his boss walked through the door; he hadn't forgotten his manners.

"You don't need to be here" James started. "Why don't you take some time off?"

Lieb looked at James, looked deep into his eyes with that new steel intensity he had donned as part of his armour and replied, "I've just been off for a week."

James looked into those eyes; he didn't see pain, he didn't see torment, he didn't even see a demented desire for revenge. All James could see was a steely resolve; it chilled him to his core. "All right, but if you change your mind, let me know."

James left and Lieb got on.

Episode 2

The Iceman

Chapter 15

The late August morning glow was a promise of another glorious day and it matched Marcus' mood perfectly. Ophelia and Fuzzbutt had greeted him enthusiastically and Marcus had stroked them affectionately, using the time to reflect on his change in lifestyle and the font of utter joy that had found a home deep in his belly. The font fed him a constant stream of glee, an enthusiasm for life that at times tempted to overwhelm him. If anyone had suggested he would find this passion even six months ago he would have laughed at them. But in his bed right now slumbered a goddess: Grace had changed his world, spun it like a top and it consumed him.

Marcus thought back over his life and bemusedly asked himself how the path had taken such a dramatic turn. He was the middle of three boys; four if you counted 'Guy' and his sister always insisted you should. She could wrestle any boy who claimed she wasn't tough enough and once split Cavvy's lip for suggesting she ran like a girl.

George was Marcus' baby brother and the one he was closest to; Arthur the eldest, and somehow his mum had managed to squeeze the three of them out in twenty five months. Then there was Casey, who got the nickname Guy when she insisted, hands on hip, she was as much a guy as any of them. And after a few wrestling matches to prove it, she was begrudgingly allowed to hang around. Then after splitting Cavvy's lip, no-one made comment again.

And hang around they did; they walked to and from school together, ate lunch together, shared birthdays and summer holidays. They even shared tragedy and trauma together: like when Bernard's dad was killed at the rail yard on the docks and his devastated mother took the children south to Devon. Or when Cavvy fell from the top bunk of the bed he shared with his brother and broke his arm. He was a hero in his plaster cast at first, but no-one offered to sit on the bank with him whilst everyone else swam that hot summer away.

Casey was south now; in Essex working as a paramedic from Southend station. She always sent gifts at birthdays and Xmas but it had been an age since he'd actually sat down for a conversation with her.

George was a very successful carpenter living in a loft conversion on the banks of the river Clyde in Glasgow; his workshop and display centre taking up the ground floor. His success never amazed Marcus as he'd shown lots of early talent; he'd even built their clubhouse when he was barely nine-year-old. Now he was twenty-nine, married to Elena and with two daughters Helen and Margaret.

George and Marcus made a point of catching up at least three times each year: both birthdays and Xmas. Usually Marcus drove to Glasgow as there was then only one to uproot: plus it meant Marcus wasn't close enough to call back from leave if the fancy took Detective Superintendent Declan Macdonald.

Arthur had immigrated to Australia; to Perth in Western Australia actually. It was a standing joke that they were both in Perthshire, just 14,675 kilometres apart.

Marcus wondered how he could get Grace to meet them all.

He placed a bowl of food down for the girls, as the coffee finished brewing; Marcus carried two mugs to the bedroom. The sun had crept in and was spilling over the bed, basking Grace in its soft glow. She lay naked, stretched out before him with a cotton sheet tumbled over her hips and lower legs. Marcus gazed at the Athena on the bed: she wasn't reed thin or waif-like, there was a substance about her. But whilst she was shapely, it was sculptured; full round breasts, strong and long shapely legs, full hips but with a cinched waist that gave her a true hour-glass figure.

Marcus felt the passion within him build as he drank in her loveliness and his erection stretched his shorts. He placed the mugs of coffee on the dresser and bent over and began nibbling affectionately on the cleft of Graces' neck; she moaned softly. Marcus continued nibbling affectionately as he drifted his lips down to Graces' nipple and here his lips tugged and sucked ever so gently. Grace responded, her moans increasing and her hips slowly rising and falling in rhythm to Marcus' rhythm on her nipple.

Marcus let go of her nipple and skipped kisses across the skin of her belly, his nose connecting with the line of sheeting. He continued his trajectory south pushing the sheet before him. Grace started panting and rolled onto her back, letting her upper leg fall from the hip onto the bed, exposing her womanhood. Marcus accepted the invitation and skipped his lips onto her labia, his nose parting the labial folds and exposing her clitoris. He used his tongue to lick her labia in a soft stroking fashion; Graces' moans became sonorous and she arched her back and rolled her pelvis as if the tongue had her tied to it. Marcus shifted his attention to her clitoris and started sucking; Grace writhed underneath him, her hands clenching the sheet as she tried desperately to not lose the connection. Marcus continued to suck and tease until Grace was grunting and writhing as if gripped by a grand mal seizure; then he released her clitoris and plunged his tongue into her vagina, flicking rhythmically until she climaxed and sprayed him with her juices.

Marcus walked around the bed pulling his shorts off as he went; his erection was huge and his desire humungous. He climbed onto the bed and rolled Grace onto her belly then slipped an arm around her waist, hauling her onto her knees but with her head and shoulders draped on the bed. He dragged her fanny onto his erection and taking hold of her hips in his bear-like hands he pumped her hard and rhythmically until they both climaxed; Marcus managing to maintain his control until Grace lost hers – again.

Spent, Marcus flopped onto the bed still holding Grace around her middle, and pulling her close into him they lay there spooning whilst their pulses settled and their hearts stopped hammering. Marcus felt overjoyed and overwhelmed. That font of joy bubbled over and he found himself pondering how addicted he'd become to having Grace in his life. He realised he couldn't imagine life without her in it; that his soul was inextricably entwined in hers and efforts to separate their souls would not only be extremely painful, it would probably kill him. He had to tell her so.

He nibbled Grace's ear to make sure she was listening and he said softly but clearly "I love you Grace".

Grace held herself still for perhaps four seconds, and then she shifted, turning her upper body enough so she could look at Marcus. For another long pause she looked deep into his face, swam in the depth of his gaze and then she smiled that huge happy dog smile she kept for special occasions and said "why detective Marcus sir, I do believe I love you too."

Marcus scooped her into his embrace and they sealed their declarations with a deep passionate kiss.

Ophelia called loudly from the doorway and Fuzzbutt bounded onto the bed. Marcus laughed "it seems the girls feel the same."

They rolled apart and sat propped in the bed drinking the cooling coffee and discussing what their revelations would change in their life.

"Well it seems a shame to lose the apartment in Dundee; it's close to work so it makes a great crash when we've only got a couple of hours to take a break. But the girls can't go there." Grace said.

"Agreed, so how about for now we keep both? If one of us needs a short stay we'll stop there and if we have a nearly full day we'll come back here?"

"Sounds like a plan". Grace paused thoughtfully, then added "There is one other item to consider - working together. I have that appointment this afternoon with Mac to see about my moving into the Major Crime Support Division and continuing my education as a detective. I guess there's a rule about partners being bed-buddies"? Grace enquired.

Marcus groaned. Grace was right but he hated the idea they'd be working separate cases which could keep them apart for days at a time. "We could try to deny it but I don't know if I can keep my eyes off you in the squad-room."

"Best I let him in on the news then, if he offers me a posting. I'm never really sure about Mac."

Their life sorted for now Grace finished her coffee and climbed from the bed. Bundling her hair on top of her head she walked toward the bathroom, tossing back over her shoulder "it's not often we're given the morning off so let's not waste it. How about you organise some scrambled eggs whilst I shower and then we can go for a hike?"

"Only if you're certain I can't talk you back to bed?" Marcus replied.

Grace started the shower then stuck her head back out the door "if you're a good lad and we have time left over after our hike, well just maybe."

Marcus bounded from the bed and found his shorts. "Yes ma'am" he tossed back as he scampered from the bedroom and headed for the kitchen. They had been presenting the evidence of the 'bodies in the barrels' case to three judges late last week. The new Lieb's sullen disposition made his testimony clipped and curt and the judges often found they needed to prompt him to explain further. This has meant the two days allocated was insufficient and the hearing spilled into Saturday. There may not have been a person to prosecute but the three judges wanted to ensure all the evidence was heard and a verdict could be recorded.

Mac had given them Monday morning off in lieu of the Saturday court work. Coupled with a rostered Sunday off they had cobbled together a sinful forty nine hours; and hadn't wasted a minute.

Marcus whisked farm-fresh eggs with chives he snipped from the garden pot outside the back door. He then tossed in some strong cheddar and listened for the shower to switch off; pushing the slide down on the toaster and gently firing the gas under the eggs. Perfectly timed the toast popped as the eggs began to thicken, so Marcus switched off the eggs and left them to finish cooking in their own heat as he buttered the toast. Grace entered the kitchen just as Marcus was serving, so she grabbed the flatware, set the table and sat.

There was a quiet comfort as they ate, each exploring their own emotions and thoughts. Ten minutes later as they finished eating, both were smiling and exuding an air of contentment.

"Back to bed?" Marcus enquired.

Grace slapped him with her napkin "No, I need to run to keep my figure. And if you keep feeding me like this, I'm going to have to increase my distance from five k to ten or I won't fit through the door" Grace responded.

They dumped their dishes into the sink and exited the kitchen through the conservatory and into the domain of Ophelia and Fuzzbutt. This was the enclosed garden Marcus had covered in birdcage fencing, so Ophelia and Fuzzbutt could be allowed out into the garden without being able to wander off. They stopped at the large tree that was positioned at the rear of the enclosed garden and stretched their muscles, then opened the door of the garden shed and slipped inside, making sure the girls didn't follow: but they were already ensconced in their favourite nooks, curled up in the sunshine. A second exit allowed Marcus and Grace out into the common wooded area where they took off running at a pace.

But it was only two kilometres in when Grace called a stop.

"Are you OK?" Marcus enquired.

"Yes, but I want to talk, not run. Can we walk back?"

"Sure" Marcus replied somewhat hesitantly "Are you having second thoughts about us?"

Grace graced him with that throaty laugh "No silly, I just want to know everything about you." Grace slipped her hand inside his and turned Marcus toward home. "Tell me about your family and growing up in Glasgow and everything else about you."

"Everything?" Marcus enquired.

"Yes, even past girlfriends" Grace teased.

And together they wandered back to the house, growing evermore contented.

Chapter 16

Grace and Marcus had filled the rest of the morning looking at photos with Marcus drawing her into the family. Three knockabout lads from the northern parts of Glasgow, plus Guy: Da a rail yard worker and Mother a mum who worked 'school hours' at the market so she was always there at breakfast and when they got home.

Number 5 Abercrombie Street was gone now; the government had paid well for the tenements on either side of the road so they could expand the railway. With the money, his parents had bought further down Abercrombie Street; another terrace house but more modern, larger with three bedrooms, and on the end and a corner at that, so there was a yard. It had made the boys cocky with the neighbourhood kids, until they found Guy squaring up to take on a couple of lads who'd been making their feelings known about the boys loud crowing. One of the lads had knocked Guy down and the other was sitting on her back as the first one was making her "eat dirt like the rest of us". The brothers had got a real dose of humility that day.

Grace also learned Da had died at fifty seven from asbestos lung disease contracted in the rail yard. Mother had been devastated and Arthur had shouldered the responsibility for both the income and the parenting. And he'd done a fair job although it had cost him his chance of following his dream; to be an architect. Instead he'd got an apprenticeship in the government, working his way up from clerk to junior manager at twenty two. Between the small industrial payoff that paid Mother a small monthly wage and the fair wage Arthur got, Marcus and George finished high school and got to choose their career path. Guy got almost everything she wanted – none of them could say no to her.

And Arthur continued on, staying at home to look after Mother who eventually smoked herself to death at sixty two, ten years after her beloved. Marcus was fourteen when his Da died, twenty four when Mother had passed: Arthur was six weeks shy of his sixteenth birthday when Da died and he had to step up. At Twenty five when Mother passed he struggled to pick up the pieces of his lost youth. Eventually he took a six month break from his job and 'left to find himself'; and he had succeeded, coming home from Perth Australia with renewed vigour and a fiancé in tow.

After living in the family home for six months, including a Scottish Xmas, Arthur and Vivien decided Australia was their preference and with Marcus, George & Guy's blessing, he sold the family home.

"Now that's a story to tell" Marcus mused.

"Well go on, don't stop there."

"In the car, we're due on shift and you have that appointment with Mac."

And on the way to work Marcus explained: "we'd met at the pub without Arthur knowing, and I can't tell you who had started that particular ball rolling, but it was as if we'd all felt we needed to somehow say thank you to Arthur. So an easy agreement was reached; we'd accept the cheque Arthur wanted to present each of us, our share of the sale of the family home, and make plans for a wedding celebration even though they were planning to wed in Australia. And at that celebration we all, simultaneously handed Arthur back half of the value of our cheque."

"So effectively you only got $1/8^{th}$ of the property sale each and Arthur got $5/8^{th}$?"

"It was right: we all feel that way."

Grace squeezed his arm, acknowledging her understanding and her pride. "What an amazing family I have found."

"I hope you get to meet them all one day soon."

Marcus pulled into a parking bay in the basement area of the Tayside Police. When they reached the door to the inside lobby, Marcus reached around Grace and opened the door. Grace flashed him that enormous smile and they tumbled through the door together: and bumped into Detective Superintendent Elise Scott and two junior staffers. Elise, Graces' big sister made a very obvious appraisal of Marcus and Grace and said "professionalism please detectives; remember where you are."

"Yes Mam" Marcus responded and elbowed Grace who mumbled the same.

Elise nodded and smiled at Grace and walked on with her two charges.

"Should we go upstairs separately?" Grace asked, somewhat bemused by the restraints put on them.

"No, but it's best we don't hold hands."

By the time they had climbed to the first floor Grace was trembling, her palms sweaty. Marcus touched her on the arm and said "You'll be fine, just answer Mac honestly." Then he walked to his desk pointedly ignoring the looks Grace's presence had created.

Grace walked to Mac's office and knocked.

When Mac called her in she took a deep breath to calm her nerves, stood straighter and tucked a stray wisp of hair behind her ear. Marcus has already noticed this nervous habit of hers.

As she approached Mac's desk she found he was seated behind his desk reading a file of notes before him. Without looking up, he instructed her to sit: she complied.

After what seemed an age Mac raised his head and looked deep into her eyes: Grace found the scrutiny unnerving.

"That was an impressive report for the Barrels case"

"Thank you Sir" Grace responded.

"The three court judges have also written they were very satisfied by your thoroughness and focus under questioning."

Grace said nothing but allowed a small smile and gave Mac a nod to acknowledge she'd heard.

"I understand you've made a request to continue your detective training with more front line cases?"

"Yes Sir."

"The name's Mac."

"Yes Sir."

"Hmmm." Mac went back to reading. "If I were to partner you with a senior inspector would you have any objections?" he raised his head and eyeballed her as if the wrong answer would terminate the conversation immediately and relegate her to baby-sitting cold cases for eternity.

Grace tried to swallow, scrunched her fists tighter so her nails bit into her palms. Then, letting her fire loose she tossed her head and spoke directly to her antagonist. "I've read the staff policy on fraternisation, and it says I must alert my Commanding Officer if I am in a relationship with a colleague. So I must dutifully report I am in love with Marcus Campbell."

Mac raised his eyebrow, just the left one, and successfully hid his amusement. "Your Commanding Officer; I wasn't aware I had offered you a job?"

Grace spluttered, the fire in her eyes sputtered out and her shoulders slumped. Mac continued "He was to be my suggestion seeing you had worked so well together: obviously better than I'd imagined." He dropped his head again and turning the pages before him, continued to read the file before him.

Grace sat opposite and drowned in her emotions which swung from mortified to incredulous and back again. Finally Mac rose from his chair and walked around the desk. He stopped at Grace's chair and said "wait here, I won't be long."

And then he left his office, closing the door behind him. And so Grace sat, for twelve minutes although she was sure it was over an hour. Finally Mac came back in, closed the door and resumed his seat behind the desk. He laid his arms across the desk, his fingers intertwined and his posture leaning forward in a more engaging manner with Grace.

"Grace, I could use a skilful female detective to partner a senior inspector, and you have all the skills I believe we need. But this is a particularly heinous case and if you declined it I would not think less of you."

"The pack-rape and murder case? It would surely test my fortitude but I would be proud to be the female detective who stopped this bunch of mongrels."

Mac just looked at her, caught up in his own thoughts. Finally he said "welcome on board detective; come meet your mentor and new partner."

Grace could not hold her excitement and a huge grin spread across her face.

"I can see why Marcus is so captivated." Mac said, leaving his office and walking into 'the D-zone' with Grace following.

"Detectives let me formally introduce Detective Grace Scott, Adam's new partner: and..." Mac paused for effect..."Detective Superintendent Elise Scott's baby sister. Mess with her at your peril."

Adam McAdam walked over and shook Grace's hand. "Great to meet you Grace. I've cleared the desk opposite mine for you. Come dump your stuff and I'll give you introductions to the team and then catch you up to speed with the case to date."

Grace followed him to 'her desk', where she dumped her satchel and turned to the room for introductions.

Adam didn't just 'go around' the room; he explained the structure and then introduced the players.

"We have three Senior Inspectors currently on the roster: Marcus Campbell whom you ably assisted in bringing the body in the barrels case to a close; Senior Inspector Hamish Dudley the carrot top over there, and myself.

Ably partnering Hamish is Detective Gloria Hanson; sadly no-one wants to work with Marcus seeing the last three lassies to do so have ended up on maternity leave." There was a chorus of guffaws and Grace was certain Marcus blushed; she intended to quiz him about it later.

Adam went on "we have a further pool of three detectives who are responsible for category two cases, which means everything without the glory: theft, burglary, assaults. They also toss a coin to see who's next to work with Marcus." Adam waited for the jibes to die down. "So you have Scott McDermid, Hamilton Dunn and Joyce Mainwaring." The three raised a hand to allow Grace to identify them.

"Then we have a highly skilled team of supporting constables, lead by Jon Addams, Shiela McMurtry, Ben Hamilton, Glenda Goodrich, Deena Storey and Neil Johnstone."

His task done, Adam walked around to his desk and sat down: Grace followed suit and sat in 'her seat', feeling like she was first day in a new school. Adam looked across at her and said, with a hint of caution in his voice, "Are you sure you want this as your second case? The first crime is beyond horrendous and we haven't caught any of them yet. They're bound to strike again before we catch up to them."

"I know of the case: Marcus is Lieb's best friend and we're close so he shared the bones of it."

"OK then. But please don't feel you can't voice your dismay. Don't think less will be thought of you if you need a time-out on this one. Speak up."

"Will do: should I call you Adam?"

"That's my name." Adam stood up "How about you read through the case notes? I've got a number of tapes from the tip-line to listen to: when I'm finished we can compare notes and discuss next steps."

"Sounds like a plan" Grace replied and she watched Adam walk away, then dragged her e-notebook from her satchel and opened a new note folder. She used the stylus to write a title, and then got down to reading the file and taking notes.

It was nearly two hours later when she joined Adam in the small conference room to drink coffee and plan their next steps.

"OK, so you now know how bloody awful Lieb Canavan feels. I don't know if Marcus knows Rose was pregnant; hell I don't think Lieb knew." Adam explained. "The scene was worse than we described it because there was no way to write down the emotional devastation that was such an integral part of the scene. And that is a key point for you. Rape is about power not sex: this was sport for them. But they successfully destroyed DNA evidence and most of our fingerprints are partials or too smudged to match anything we have on the databases.

So with so few leads we've started a two-pronged public help campaign: one that showed the photo of Rose and asked if anyone could remember seeing her or her car that day in April. The second is the tattoo: we've sent it to every tattooist in eastern Scotland to see if someone will own up being the artist. Maybe they saw something."

"Did you get anything from the tip-line tapes?"

"Only sightings of her in Inverness, Glasgow, Edinburgh oh and London. I'll get Jon Addams team onto them."

"The other lead is the drugs" Adam continued. "Whilst they are somewhat unique, they are imported as herbal medicine so there isn't the comprehensive checking and reporting going on. Again, we've been canvassing herbal stockists but they're unlikely to be forthcoming if they're involved. Shiela McMurtry and Glenda Goodrich are searching through import manifests to see if they can find anything."

Adam looked at his watch, it was 18:15. "Let's call it a night and start fresh tomorrow? Shall we say 08:30?"

"Sounds good. Here's my mobile number" Grace handed him a slip of paper. Adam took it and keyed the number into his phone, then he hit dial. Grace's phone rang and she accepted the call. "OK now we've captured each other's number. Let's call it a day, cos sometime soon our world will become endless days of torment and sleeplessness" Adam concluded.

They parted ways as Adam headed to Mac's door; probably to apprise Mac of his first impressions; and Grace grabbed her satchel from the desk and looked to Marcus. He nodded and settled his desk for the night, then got up and followed Grace across the room and down the stairs.

Chapter 17

Rosy Garden woke to the chirruping of her phone alarm, threw back the duvet and swung her legs over the side of the bed: she was not an early morning woman. She padded across the room to the little table by the door where she kept her keys, her watch and her phone: far enough away that she had to get out of bed to turn the alarm off and not reach for it from her comfortable bed where she could just snuggle down and go back to sleep.

She carried the phone with her into the small bathroom and placed it on the window sill whilst she attended to her early morning toileting. Then she washed her hands and face and left for the kitchen, where she turned the kettle on. Whilst waiting for the kettle to boil she wandered into the shop and over to the front window to check the front parking area was clear. She'd lost a couple of clients because the local trash had decided it would be fun to fill her three small parking bays with branches they'd hacked off the trees in the local park; clients couldn't park so they went elsewhere.

Rosy hated mornings but her clients felt otherwise. She collected the junkmail from the floor under the letterbox slot and returned to the kitchen to make a cup of tea. She mused how she thought running her own tattoo parlour would mean she could make the rules. The truth was very different: clients provided the money that kept her in the luxury she'd become accustomed; her own work area with a small flat attached, all in her own name. And she had an 07:00 client this morning, a sailor calling in after his shift and before the pub opened at 09:00.

She yawned and stretched and told herself again how she hated early mornings; then she settled down at the small table to drink her tea. Looking through the junkmail she'd collected from the front door she came across a flyer that had apparently been dropped by the local police. 'Attention tattoo shop owners and tattooist' she groaned; tattooist was someone she thought you'd find in a circus, she was an artist. 'Do you recognise this tattoo?' 'If you do, please contact Tayside Police on this number and ask for Senior Constable Jon Addams'.

Rosy looked at the scanned photo that was provided and chewed her lip. She surely did know that tattoo, she done it herself. A pretty little blue yacht: she remembered the other Rose who'd come in with the design and had her place it above her left breast not three months previously. She put down her mug of tea and carried the flyer into the shop again where she put the flyer on the counter, went around behind and opened the drawer that contained a catalogue of photos of her clients and their tattoos. She was standing behind the counter looking at the flyer again when she suddenly realised someone was standing in front of her.

Before she could compute who it was, or respond to her inner warning alarms, her brain exploded in a mountain of pain after being slammed with a small wooden bat. Rosy collapsed to the floor unconscious: she didn't hear the striking of the match or the smashing glass of four Molotov cocktails as they were thrown around the room. She didn't hear the car engine start or the diminishing noise of the departing vehicle.

She remained unconscious as the flames took hold with all the sound of crackling flames and popping wood and as the heat intensified, she remained unaware as her skin started to blister and her night clothes to smoke.

The ink pots exploded as the inferno built and the temperatures climbed, but Rosy's trauma happened slower as the counter protected her initially; but it did happen. The blisters enlarged, burst and the skin pealed back exposing the deeper dermis layer which then allowed the blood vessels to thrombose and the surrounding tissues began to die. This started with her exposed feet, hands, neck and face and then as her clothes disintegrated, her legs, arms and torso. The tendons of her hands contracted into claws and the photo she held became cocooned within.

Her lungs began to burn as the breaths her automated responses kept up sucked in the superheated air and toxic fumes. She was minutes from death but she remained oblivious to her fate, until an emergency care worker lifted her from the floor and rushed her outside. He was doing what he'd been trained to do, save lives. But Rosy's life was beyond saving and the EMT would reflect later, in those cold dark anguished hours before morning, that maybe she would have been better served if he'd let her be.

They provided oxygen and heart stimulation until Rosy's haunted eyes opened to take in the horror of it all. She moaned in pain and shock, looked into the eyes of the EMT ministering to her and used her last strength of will to raise her right arm to him and whisper two words.

Then death provided her the peace her rescuers had delayed.

The emergency team controlled the blaze and the EMT called the attending Officer over to report Rosy's death and her message, handing the Officer the photo she'd had clutched in her hand. The photo was a polaroid instant, scorched around the edges and curled from the heat but sufficiently intact to be obvious. The Officer looked at the photo and turned it over to read the back, then sharply inhaled and said to the EMT's "this young lady needs to go straight to the autopsy room of the Procurator Fiscal. Please see to it."

He then walked away from the noise of the scene and placed a call through switch to Senior Inspector Adam McAdam.

Adam awoke to the ring of his phone, taking note of the time 05:43 "McAdam?" was all he managed as he swung his legs over his bed.

"Senior Inspector, it's Constable Douglas; I'm at a scene in Arbroath I believe you'll want to attend with urgency sir. It's a suspicious fire and death, and there's a message been left for you Sir."

"How intriguing, text me the address, I'll collect my new partner and be with you immediately."

Adam stood and checked his phone. Damn he'd taken Grace's mobile but not her address. He needed to know where to collect her before he left. Oh well, she was on the team now, so he hit the call button.

Grace responded on the second ring "Grace Scott".

"Grace, we have a callout – where do you live?" Grace was initially confused, taking a full three seconds before she recognised the voice: and all that early morning thinking made her forget what Marcus' address was. Fortunately he was now sitting on the side of the bed looking at her, so when she said "Barnhill" into the phone and look at him desperately, he gave her the rest of the address which she repeated into the phone.

"Great, I'll be there in ten minutes. Can you make coffee for the road?"

Grace asked Marcus and he said "sure" and took off for the kitchen. "I'll be out front in ten" Grace said lastly to Adam and rung off. She could see Marcus managing the coffee so she toileted, washed her hands and face and quickly dressed. She was tumbling her hair into a loose pony tail as she stumbled into the kitchen: looking at Marcus sheepishly she gave him her award winning smile "thanks" and a long kiss on the lips. "That may have to last you all day by the sounds."

Marcus handed her two thermal mugs of coffee as they saw headlights coming up the road. "Wish me luck."

"Sweetie if you've been called at this hour someone's luck has run out. Stay safe and call me when you can. I love you" Marcus added.

"I love you too."

"I'll tell Mac shall I?" Grace groaned, grabbed her satchel which was always prepared and by the door and trotted out to meet Adam.

"Coffee" Grace said as she opened the door and climbed in.

"Nicely met, and thanks" Adam responded. He turned the car round and headed back to the A92 and sped toward Arbroath.

"What's the call?" Grace asked.

"A fire, a suspicious death, and a message for me apparently."

"That doesn't sound like our SAT Pack" Grace looked at Adam who was speeding, one hand on the wheel the other sipping coffee.

"SAT Pack?" Adam enquired, offering Grace a brief quizzical look.

"Sexual Assault & Torture Pack" Grace proffered.

"OK then. Just don't let the press hear you say it."Adam didn't seem to have anything more to say on their callout so Grace asked "did you have to back-track to collect me?"

"No, I live north of Dundee, between the A90 and A92 so it was actually on the way. Tell me, do you often not know your address?"

Grace flashed Adam a smile, friendly but with just a hint of malice: a clear message of don't mess with me layered through it.

Adam noted the reaction, grunted and returned his attention to the road: which was just as well as Arbroath township was coming up fast. They turned right at the roundabout toward the world-renown harbour and followed the one-way street plan until they arrived on Old Shore Road, just down from the Old Brewhouse. Their destination was obvious with a fire crew and police cruisers still lighting up the predawn morning.

Adam parked and he and Grace climbed out and headed to the police Constable they could see standing by his vehicle watching the fire crew finish dousing the property. Adam's interest piqued when he saw what was left of the shop sign 'Rosy's Signature Tattoos'.

"Constable, Senior Inspector Adam McAdam and this is my partner Inspector Grace Scott" Adam introduced them and took out his notebook. Grace was already taking notes & photos on her e-book.

"Simon Douglas Sir, Mam" the Constable replied. "The fire appears deliberately lit the Fire Marshall says, evidence of Molotov cocktails being used. Also a side window is broken so entry appears unlawful. One person recovered, woman about thirty, head trauma and severely burned. But she had this in her hand" and Simon handed Adam the photo.

Adam looked at the photo of the little blue yacht: it was different in that this had been taken on live skin, his photo on dead skin. He turned it over and written on the back was 'Rose Canavan, 25 April 2012'. Adam handed the photo to Grace, looked at Simon and asked "anything else?"

"The poor lady was revived for just a moment and she said two words 'his birthday'. Does that mean anything Inspector?"

"Unfortunately I believe it does, and it's not nice news. Thanks Constable, good job. Let the Fire Marshal know we'll be around for a report later this morning will you?" Adam added, looking over at the firey busy about his task.

Adam walked toward the car and Grace kept pace. When they were back onto the A92 and heading south Grace asked "Where to now?"

"We need to see Lieb Canavan and then an autopsy."

"I take it the birthday message was personal?"

"Rose was killed April 25th, Lieb's birthday is April 29th, and his favourite pastime aside from Rose, was sailing."

"Oh, so she was likely in Arbroath getting the tattoo when she was taken. And Lieb didn't know about it because she was going to surprise him."

"That's sure how it looks. This is only going to add to his burden."

Chapter 18

Lieb sat in his office working through case papers awaiting the day. He knew his second, Martin Ashton was in preparing the autopsy suite for a victim being delivered by a paramedic team. Some time it worked like that; sometimes they got the call to attend and a recovery crew would accompany them, sometimes the scene was such that the Fiscal needed to see the scene second hand if at all: fire scenes, road collisions and the like needed expert cleanup and the Fiscal team only added to the confusion. Other times it was helpful to be on scene and collect trace evidence and view the scene undisturbed such as homicides and suicides.

It was here Adam and Grace found Lieb just after seven o'clock. The Office Manager Marianne greeted them as they signed in; she searched Adam's face and asked "battle stations?"

Adam nodded and Marianne walked down the corridor toward Lieb's office with them, stopping at the intersection to the laboratory area. She stationed herself in a doorway that gave her a view of Lieb in his office and the intersecting corridor: this allowed her to watch for traffic with intentions of speaking with Lieb and turn them away. Marianne had been practicing this manoeuvre for the last few months in an effort to maintain some harmony.

Lieb looked up and saw Adam and Grace approaching and noticed Marianne in her intercept position. He had chastised himself on occasion that his demeanour had become so dour she felt she needed to do this and at other times just mumbled 'whatever' to himself and continued on being surly. But Marianne's intercept mode had become a good indication when bad news was on its way and Lieb actually appreciated the heads-up.

Adam tapped on his door and walked right on in. Grace followed him and Lieb took a moment to drink the sight of her in. He'd heard pieces of conversation between police officers that suggested his friend Marcus was quite smitten over Grace, but Lieb had never taken the opportunity to ask him. Lieb made a mental note to do that next time Marcus was in front of him.

"Morning Lieb; you know Detective Grace Scott?" Adam opened the conversation.

"Yes, from the body in the barrels case, hello Grace".

"Hello" was all Grace answered. She had suddenly become reticent in front of Lieb: this was Marcus' best friend and her only previous encounter with him was when they were concluding the barrels case, and then he'd been warm and charming. Grace had heard the comments in the stationhouse about his huge personality shift, his surliness, even downright venom and she'd heard Marcus bemoan his inability to lighten Lieb's emotional load. And here she was probably adding it to it big time. They didn't sit down.

Adam took the lead "it seems we found the tattooist" Adam paused to let Lieb process this information, and then he continued "Rosy Garden was on the waterfront in Arbroath."

"Was?" Lieb responded.

"Yes, unfortunately she's visiting your autopsy suite as we speak." Lieb just kept looking straight into Adam's eyes, trying to extract the information that wasn't being shared. But Adam shifted the focus forward by next explaining what the information about finding Rosy meant "so Rose was in Arbroath when she was taken." He was very careful with his words. "And the tattooist must have some connection with our pack because they didn't want her talking. So that gives us further leads; Grace and I will now dig into Rosy's life and use the CCTV footage of Arbroath to look for further information."

Lieb nodded but never allowed Adam's eyes to break the connection; he just knew there was more. Why else was Marianne hovering?

Adam noticeably inhaled deeply and extended his hand toward Lieb, who hesitated initially, not allowing Adam to break the eye-to-eye they were having. Adam looked back at Lieb and nodded slightly, offering Lieb the information that he wanted to take what was being handed to him. Lieb looked down and then took the photo from Adam's hand.

Grace found she was holding her breath.

Adam spoke softly and personally to Lieb "the message Rosy Garden stayed alive long enough to ensure you received was, that your Rose had arranged the tattoo as your birthday gift."

Adam motioned to Grace and they turned and quietly left Lieb's office. On the way passed Marianne, Adam stopped and said "One more piece of the puzzle: not sure if it will help or increase his pain."

Marianne nodded and looked toward Lieb who had crumpled into his chair. "You two have a good day" she said as she hurried up the corridor to let Martin know he was taking point today.

Lieb's legs buckled and he crumbled into the chair. Adam had handed him a photo, a polaroid singed around the edges and curled from the heat but with the majority of the image unharmed and very clear: a beautiful sky blue yacht. His Rose's left breast was the canvas and she had intended for him to find it when he unwrapped her after her time with sister Heather; his birthday gift.

He sat and stared at it for the longest time, running the gamut of emotions from loss through love and slamming into anger and rage and bouncing back to loss to start over. He hadn't felt such upheaval since his father was taken from him. Lieb relived that period as if he was fifteen again; the emotion so overwhelming he grabbed his overcoat and bolted from his office, down the corridor and out into the throng of the university organism to lose himself in all that humanity.

His father had been a pharmacist, very successfully working his own store in Stirling. Alasdair Donald Canavan was a firm but friendly father, one of those who had rules and ways he liked things done, but if you abided by his code, he was supportive even fun. He married his schoolgirl sweetheart Fiona and they lived as kindred spirits. Along with Lieb's younger sisters Jinty and Rona they had a family Alasdair was not only proud of, but enamoured.

Everyone heard stories of families fractured by drugs and other social ills, but the Canavan family was happy, enjoying each other's company and sharing each other's triumphs and joy. Which was probably why Alasdair was taken from them that day; he never sensed the danger in opening ten minutes early for a customer.

So he was robbed and killed by a lesbian girl for her junkie partner: a seventeen year old who was unconcerned for the consequences of her actions.

Fiona was devastated at her loss, broken even. Everything was sold up and the family scattered: Lieb to a boarding school in Edinburgh, the two sisters to another boarding school in Perthshire. Mother took herself to the wilds of Lochgilphead south of Oban on the Scottish west coast. 'Just 2 hours by car along the scenic coastal road' the tourist website said; getting 'home' for the holidays was unimaginably difficult for a young sixteen year old Lieb. Firstly he had to train to Glasgow and then take the coach from there. And mother had found a 'quaint seaside cottage' that was actually forty-five minute walk from town, seeing mother forgot to collect him from the station.

Hence he spent so much time doing nothing more than his studies, Lieb had no trouble getting the marks that scored him a first round option to do medicine at Edinburgh University. But he was changed too: he no longer wanted to 'follow in his father's footsteps and take over the pharmacy one day'; he wanted to become a Procurator Fiscal and help solve the heinous crimes. And so he had thrown himself into two consecutive degrees, law and medical science, scoring honours in both. Then twelve months in the Crown Office in Edinburgh and a two year traineeship with the Procurator Fiscal Service. So by twenty eight he was well prepared and well sponsored for the role of Procurator Fiscal. Now thirty three he was well established and respected, although his manner over the last four months was wearing down even his most ardent supporters.

Lieb sat on a bench in the middle of the campus and tried to breathe, but his chest was so constricted all he managed were small rapid gulps, and then, when he gathered his wits, he realised he was hyperventilating and instead of complicating his life further and fainting, he cupped his hands over his mouth and forced himself to slow his breathing and increase his body's carbon dioxide levels to near normal.

Lieb realised he needed to talk: he fished his wallet out of his pocket and his cell phone. Inside his wallet was a card for a clinical psychologist, Anne Haggarty. Lieb had made an appointment when his boss insisted, but only one. And that had taken some time as he initially struggled with a dilemma: did he choose a man who would understand his hidden angst or did he choose a woman who might be able to explain Rose's pregnancy and why he should forgive her. Finally he had chosen Anne and given her enough information to start a conversation. Unfortunately he hadn't given her enough: hadn't shared the gruesome details of the remains he'd received to autopsy, and hadn't managed to get to the pregnancy / sterility complication before Anne had suggested a coping mechanism that had him bolt with terror and have the nightmares return in full glory: she'd suggested Lieb 'just think of Rose's face, how she'd looked...' and before she could finish there was the slamming of her door and Lieb's footsteps running away down the corridor and then down the steps.

Three days later, after dodging Anne's follow-up calls, Lieb faxed over the autopsy report. Only then did Anne understand that when Lieb thought of Rose's face he remembered the soft gauze draped death mask, under which was the absence of all flesh and beauty; all soft tissues eaten by rats.

Now however, he had found an image he could focus on; the tattoo of a perfect blue yacht on the canvas of Rose's soft breast. His birthday gift. So he concentrated on that and he rang Anne. Yes she could see him right away, come on over.

While Lieb was driving to Anne's office, Roger was completing his carefully arranged plans. He'd left for work as always, kissing his wife long and ardently and wishing her Happy Anniversary for the umpteenth time. They had agreed dinner plans for that evening and both were on a romantic high as they parted for the day: Roger to his plumbing job and Janine to her reception role at the local doctor's surgery.

But after they had separated, Roger drove around the block and stopped to clandestinely watch Janine catch her bus. Then he drove home and put his plans into action. Firstly he rang Janine's colleague to check yet again that all was in order and that Maree could keep the secret. Then Roger showered and changed into his weekend clothes: cotton slacks, button-up shirt and light-weight pullover. He packed the picnic set and grabbed the out-door rug, candle & lighter and the camera.

He headed off for the second time that day but this time headed into town where he had some shopping to do. He pulled into Marks & Spencer's supermarket and shopped for cold champagne, strawberries, pate, cheese and cold-cut meats plus a decadent dessert. He also visited the florist and collected the dozen pink roses he'd ordered: by the time he was done it was nearing ten o'clock.

Humming jovially to himself he drove to the doctors surgery, collected up the roses and went inside to collect his bride: "we're still on our honeymoon" he'd answer anyone who challenged him, reminding him they had been three years married now.

Janine was gobsmacked when he presented at the desk in front of her, smartly dressed, a dozen of her favourite roses in his arms and a huge grin on his face. Her colleagues clapped when he presented himself to her; one of the waiting male patients even wolf-whistled them. Janine was flustered when Roger announced he was taking her away from it all for the rest of the day. But Dr Harper, who had been pre-warned, nodded his approval from the doorway, so Janine joined Roger and the two left the office hand-in-hand and giggly.

Chapter 19

Roger drove Juliette northwest along the Old Military Road out to the Cairngorm National Park, to their favourite picnic spot, the Tullyfergus circuit near Blairgowrie. The circuit was an enjoyable walking loop starting in the dense forestry plantations of Drimmie Wood and leading on to the lovely Tullyfergus estate which had fine old drove roads with ponds, woods and wild flowers.

Roger's car was a small fastback that was used to driving onto building sites, so instead of stopping in the parking area, Roger carefully bumped his car over the kerb and drove down the unsurfaced road which ran almost parallel to the road and along the edge of the forest. About half a kilometre in he pulled the small car into a clearing beyond the line of Sitka spruce and alongside the weir, with views across to the church.

"I feel like we're playing hooky from school" Juliette giggled.

Roger laughed out loud, Juliette's giggles infectious. He grabbed the picnic blanket and spread it out on the grassed ground and then grabbed the picnic basket. Juliette grabbed a bucket from amongst Roger's plumber's kit in the boot and headed off to the weir to get water to keep her roses in.

Roger laid out the spread he'd prepared and as Juliette settled on the blanket he popped off the champagne cork and poured two glasses of bubbly liquid. He raised his glass and toasted "to my beautiful bride, let me celebrate your beauty, your friendship and your joy for life. May we celebrate thusly for eons to come?" Juliette chinked glasses with Roger and sipped deeply, then reached for ripe strawberries, followed by pate' and cheese. Roger followed suit and for the next hour they laughed, and ate and drank in celebration.

Roger pulled out the camera and took photos of Juliette, the two of them holding champagne flutes and then of their little patch of bliss. Juliette returned the favour and took photos of Roger hamming it up for the camera. The late August light was softened somewhat by large fluffy clouds and they spent some time interpreting the scenes the clouds formed. So caught up were they in each other and the moment, they didn't hear the other car approach and park.

The five men in the SUV sat quietly, drinking water and watching their prey. They took note of the quietness around them; no vehicle traffic out here on a Tuesday. And they drank more water and a bottle of sports drink each. The 'chemist' had successfully instilled in them the dangers of taking other substances before using his magic potions, but despite his warnings about dehydration, the first time they hadn't drank enough water. The 'chemists' magic potion gave them unbelievable stamina and an erection that could last hours but they had become so dehydrated that after their first game, they had cruel stomach and leg cramps that rejected all attempts to overcome. Two of them had curled into a foetal position for days waiting for their muscles to unbunch.

For half an hour they sat and drank water and watched: 'the Chemist' who supplied the drugs and 'Wheels' obviously the driver, in the front; 'Dog' cos he liked the anal entry, 'Fangs' who was a biter, and 'Import' the Englishman, on the back seat. Satisfied they were unlikely to be disturbed, the chemist handed out a parcel of pills to each of them and they all washed them down with the last of their water. The driver grabbed a short barrelled gun from under his seat and they all got out the car and moved quietly toward Juliette and Roger.

Juliette put the camera down and picked up her glass of champagne: they were in the middle of a conversation about whether to get a cat or a dog when Juliette noticed the five men appear behind Roger and she stopped talking mid-sentence.

Noticing Juliette's gaze rise over his right shoulder, Roger asked "what?" and was answered by the loading ratchet of the short barrel gun. Roger tried to turn his head to see who was behind him but the barrel of the gun was placed under his right cheek, digging deep enough into the flesh that Juliette could see a trickle of blood escape and run toward Roger's chin.

"Well, look what we've found fella's, play time" Driver announced. To Roger and Juliette he said "get up." Juliette started to whimper but they both complied. The driver maintained the pressure of the gun against Roger's cheek and grabbed his upper arm and tugging him forcefully he said "This way my man." Driver pulled Roger to the back of his car, and when they arrived he instructed Roger to undo his trousers and drop them around his knees. With fumbling fingers Roger complied.

The Chemist started laughing, a high-pitched manic-wrapped noise that grated on Juliette's nerves. He grabbed a handful of Juliette's hair and marched her to join Roger at the rear of their car.

Driver spoke "see this here shotgun? I've taken some of the length of the barrel off so it delivers a wide spread of pain and carnage. Now Dog is not going to aim it at your little man's head, he's going to aim it at his belly. If you give us any trouble, Dog will fire the gun and blow a hole in your man's belly. The bullet will rip through the muscle and intestines and spill a toxic soup throughout his insides. It will hurt like hell but it won't kill him, not for a long while. Capisce?"

Juliette nodded as best she could with the Chemist tightly holding a handful of her hair.

Dog took over the gun and kept it trained on Roger's lower belly. Driver kicked Roger's legs as wide as his trousers would allow, unbalancing him so he was leaning with both hands on the glass window of his fast-back shaped car. The car was low enough that he had an unobstructed view of what was happening to Juliette.

The Chemist used his leverage of the handful of hair to manoeuvre Janine to the front of the car. She was standing facing Roger and the two of them looked for salvation in each other's eyes but none was forthcoming.

The Chemist now addressed Juliette "take off your top". Juliette fumbled with the buttons but managed to comply. "Now take off your panties and lean on the bonnet of the car." Juliette's whimpering increased and was joined with deep sobs that paralysed her.

Roger could watch no more, so he shouted "leave her alone!"

The Chemist's head whipped around, his eyes intense and full of venom "shut him up".

Dog lifted the gun and slammed it into Rogers face, smashing his way through teeth, and then he fired a single shot. Juliette screamed. Roger heard the roar of noise that filled every cavity in his skull and tried to separate the bones. He felt heat and intense pain as the bullet smashed through more teeth, the bones of his jaw, shredded his tongue and cheek and left him laying across the back of his car, panting. Dog grabbed a handful of hair and pulled him upright, then relocated the gun to its position against his right flank.

The Driver grabbed Juliette by the hair and shook her head. "Last warning, do as you're told or the next bullet will rip his belly apart."

Juliette couldn't look at Roger but she could hear his moans of pain: she lifted her skirt and hooked her thumbs into the lace at the top of her panties and pulled them free; dropping them around her feet and then stepping out of them. The Chemist pushed her between the shoulder blades so she fell forward onto her hands, and then he kicked her feet apart so she was positioned spread-eagled over the bonnet of the car.

He reached around and took her left nipple in his finger and thumb grip and squeezed and tugged it. Juliette stopped herself crying out by biting her lip. The Chemist stood behind her and took both nipples in his fingers and thumbs and squeezed and tugged; and Juliette could feel his erection hard and eager pressing into her buttock. She started to panic breathe, waiting for the inevitable penetration but the Chemist was cackling his maniacal tune and he grabbed her hair again and jabbed a needle in her neck.

Unprepared and restrained as she was, Juliette had the potion injected into her neck vein before she realised what was happening. The drug screamed along her vein and her body racked in response. As she struggled with the chemical onslaught, Driver slammed his erection into her vagina.

Juliette screamed and Roger moaned, but the packs party was afoot and nothing was going to stop them now. And thanks to the Chemist's potions, the party continued for ages. They took turns and each turn took was accompanied by chanting and encouragement from others in the pack. After an eternity, Dog came forward from his guard post, handing the gun to Import. Roger realised with dismay he'd lost any chance of disarming the gun holder and saving his bride.

Dog stood poised behind Juliette and the Chemist squatted on the bonnet over her and cackling maniacally, he injected Juliette again. As she screamed and writhed in pain and despair at the substance scorching its way toward her brain and around her body, Dog mounted her through her anus and tore his way upward through her rectum. He grabbed a purchase in the skin of her hips and kept pushing and then rhythmically withdrawing and pushing forward again.

Juliette's body convulsed: she fell onto the bonnet and her Saint Vitus' dance kept time with the Dog: all the while the muscle of her heart, starved of life-giving oxygen, screamed and died, small patches at a time.

Dog didn't stop till he was fulfilled.

Roger realised he was on the ground with a headfull of pain: he also realised he was no longer restrained and that the noise from the other end of the car was no longer. He swung his body up into a crouch and stopped as the pain in his head screamed and his visioned dimmed, with unconsciousness threatening again. Finally he managed to stand and steady himself on the back of the car: he touched the top of his head from where the pain was emanating and felt the sticky mass of blood and his hair. He closed his eyes and controlled his breathing, then looked over the car toward the front but couldn't see Juliette; nor could he see their tormentors. The sun was much lower in the sky, hours lower he judged. Roger turned and moved to check on Juliette, but forgetting his trousers were down, tripped and fell.

There was an explosion of pain from his mouth and face and head and he dragged his knees up to his chest and hugged them until the pain subsided. Then he reached down and untangled his legs: free he resumed his passage to Juliette.

He found her crumpled at the base of the car. He found she still had a pulse, but her skin was pasty-coloured and cold and she did not respond to his words or touch. Roger sat in the dirt beside her and pulled her into his embrace. He rocked them and cried, trying to fathom how he could live without her: how he could live with the knowledge he didn't save her. For an age he continued just sitting in the dirt holding Juliette, and then he made a decision.

Roger gently laid Juliette back onto the ground and went back to the car. He slid both front seats forward to allow greatest access to the rear seat. He then went into the plumbing tools and equipment in his boot and secured a length of tubing and tape. He smashed the housing of his brake light and secured the tubing to the exhaust pipe, pushing the pipe back through the light housing into the cabin.

Then he collected Juliette from the ground in front of the car and carried her to the passenger side door, sitting her in the space behind the front seat. Roger then went round to the driver's door, started the engine and climbed into the rear seat area. He pulled the door shut and reached over and pulled Juliette onto the back seat beside him. Then he closed and locked both doors.

The exhaust fumes were already filling the cabin, so he sat back and pulled Juliette into his embrace. He spoke quietly into her ear as she lay slumped against his chest: he told her over and over again how much he loved her, how beautiful she was, how he could not live without her. He spoke until the effects of the carbon monoxide overwhelmed him and he joined Juliette in death.

Chapter 20

"So Lieb, can I take it you forgive me my gaff and we'll continue on with my more informed observations? Dr Anne Haggarty asked.

Lieb sat before her, on the edge of his seat and with his hands clenched together and tucked between his knees. He nodded to Anne's question.

"I understand there has been a development you wish to share?" she asked.

Lieb nodded again.

Anne made no attempt to extract the information from him; she was acutely aware he had uncorked his emotional bottle and when he started the flow of emotion and information would be effusive.

Lieb started by showing Anne the photo: she examined the tattoo of the pretty blue yacht and noted the scorch marks and heat damage. She had heard on the radio in her car, of the fire and death of the tattooist in Arbroath this morning.

When Lieb remained unforthcoming she tried "so, why a yacht?" and the floodgates opened. Lieb's diatribe ran like water down a fast flowing stream, bubbly and explosive at times, mired in eddies at other times. But he told it all, finishing with "and she was pregnant."

Anne looked at Lieb, looked at the emotional storm that ebbed and flowed over his features and noticed the storm that remain behind his eyes; a tempest not yet breached. She always considered her responses, but today she was overly cautious, not wanting a repeat of their last encounter when a wrong suggestion had sent him fleeing.

"The whole episode has been tragic; in hindsight it was totally inappropriate for you to have been asked to attend the scene or undertake the autopsy. But I'm sure you do not hold anyone responsible for that: no-one knew." Anne looked at Lieb and saw him nod in agreement, so she continued "And I'm sure you do not hold Rose responsible for her demise?" Anne saw Lieb flinched and made a note of this reaction; she changed her line of commentary, exploring Lieb's response to Rose's culpability.

"So Rose was supposed to be visiting her sister in Aberdeen?" Lieb nodded. "And we now know she made a diversion to Arbroath to get a tattoo; the tattoo of a yacht for your birthday, to celebrate your love of sailing?" again Lieb nodded. "But there's more here isn't there?" "More about Rose and her actions?"

Lieb's shoulders sank visibly and he sunk into himself as if a turtle withdrawing from danger and Anne knew she would get little more from him today.

"OK, so let's explore that next time? For now, whenever you feel angry toward Rose I want you to think on it and try to identify where that anger is directed. Then I want you to look at the little blue yacht and remember Rose loved you. She made an effort to have a permanent declaration inked on her skin so every time you unwrapped her, the reminder was there for you to see. Can you do that?"

"Yes" Lieb answered in a quiet monotone: then he stood, shook Anne's hand and left the office of Anne Haggarty *BPsych, MClinPsych, PhD.*

Lieb walked back to his car, stopping to buy a coffee and Danish on the way. As he sat in his car sipping the coffee his phone chirruped with the tone that alerted a case had come in. Feeling somewhat guilty of bugging out without explanation earlier that morning, Lieb responded he would take the call. Marianne text replied she had allocated it to him and provided the address. The address was near Blairgowrie, a good hour away which Lieb thought gave him enough time to climb back into the emotional suit he had been wearing to protect him from the pity and the cloying concern from the people he encountered.

As he fired his vehicle into life he wondered yet again how long it would be before he was told 'enough was enough'. And he actually spent a moment discovering he did feel better after speaking with Anne; having the opportunity to uncork his emotions and damn the consequences. For the first time in four months he felt there was somewhere ahead that he could drop a new anchor.

And so he drove northwest along the Old Military Road to Blairgowrie and Rattray where he stopped to refresh his coffee and something more to eat: he felt like he hadn't eaten in months, and truth be told, he hadn't.

After Blairgowrie and Rattray he continued on along the A93, to the small hamlet of Lornty and then he took the Bonnington Road, finally seeing the turnoff for Drimmie Wood. He noted how isolated the spot was and how quiet.

When he arrived the Fiscal recovery team had already set up and were awaiting direction. Lieb noticed the nervous shuffles and dropped gazes when the team spotted him and his mood soured. So after he exited the vehicle, he targeted the female detective standing waiting, with his eyes and long strides. Inspector Beth McAuliffe introduced herself and explained the sit-rep (situation report) to Lieb as he stood listening and not commenting.

Beth explained 'the patrol had found the car down the little-used track in the Drimmie Wood; in a quiet grove, a perfect picnic spot. It was quiet and peaceful and apart from the car it was completely deserted. They had walked to the car calling out but heard no response. The car windows were fogged over and they guessed someone was taking an afternoon sleep after a picnic: one of those dalliances where the mood is high, the company exquisite and the food superb, so superb one over indulges and the body slows to concentrate on digestion."

Lieb offered no comment so Beth continued "When they had reached the car it didn't 'feel right' Stanley Fullerton had tried to explain when she arrived". "They had rung dispatch and checked the number plates and that had raised no flags, but something appeared 'wrong'. So Henry McKay had smashed the rear passenger window and they saw the couple inside. Then they backed off and called it in."

Again, Lieb offered no response so Beth motioned for the response team to move in and get to work.

"STOP! Lieb called "nobody moves." And as no-one wanted to crack the egg-shells, no-one did.

Everybody had been walking on egg-shells around Lieb these last months. No longer did they find their Fiscal the communicative commander-in-chief they were used to; no longer was the office door open and welcoming, it was kept closed. Most of the communication was done through the email system; they submitted their findings and watched obsessively in case Lieb sent back a query.

He had become cold, ice cold. Someone had even taped a note to his door 'Ice Man': no-one owned up to it and Lieb hadn't taken it down. It was there for three days before someone removed it as quietly as it had gone up.

It was rumoured even the detectives tried to avoid callouts that would include meeting the cold eyes of Lieb Canavan.

Not everyone was hesitant around Lieb of course; Marianne, his personal assistant kept up with her charming professional nature although she toned down her bubbly enthusiasm in respect to Lieb's period of mourning. And Leon would talk down anyone who voiced objections to Lieb's change of personality: he'd been there, at the site where the victim had been found. He'd seen the state of the body, especially how the rats had chewed the face off. How anyone could be expected to face such gruesome sights as part of their job was bad enough, but when it turned out to be your wife? Well, people had a right to be sullen and uncommunicative; and he told his colleagues that.

"And Lieb's never shirked his responsibilities at the table" Leon continued. He still fronts up to each new horror and does the autopsy's and visits the families; he never asks someone else to take a case, and we've had some really bad ones these past months."

Inspector Beth McAuliffe walked to Lieb's side and asked softly "what is it?" in response to the order to stop.

Lieb looked at her as if seeing her for the first time today. "I want you to stand right here" and Lieb stepped back and slightly to his left; Beth stepped to where Lieb had vacated and looked at him askantly.

"I want you to look through the break in the window and line up the rear-view mirror so you can see the bodies in the back" Lieb instructed. Beth shifted position slightly until she could see the bodies in the back like Lieb wanted. "There's something on the man's cheek" she said.

"Yes, the exit wound of a low velocity firearm. Now why would someone gas themselves when they had the balls to shoot themselves?"

"I don't know?" Beth replied.

"I bet we'll discover they were victims of foul play first" Lieb explained. "And as we're still hunting the pack of monsters that killed my wife, I think this site deserves Adam McAdam's attention".

"I'll get him out here" Beth answered and backed away to make the call.

"Without taking another step forward, I want everyone to get into two groups; one at the rear of the car and one at the front. When you have done that, I want you to tag the start position and then I want everyone to advance carefully in single file to a point one metre before the vehicle. And then I want photos of the vehicle and the ground around it from that one metre position. When I have sufficient photo's I want you to carefully approach the vehicle and take plaster moulds of the footprints there. Dust the vehicle end for prints and scour for trace evidence. When you're finished, walk back to your start point, again in single file." Lieb looked at every technician for an acknowledgement of his instructions; they nodded one person at a time.

"Constables McKay and Fullerton, can you carefully walk back along the track and look for evidence of another vehicle please. Take some flags and just identify items for photos and collecting." Lieb continued with his instructions. The constables nodded their understanding and moved away to complete their assigned tasks.

Lieb then stood and watched the technicians work; watched where they stood, what they touched and where they collected evidence. He watched until SI McAdam and Detective Grace Scott arrived and then he showed them what they had found.

Chapter 21

"Lieb, what have you got?" SI Adam McAdam asked when he had approached Lieb and stood beside him. Lieb looked over to Adam and to Grace and acknowledged them with a nod.

"A car with two deceased inside and we're carefully examining the scene so we can give you a clearer picture shortly."

"Beth says you've made a significant visual discovery?" Grace asked. "Can I see it?"

Lieb looked at Grace and smiled; it wasn't a happy broad grin but it was far from the dour grunt everyone had been getting of late. Grace and Adam both noticed it and hoped it was a sign of recovery: Grace made a mental note to share it with Marcus later.

As he had with Beth earlier, Lieb had Grace stand where he was standing, and line up the break in the rear window with the rear view mirror so she could see the man on the back seat.

"That looks like a gunshot wound to his face" she exclaimed. Lieb nodded.

"My turn" responded Adam: he was taller than Lieb so he needed to squat somewhat to achieve the same visual expose.

"Well I'll be damned" Adam summated.

"I've sent the crews in to investigate in single file as you can see, starting from those flags. I have been here watching their movements so I can reconstruct the activity around the vehicle for you later. There seems to be a heavy concentration of activity at the front and rear of the vehicle, although Jon Addams has identified a picnic area beyond and he is documenting that scene and collecting evidence from there. Constables McKay and Fullerton have walked back along the track and have identified clear fresh tyre marks in the parking lot and Johnstone is taking casts for us. Constables McKay and Fullerton are now inspecting the area between that vehicle and this one. That was the noise you heard when you walked up, they called for MacEe to collect photos and evidence."

The two-minute diatribe from Lieb was not lost on Grace and Adam; it was more words they'd heard Lieb speak in all the months since Rose's death.

Just as Lieb finished briefing Adam and Grace the Fiscal team started single-filing back to their start flags, hovering in their groups awaiting Lieb's instructions. When they had all gathered, including Constables McKay and Fullerton, and stood in front of Lieb, Adam and Grace, Lieb spoke to them collectively "good job team. Now starting with the rear team, can you describe to us your observations and findings." And after some furtive looks between the team members, Lieb added "please."

Leon started, and following him, his colleagues took up the mantle and followed on.

"There are only four distinct footprint sets at the rear of the car, with the greatest concentration directly behind the vehicle facing forward toward the front of the vehicle. And there is some sign of a struggle, although it doesn't appear long-lived. All the footprint sets are large with square heals suggestive of four men having been there."

"There is also blood and tissue spatter from the vehicle, away to the left, consistent with a single shot. In addition is blood drops from a steady drip in a stationary position from the rear of the vehicle.

"And there is blood smearing on the rear window of the coupe, but I didn't identify any hand or fingerprints with it, suggesting it was directly from the wound."

"There is however, multiple hand prints on the rear window, all appearing to be from the same person."

"And there is tubing taped to the exhaust pipe and pushed back through a broken tail-light. And this has been resealed with foam filler."

Lieb asked this group of staff "Can you see the front of the vehicle from the rear?"

"Most definitely" Leon answered. The car's fastback shape and low height gave us a very clear view of the activities happening at the front of the vehicle."

"Thank you" Lieb continued. "Front team?"

After the ease in tension from the 'rear team' this information flowed easier.

"There are many overlapping footprints at the front of the vehicle, but we believe there are six sets of male prints here and one female; and as with the rear prints, these predominantly face the rear of the vehicle. One set was without shoes"

"There is lots of fluid evidence here Sir; urine, blood, sweat and semen. The distribution is predominantly sweat and semen on the bonnet and urine, blood and semen on the ground in front of the vehicle and on the grill. I've taken lots of samples."

Lieb Adam and Grace all looked at each other, silently acknowledging their collective agreement this was the pack again.

Then Jon Addams spoke up "There are a pair of men's trousers discarded near the rear of the vehicle; I've bagged them. The picnic area seems just that, a celebration picnic lunch for two, champagne included. The interesting find was a small camera; it seems they were taking photos of the occasion."

"Jon, give that your priority please. Let us know if there's anything helpful on it" Adam directed.

Constable Stanley Fullerton then spoke up "Sirs, Mam we found evidence of a single vehicle parked since the rain we had three days ago. They've taken tyre casts of them."

"They don't go beyond the parking lot" Constable Henry McKay added.

Stanley continued "when we walked back to this scene from that carpark we could identify ground disturbed by recent movement, and we found a discarded drink bottle: that's been collected."

Henry added "the path from the vehicle back to the scene provided clear observation of the activity going on: we even stopped and waved at Jon Addams a couple of time when it appeared he was looking straight at us but he never responded."

All eyes turned to Jon who had drifted off into his memory: Jon then responded "I never noticed them."

"OK, can those with evidence get back to their labs and get onto examination and reporting. Leon, can you and your partner help us extract the two people from the vehicle please?"

"Yes boss, I'll get Barnie to bring the wagon to here shall I?" Lieb nodded his approval.

"Jon can you call forward and get a vehicle extraction team out here please?" Adam asked.

"Already on their way."

"Great. Henry and Stanley can you wait for it up by the parking lot and direct it down here please. Can you also tape off the parking lot and send any inquisitive members of the public on their way?" Adam added.

With the Fiscal team and the constables departing, Lieb, Adam and Grace turned and walked to the vehicle. They stayed silent, each putting images to the information they had received; Grace drawing scene diagrams into her e-book.

The three gathered at the rear of the vehicle and looked at the struggle that went on there.

"They made him stand here and watch" Grace spoke in hushed tones.

"They're truly animals" Adam added.

Lieb just nodded, his fists clenching and unclenching. Adam knew better than to ask Lieb if he wanted to pass this case on; he simply placed a hand on Lieb's shoulder to announce his support.

Leon joined them and they discussed extraction options.

"How about we open the rear door and remove the seats?" Leon suggested.

The detectives and Lieb nodded acknowledgement and they watched as Leon made it happen. Grace stood beside him and made notes of the interior of the car as he worked. When she was finished, Leon used the lever by the driver's seat to unlatch the rear window / door: being a fastback shape the window lifted creating a large unobstructed opening. Leon and Barnie emptied the plumbing tools from the boot compartment and then extracted the tubing that linked the exhaust to the interior cabin through the centre armrest.

Leon then took some tools from his kit bag and climbed into the boot space and cut the cover from the rear seats exposing the underlying structure. He removed the retaining bolts and the seat backs sagged. "Are you ok for me to pull these seat backs off now?" he enquired. Again the two detectives nodded and Lieb responded "yes please."

Leon juggled each seat frame, disconnecting the seat from its fixation device, and then passing the seat back through to Barnie who took each in turn and placed them on the ground. Now everyone could clearly see the last moments of Roger and Janine Hartfield: Roger had pulled Janine into an embrace and held her there until they had both died.

"He must have been devastated about not being able to protect her; couldn't live with the memories of it" Grace postulated.

"I wonder if she was even alive when he pulled her into the car with him?" Adam added.

"Let's get them out of here and find out that and everything else we can" Lieb responded.

Behind them they could hear the sound of a heavy vehicle: "OK Leon and Barnie, when you finish up here can you instruct the vehicle recovery team to bring the vehicle to the lot? Thanks" Lieb added.

Then Lieb Adam and Grace left the recovery teams to do their job and they walked back to the parking lot to collect their cars. "Meet in my office for a briefing before we complete these autopsies?" Lieb asked.

"We just need to brief Mac on the way through and pick up the Fire Report" Adam replied.

"OK, I'll get on to the scene reconstruction and see you later this evening."

The three climbed into their two vehicles and departed. It was already after 18:00; this was going to be a long day.

Chapter 22

Lieb relaxed into the drive: the A93 terminated at Rattray and he'd crossed over the river Ericht and through Blairgowrie and was now heading south on the Old Military Road to Dundee.

Much of the original growth of the town of Blairgowrie in Scotland was a direct result of the town being strategically located along the river, enabling the linen weaving industry in the late 1700's to enjoy massive success. It had always been one of a pair with Rattray, which sat on the opposite bank of the River Ericht.

Now Lieb drove through undulating farmland, bordered by dense hedges and dotted with small lochs; he breathed deeply and exhaled slowly, and congratulated himself on the ability to do so. For four months it had been like holding his breath, or rather, having the breath squeezed out of him; where inhaling was constricted by tight bands that simply refused him room to breathe. Finally he thought, he was moving forward.

He placed a call to Dr Anne Haggarty "Good afternoon, Dr Haggarty's rooms" the voice answered.

"Dr Haggarty, Lieb Canavan; can you talk?"

"Why yes Lieb, I was only completing paperwork and I'm sure you appreciate how long I'm going to be here. How are you feeling?" she enquired.

"Better" he replied, then hastily added "not good, but definitely an improvement on before we talked. Thank you" he concluded.

"You're most welcome. Where are you now? You sound like you're in an empty room."

"In the car, driving back from a case." Lieb explained.

"Are you alright? Was this another attack by those men?"

"Actually yes, but that's not why I called. I wanted to say thank you; ever since you taught me to focus on the blue yacht tattoo I have been able to take a step forward. I can speak to colleagues without clenching my teeth to contain the screams. And I can breathe; you did that."

"Well I'm glad to hear that Lieb: one step at a time and we'll take those together."

"Dr Haggarty" Lieb started again, his brow now filling with sweat..."Anne please; one doctor to another?"

"Anne" Lieb said and swallowed the bile that filled his gullet, determined now to say this gall he kept inside: "Anne, Rose was pregnant."

"Yes Lieb I know, it was in her autopsy report."

"But Anne, I had testicular mumps when I was fifteen: I have azoospermia." There, the words were finally spoken; his gall discharged.

"Oh" was all Anne's initial reaction; then "we do have a lot to work through. But not over the phone; ring me when you get to the office and can give me some times you can be free to talk. But make it soon Lieb, very soon."

"I will Anne: thank you, I already feel somewhat more unburdened." And Lieb rang off.

Anne stood with the phone in her hand, looking at it as if it had just bitten her and she was wondering if it would strike again. Lieb may well feel unburdened; he'd just piled it on top of her.

Whilst Lieb was on the phone talking to Anne, Grace was on the phone talking with Marcus.

"Hi Sexy Man, what are you into?"

"Sexy Man?" Adam asked from the driver's seat.

"Shhh, private conversation: just drive" Grace hissed at Adam. Back into the receiver she listened to Marcus explaining he was sitting thinking about an intriguing conversation he'd just had and wondering what his best next steps were.

"Well, we've just left a scene where Lieb actually spoke to us for two minutes in one stint" Grace paused for impact and then added "And then he spoke with members of his team in an actual dialogue that wasn't just nods and grunts."

"Really?" Marcus came back. "He's done something to reconnect himself with the world: how encouraging. Actually, I could use this recent intrigue as an opening into a conversation. How long are you out? And are you going straight to autopsy?"

We're still forty five minutes out and no, we're coming in to brief Mac before going to the Fiscal's office."

"Great, I'm going to give Lieb ten minutes in his office and then I'm going to take my intrigue to him. If you come as planned that will give me an exit if I need it. I promise not to keep him from you." And then Marcus changed direction and asked Grace her plans for later.

"It's 18:I0 now and our ETA into Dundee is 19:00; after speaking with Mac, I guess we'll be in Lieb's office at 19:30 starting autopsy about 20:00. This is going to be a long evening."

"OK, so you stay in the apartment tonight; I'll go home to the girls. Just remember to eat something and don't drive tired."

"Adam's the driver" Grace said looking over at Adam and noticing the strain around his eyes. "But yes, I'll get a patrol to drop me off at the apartment; sometime around midnight I suspect."

Grace rang off and looked over at Adam "do you want me to take the wheel for a while?"

"Thank you, yes I would appreciate a break" Adam replied and pulled into the roadside bay and they swapped places.

Marcus sat in his vehicle and watched Lieb walk through the maze of buildings on campus toward his office complex. Grace was right; there was something more positive about Lieb's presence. He was walking with his head up and his stride more affirmative whereas he'd been walking with his eyes downcast and he stomped the ground as if punishing it for its existence. Marcus mused over this information for a couple of minutes and then rang Lieb to announce his presence.

"Hi Lieb, its Marcus: I was hoping I could call in for fifteen minutes to chew a bone with you?"

"I'm expecting Adam and Grace shortly, but I can spare fifteen minutes for you."

"Great, I'll be there directly."

Marcus had decided to buy coffee and pastries before walking to meet Lieb: was actually at the counter having already placed the order and was simply waiting to collect the coffee. When it was ready he walked the short distance to Lieb's office and signed in at reception.

Marianne was leaving as Marcus walked in "Another one working late?" she enquired.

"This is my last stop for tonight" Marcus replied, and dropped his voice so only Marianne could hear, "How is he?"

"Better every day. Don't you stay late now and don't the two of you think for one minute that constitutes dinner" Marianne added, pointing at the pastry parcel Marcus held.

Marcus wandered down the corridor towards Lieb's office and the first thing he noticed was the door was open: Grace was right; there was a fundamental shift in Lieb's persona and a positive one it seemed.

He tapped at the open door and Lieb looked up and motioned him inside.

"Great, food and coffee; can we eat whilst we talk?" Lieb started.

"Let's" Marcus agreed and the two of them moved to the small seating area to the side of the desk and sipped coffee and munched on pastry.

"OK, don't keep me in suspense; what's your bone?" Lieb enquired.

"I got a visit from Margaret Marshal, Executive Director of Governance at Ninewells Hospital. She's actually my sister-in-law Elena's sister so that's why she came to me. It seems her governance team were doing the legwork for a national audit on the Liverpool Care Pathway, which is used for end of life care." Lieb nodded, as a clinician he was well aware of the protocol: when there was no hope of recovery a patient was kept comfortable and a regime of medicines was administered to alleviate pain, ultimately ending life.

"Well, they discovered some irregularities in the documentation of some patients; gaps actually and they all involved the same doctor. And when they spoke with the Nurse Manager of the ward they got evasive comments. They spoke with their manager who in turn asked some of the ward nurses in a conversational manner and got comments that raised red flags."

"What sort of comments?" Lieb asked as he sat back and sipped coffee.

"We're not sure what he does behind the curtain: whenever he gives the meds the patient dies moments later: you can't trust a doctor who disposes of his own medication giving set." Marcus read from his notes. "Oh and this gem: I told the charge nurse he was playing god; I told her I had caught him administering meds that weren't written on the patients chart."

"Anyway" Marcus continued, "The Governance Manager spoke with her Exec Director, who in turn spoke with the Chief Exec and the Board's Clinical Governance Lead. They instructed her to look at the audit herself and bring her findings to them: this she did and the doctor was questioned. He answered all the questions put to him, grudgingly apologised for his tardiness in documentation and was allowed to return to the ward."

"Margaret doesn't feel the matter is fully uncovered but having put her case to the highest power feels she has no further options: what do you think?"

"It's interesting that the hierarchy in clinical care persists even after the myth was exposed and published, that doctors are not gods and made mistakes. And the Shipman enquiry shows us doctors are not only human, they can be serial murderers just as much as anyone else. Scary that lesson hasn't galvanised a more radical response." Marcus was satisfied: this was the most Lieb had said in four months and he found it most encouraging.

"So" Lieb continued "what have you got other than a story?"

"Margaret gave me all the evidence on a thumb-drive" Marcus replied, fishing the small data device from his pocket and handing it over,

"You know, regardless of the outcome, if I get involved Margaret's professional life will suffer. She may be protected in Whistleblower legislation but that can't protect her from being a pariah amongst her colleagues."

"She's very aware but she also knows she can't just let this go."

"OK I'll look over the findings and see where that takes me. Did you let her know I'd be looking at it?"

"Yes" Marcus answered "I promised I'd keep her in the loop."

Lieb and Marcus looked up as the sound of voices announced the arrival of Grace and Adam. "You have us queuing at the door, so I'll let you go" Marcus said standing up.

"Yes, I'm afraid these two have priority tonight, but I'll let you know as soon as I've investigated the information on the data file. And Marcus, great to see you" Lieb finished.

"Too right, let's catch up for a drink one night soon" Marcus collected the paper coffee cups and paperbag rubbish and left the office to Lieb Adam and Grace. Looking back as he walked down the corridor he was overwhelmed by emotion: his best mate was surfacing after drowning for so long, and he was talking to the woman who took Marcus' breath away.

Chapter 23

Lieb ushered Adam and Grace into the chairs across from him and then got up and collected the files that he'd been working on when Marcus had visited. Seating himself across from Adam and Grace Lieb spoke to Adam "what does the fire report give us?"

"About as much as we expected: hot fire, started by four Molotov cocktails. Fortunately, at least for us, the counter protected Rosy Garden from the initial conflagration and we had the opportunity to speak with her before her demise."

"OK, here's the autopsy findings" Lieb said, handing them both copies.

Lieb started walking them through the autopsy findings: he'd taken the liberty of highlighting key pieces of information so they could follow his channel of communication.

"The autopsy was completed by Martin Ashton on Tuesday August 14 2013 at 07:15. The external body was burned third and fourth degree, to 74 percent, with lighter second degree burns to the remaining 26 percent. The lower torso and limbs were most extensively burned, with lighter burning to the upper torso and head. Is that congruent with scene photos?"

Marcus and Grace nodded the affirmative, so Lieb continued.

"The attitude of the body was pugilistic as a result of heat-related contractures" Lieb looked up and imitated a boxer with flexed arms in a typical boxer stance. Then he continued on "Close examination shows a depressed skull fracture over the supraorbital margin" he tapped his head just above the left eyebrow "with underlying haematoma."

"On opening the skull there is an extradural haemorrhage related to the skull fracture."

"So she was knocked unconscious and left to burn to death?" Grace clarified. Lieb just nodded; then continued.

"The rest of the autopsy shows no sign of chronic or acute disease processes other than those associated with the burning. A blood sample estimated the carboxyhaemoglobin (CO-Hb) level at 78 percent; coupled with the presence of soot in the airways, particularly below the level of the vocal cords, and mixed with mucous in the distal airways, is additional evidence supporting the view that the deceased was alive at the time the fire started."

“Damn” was Adam’s comment; Grace just screwed up her eyes in a pronounced wince, looked up at Lieb and said “so cause of death in inhalation of fire gases?”

“Yes, that is Martin’s conclusion” Lieb answered Grace.

“Well that fits with the scene photos, the fire report and the statements taken from officers at the scene” Adam concluded.

“The only other information from the labs is a footprint taken from under the window at point of entry. Interestingly it matches a print taken from our other scene.”

“So that definitely links the crimes?” Grace asked.

“It confirms one man was at both scenes” Adam explained.

“OK, if you two are ready, there are two autopsies waiting” Lieb said as he stood. Adam and Grace followed him out of the office and into the autopsy suite.

“Do we have identifications” Lieb asked?

Adam looked at his notes and read aloud “Roger Mackie 31 years and his wife Janine, 28.”

“OK, let’s start with Roger” Lieb said, his tone not suggesting it was open for debate. And then he switched on the laboratory recording tape and began “this is autopsy G762, performed Tuesday August 7th 2013 at 20:07, in the presence of Senior Inspector Adam McAdam and Detective Grace Scott, both of Tayside police. The decedent is Roger Mackie, male, 188cm high and, how old?”

“Thirty one” Adam provided” “thirty one years old” Lieb repeated into the recorder.

Lieb continued, describing the external skins bright, cherry red colouring “This indicates he has had significant carbon monoxide exposure: I’ll take blood samples to confirm.”

Lieb turned his attention to the macerated cheek, and taking a scalpel he neatly cut the damaged tissue free from the face. Adam ducked his head and pretended he was making notes; Grace looked on in fascination. Lieb turned the cheek over to examine the inside tissues and pointed out to his audience the dark staining that was clearly apparent. “This tattooing or staining is caused by close proximity firearm discharge. And looking at the damage to his teeth at the same spot, as well as the laceration to his lower lip and bruising to his tongue, I’d conjecture he had the firearm shoved into his mouth and fired.” Lieb concluded.

Grace looked puzzled so Adam added “To stop him from protesting I guess.”

“Bastards” was Grace’s only response.

Lieb continued his examination, taking photos and sharing any finding: bruising to the lower right abdomen, abrasions to the knees and fractured nose.

“This is interesting” Lieb exclaimed whilst holding Roger’s head in his hand. Roger was staring up at him, not looking. Lieb pulled an overhead light to an angle to light the back of the skull. Help me roll him over he asked of his audience, and Grace stepped forward to help. Lieb directed the light low over the back of the skull, shining up and over the top, and then he grabbed a shaver and removed the hair over the area he’d illuminated.

Grace and Adam watched as a dark purplish bruise emerged from under the mat of hair. “He was very lucky, or not, to have died from this injury. If this depressed fracture had occurred just 2cm lower, it’s most likely it would have damaged the anterior division of the middle meningeal artery and he would have remained unconscious and died of a cerebral haemorrhage” Lieb explained.

Lieb took lots of photos and then applied a paste which, when he peeled it off, showed a true likeness of the shape of the item used to club Roger. He then got Grace to help roll him onto his back and he continued with the examination.

The internal organs did not identify any chronic disease or further trauma, so Lieb finished up and moved Roger to a trolley. He washed down the autopsy table and pulled Janice's body onto it.

He began the same way as he had for Roger, providing the autopsy recorder with all the information on identification, description and witnesses. Then he looked up at Adam and Grace and asked "ready?"

"No" Adam answered "Not ever will I be ready to witness this cruelty." Lieb nodded in response and began.

"There is cherry red colouring of the external skin but not as distinct as that of Roger Mackie with whom she was found: blood taken for haematology. Examination of her neck shows three distinct puncture wounds consistent with an injection site: Blood taken for analysis."

"Nipples are intact and no obvious injuries to the frontal torso. The front of both legs shows extensive contusion" he looked up and added "bruising" for the benefit of Grace "and abrasions across both lower thighs. Incision of the contusions shows hematoma maturation, inflammation, necrosis of damaged myofibrils, and phagocytosis of the necrotic debris. In addition both femur bones show comminuted fracturing."

"So the attack went on for so long they managed to break both her legs?" Adam enquired.

"Yes, I'm afraid so" Lieb answered, then continued "The skin from the digits of both feet show extensive abrasions."

Lifting Janine's shoulder Lieb said into the recorder "The back of the torso shows numerous bite marks." Lieb stopped and asked Adam to help him turn Janice onto her front. Then he carefully excised three bite marks and placed them in containers for later ascertaining dental patterns.

Lieb took a shuddering breath and then carefully lifted Janice's legs at the knees then let the legs fall open. As the legs parted to show the extensive damage, there was an audible groan from the three witnesses. Lieb lifted his face toward the ceiling and pictured a little blue yacht: he held that image for a long moment before dropping his head back to the task at hand.

"Examination of the external genitalia and colposcopy examination with digital image capture shows an injury pattern consistent with rape. There are extensive lacerations to the external and internal organs and anus and rectum."

Next Lieb picked up a reciprocating saw and opened the chest cavity. "Now this is interesting" he said, and he took a scalpel and with a few deft strokes, he extracted the heart from its foundations. He held Janine's heart in his hand and showed them a large pattern of discolouration. "This is acute myocardial ischemia."

"I don't follow" Adam said and Grace added "me neither."

"Janine suffered a heart attack, but not from the occlusion of a coronary artery in the usual way. We see this pattern and distribution when the blockage is caused from coronary artery spasm. With proper and emergency care it's usually survivable" Lieb explained.

"So, how did this happen?"

"Extreme emotional distress, or a reaction to the drugs are both reasonable explanations" Lieb postulated.

Lieb examined the abdominal cavity next and gave it a "healthy' report. "Not pregnant?" Adam enquired: Grace gave him a hard look and then turned to see Lieb's reaction.

"Thankfully not" was all Lieb said but the tightness around his eyes carried his message. "Let me finish up here and I'll join you in my office." Adam nodded and turned toward the door: Grace placed a hand on Lieb's arm and he raised his eyes to meet hers. She didn't need words; Lieb could see the comfort her gesture portrayed.

Lieb closed the y-cut made in the chest and wrapped the body and pulled it back onto the trolley. He wheeled it into the storage and left it alongside Roger: they could share this last night together until claimed by a loved one.

Leon appeared then and started the clean-down process; Lieb visited the restrooms to wash and freshen up and then joined Adam and Grace in his office.

Settled with coffee and pastries Leon had brought in, Grace, Adam and Lieb sat in quiet reflection for minutes, before Adam looked at his watch and started the briefing.

"So, between the scene reconstruction and the autopsy results, is it reasonable to conclude this is a double homicide, or do we need to consider Roger's final act and call it a double suicide?" Adam enquired.

"Whilst the attack on Janine would have eventually resulted in death, suggested by the depth of cherry colouring of the skin, she didn't die until she was pulled into the car by Roger. I feel a conviction of grievous assault resulting in death is more likely to succeed in court" Lieb explained.

"Now Roger, the carboxyhaemoglobin result should confirm he died of carbon monoxide poisoning and he perpetrated that. So his c-o-d has to be suicide and the charges on the pack, when found, can only be grievous assault."

"What: Adam exclaimed, "That hardly seems fair. They pistol whipped him and left him for dead."

"Ummm" Lieb countered "we don't know what he was struck with yet: let my team work it up first please."

"But that seems a reasonable assumption; we know he had a firearm held on him" Adam persisted.

Grace interjected "They don't know". The two men stopped their discussion over likely charges and looked at her questioningly. "They don't know" she repeated. And realising Adam and Lieb also still didn't get it she elaborated "They struck him and left him for dead, but they don't know he is dead. We could use this to lure them out?"

"What, set the hospital up for an attack by four or five mangy animals?" Lieb asked.

"Well obviously we'd be prepared" Grace defended.

"And there's the camera" Adam answered. "We could say we have photos – no that would keep them away. But we could setup a snare. Let's ask Mac".

Adam looked at his watch, it was 22:47, so he decided he would send a text and if Mac was still up he would ring back. And so he texted 'we have a break in the case, need to talk before anyone releases info, will brief at 07:30'.

"I'll let you know tomorrow what the plan is" Adam explained to Lieb as he stood up. "Come on Grace, let's get some shut eye before we brief Mac at 07:30." Grace nodded and stood also. She turned to Lieb and added "We'll get them, if it takes the rest of my life, we'll get them all." Lieb nodded and smiled. It wasn't a big smile, no happy grin, just a small satisfied curl of the lip.

As they walked out to the car Adam commented "You have a goodness about you Grace, I hope this job doesn't kill that." Grace nodded and looked into Adam's eyes and Adam silently made a pact with himself; as long as Grace was his partner, he'd go extra miles to keep her safe, physically and emotionally.

Lightening the mood he asked "Do you know your address tonight?" She barked a laugh and punched him in the arm. "My apartment in Dundee would be great." And that's where he left her on his way home.

Chapter 24

When Grace tumbled through the door of the apartment she was tired; emotionally exhausted and bone weary. But when she noticed the apartment was filled with soft music and candlelight, many of her cares fell away.

Marcus took her in a bear hug and just held her; he held her until the knot in her shoulders fell away and her head fell onto his shoulder, then he held a little while longer. Finally he lifted her face up and he kissed her long and deep and promising and when she was responding with her usual pattern, he let her go and held her by her shoulders.

"Head off for a hot shower and I'll meet you in bed. What time do you need to start tomorrow?" Marcus enquired, his voice low and soft.

"Adam's collecting me at 07:00" Grace murmured.

"OK, I'll set an alarm."

Whilst Grace showered Marcus busied himself in the small kitchen. By the time Grace walked to the bed he was sitting waiting for her, warm chocolate in hand. And as she sat on the bed and slurped at it, Marcus poured warm oil in his hands and began massaging her feet: Grace oohed appreciatively.

Marcus worked his way up one leg, then the other; all the while Grace slurped on her warm chocolate. The legs and chocolate finished, Marcus took the mug from her and then rolled Grace onto her tummy. Then he poured more warm oil and massaged her buttocks in firm tender strokes, moved up her back and onto her shoulders: Grace snored softly and he turned her on her side and covered her with the doona. Then he walked around the apartment making sure all the candles were out, before finally joining her in bed. He pulled her into his embrace and fell asleep too.

The alarm woke them at 06:30 and Grace stretched and rolled over onto her knees. She straddled Marcus and honoured him with her award winning smile. "You put me to sleep last night before I could say thank you." Marcus reached up and gently tugged at Grace's left nipple; it responded immediately. Grace moaned and started rolling her hips, massaging her clitoris on Marcus belly. Marcus shifted his hands onto Grace's hips and lifted her onto his erection, where she continued her hip rolling: he busied himself stroking a nipple under each thumb and enjoying the ride.

Eventually Marcus sat up to get a deeper purchase within her and Grace threw back her head and moaned. Marcus leaned down a licked Grace's nipple and she squealed with delight. Enough foreplay, Marcus dislodged Grace onto the bed, rolled her on her belly, lifted her hips with his arm and re-entered her doggy-style. Then the action kicked up to frenetic pace, until Grace and Marcus were trumpeting their ecstasy to the neighbours.

Time and responsibility finally barged in and Grace extracted herself and headed for the bathroom. Marcus headed for the kitchen; fired up the coffee pod, warmed milk, multiseed wrapbread and the filling he'd prepared last night and by the time Grace entered the kitchen at 06:54 Marcus was waiting with two coffee's in thermal mugs, two scrambled egg tomato and bacon wraps and two napkins. Grace threw her arms around his neck and kissed him long and deep.

"I love you Marcus Campbell": then examining the parcel he offered she added "I'm just scared Adam may steal you away." Marcus laughed.

"He'd just better keep you safe or I'll take him away; and what they find won't be pretty."

Grace grabbed her kit and the breakfasts and headed out the apartment for another day.

Adam opened the passenger car door from inside and pushed it so Grace could climb in. "Breakfast" she announced as she handed over coffee and hot wrap. "Is this what they mean when they say friends with benefits?" Adam enquired, which earned him an arm punch.

It was only a short drive to work so breakfast was still warm when they reached the desk. They took a few minutes to wolf down the food before Mac arrived.

"Who is eating real food in here?" Mac asked, announcing his arrival. He looked askance toward Adam and Grace "where's mine? You ask a guy in at the crack of dawn, scoff mouth watering food in front of him and don't bring one? Man, you two are cruel."

"OK you two, my office, now" Mac barked. Grace was still unsure of Mac's demeanour; was still unsure when he was joshing, if he ever was. She followed Adam into Mac's office.

"OK, what do we have?"

"The double suicide yesterday was as a result of the SAT pack's assault on a young couple enjoying a celebratory picnic. She was sexually assaulted for so long she suffered a coronary artery spasm that resulted in a heart attack. Her husband was forced to watch; when he objected they shoved a firearm into his mouth and blew the side of his face off. When they had finished their attack they struck him on the head and left him for dead. He came to extremely distraught, jerry-rigged the vehicle, put the two of them inside and let them die together compliments of CO poisoning."

Mac sat quietly listening to Adam's report. "Any leads?"

"There are footprints from the scene – five sets. Lieb's rushing other lab tests first thing this morning. Also, there was a camera the couple were using; maybe there are photos?"

"So why are we here?" Mac asked. Adam looked at Grace and said "It's your idea, tell him."

Mac trained his attention on Grace and she squirmed: it was like being sent to the headmaster. She took a deep breath and started "They left Roger Mackie for dead. He came to and took his own life, along with his wife Janine's; but they don't know that. What if we say he survived? Was under guard in hospital?" Grace left the question hanging, so Adam added "It may draw them out? If they thought to kill the tattooist Rosy Garden it's a fair bet they'll try to take out another witness."

Mac sat quietly summing up their information. "That's a mighty risky strategy; it would need careful planning."

"We would put an under-cover in the bed in a vest and someone in the bathroom fully loaded and watchful, plus other police in the waiting area. And we'd have under covers in nurse uniforms" Adam explained.

"And if we use the isolation room and the hospital security protocol" Grace proffered; to which Mac barked "I'm well aware of the protocol inspector, I wrote it."

"Yes sir" and Grace fell silent. Mac sat watching her for a long moment then continued "OK you two, let's try it. Any suggestion as to whom goes in the bed?"

They spent another fifteen minutes talking through the possible scenario's when John Addams tapped on the door, opened it and stuck his head in. "Sirs, Grace I thought you'd want to know; we have photos."

"Bring them in" Mac barked so John came in and stood whilst the two detectives and Mac continued to discuss the plans. When they seemed stuck on the notion of Grace playing a man in a hospital bed in an undercover role John proffered "I could do that". They all stopped talking and looked at him. "I did that undercover work at the mall last year, and you gave me a tribute sir, remember? I'd like my training not to get rusty; this would be a great opportunity to refresh my skills."

Mac looked at Adam, then at Grace; they both nodded so Mac said to John "OK John, it's yours. Grab a seat and we'll go over the plans to make sure we're all on the same page." Then Mac summed up the plan, watching each face in front of him in turn to assure himself they were working the same script "John, wearing a vest, will be Roger Mackie in bed. Grace, you take point in the bathroom: Adam, cover the waiting rooms with Marcus and Hamilton. Joyce, Glenda and Sheila can play nurse and Neil orderly. What do these photos give us?"

They looked over the photos: one in particular showed Roger Mackie hamming it up for the shot, but over his shoulder was one face and two part-faces. "Make sure everyone has copies of these and spends some time getting to know them" Mac instructed. Then he ushered them out with "You three go brief the team and I'll speak with Matron"

As they filed out, Mac flipped a switch on his phone and asked his assistant Deborah to call Vincent in media and ask him to come to the office.

An hour later, Detective Superintendent Declan Macdonald stood on the steps of Tayside Police, behind a bank of microphones and in front of a rabble of reporters and cameramen. Adam and Marcus stood to his left.

"I'm saddened to inform you another horrendous sexual assault has occurred; another young woman has died of her injuries." There was a hubbub of questions called his way, but Mac held his hand for silence. "I cannot give out the name of the latest victim because her husband, who was forced to witness the assault, was struck in the head and left for dead; and he has survived and is recovering in Ninewell's Hospital. As soon as he wakes we will talk with him and then we'll have descriptions to match to other forensic evidence. That's all for now; as soon as we have apprehended this pack of mongrels we'll let you know. For now, please send your prayers for her husband; don't however harass the hospital staff for information, the patient is being kept in isolation for peace and quiet and doesn't need your noisy banter under his window."

Mac made an obvious conclusion to his speech by stepping away from the microphone and walking back through the police headquarters front doors.

Whilst the media conference was underway, Grace and John took the rest of the team to the hospital and set up. The Director of Nursing Margaret Metcalf was waiting, along with the Security Manager Lucas Salmon: "this is not my favourite role, playing sportsmaster to the Tayside Police" was the DoN's greeting. Lucas just grunted. "However Mac has explained the situation and I understand the imperative to catch these miscreants, so you have our support, and I suppose our blessing as Janine was a healthcare worker, so a member of our extended family."

"We've set up the infectious patient protocol and all staff and visitors have been alerted. The signs are out as you can see that explains the isolation of the patient in room 4A; so all staff and visitors will use the wards south entrance only. I've volunteered Bernadette Macdougall to be your nurse liaison, so she can brief you on the nursing activities you'll need to conduct to sell the ruse. Will the police in the waiting room be in uniform?"

"Yes DoN" Adam replied, using the nursing director's title as he'd witnessed our staff do. She nodded her head at the response and so Adam took it as approval.

"OK, well I won't get in your way: it would only spoil the ruse anyway. How many miscreants are you expecting?"

"One or two only: any more would give their intentions away" Adam explained.

"And are you expecting shooting?" asked Lucas, speaking for the first time.

"We can't rule it out, but we're hoping to identify and contains the suspects before that occurs" Adam answered.

"Well the bullet proof doors installed as 'fire doors' should add an element of safety to the staff and patients, but I'd be happier if we could also lock the doors."

"That would limit the egress points to cover" Marcus added, deferring to Adam.

"I agree, but can we secure it from our side? Just to stop unexpected entry from the ward side when we aren't expecting it?" Adam asked Lucas.

"Yes, I'll show you how."

And so the trap was set: Vincent had briefed the families of Janine and Roger, Mac had used the media to lay the bait, and the hospital setting was enacted. Now all they could do was wait.

Chapter 25

They sat around in their living room laughing, eating and drinking water. The pack was still on a high from yesterday's outing: "I really enjoyed my picnic" Dog exclaimed and the rest of the pack laughed and joined in the merriment, each interjecting their highlight of the day. That two people had been the brunt of their enjoyment seemed totally lost on them.

Driver turned on the TV and switched to the local news channel; a key part of their post attack ritual was to belittle the police efforts to catch them. The morning news was filled by the horrific death of a tattooist in Arbroath, to which they clapped each other on the back and charaded their activities of clubbing Rosy Garden, throwing Molotov cocktails and the tattoo shop erupting in flames. Life, for them, was a hoot.

Then there was a news break: an interview with Detective Superintendent Declan Macdonald and they were all shouting derogatory comments at his TV being when Driver told them all to "shut the hell up". Mac was explaining how the man at the scene yesterday had survived and was recovering in Ninewell's hospital.

The party atmosphere suddenly turned nasty, with accusations and recriminations flying thick and fast. In amongst that hubbub an uneasy realisation took hold and the shouting subsided.

"Import was the idiot who was responsible for fixing the man" Dog announced accusingly.

"Yeah" Biter added, "He had the gun and he gave the all clear."

"Well Import, what about it?" Driver asked quietly; the threatening tone not lost on anyone.

"I hit him hard. He went down and didn't move and I couldn't see how he could still be alive" Import's words gushed forth like blood from a broken nose. "I think they're just bluffing; trying to get us to turn on each other" Import added.

"You bloody import, you've ruined everything" Dog shouted.

Biter added "can't trust an Englishman – ever."

Driver picked up the gun and raked the loading mechanism and aimed it at Import.

"Wait" said the Chemist. "We have no proof. That top cop may just be trying to cover his ass. Members of packs don't attack each other without proof; if we did we'd be nothing but animals. Let's go for a drive and check out the hospital; and if there's something amiss, let's give Import a chance to fix it?"

The mood of recrimination dissipated and Driver reset the guns safety and put it down.

"OK, let's pack up for a drive shall we? And maybe we'll look for some more sport later?" they all agreed with the Chemist, brightened by the prospect of sporting later on. They bundled into their usual positions in the vehicle and started off. They were staying in a remote farmhouse off the A984 just out of Dunkeld and they made their first stop at their local store to resupply on water. Drinking so much meant needing to stop for a pee many times more than normal but they needed the fluids to replace the stores lost during sporting and to flush the electrolyte imbalance from their muscles. Otherwise the cramps were crippling.

Once on the road they drove in silence, each lost in a reverie of the breakdown of their believed invulnerability. But it only took thirty-five minutes to reach the Ninewell's hospital in Dundee and scope out the situation. They found two police cruisers parked in the executive staff car park, a knot of reporters hanging around out front and when the Chemist and Import wandered into the hospital reception area they saw signs about an infectious outbreak requiring all access to ward 4 be via the south entrance. They didn't see Detective Hamilton Dunn watching them from behind a newspaper where he sat in the corner of the reception area. When they turned and left, Detective Dunn was straight on the radio to Adam McAdam "Sir, I've just spotted two men checking out reception; one looks like one from the photos."

"Tony can you see where they've gone without being spotted?" Adam asked. Hamilton, or Tony to his colleagues, walked to the glass entry doors and stood just to the side where an information board provided some cover. He scoured the area out front and saw the second of the two men climb into the front passenger seat of a large SUV and the vehicle pulled out of the parking lot by the far exit. It was too far away and too obscured to get plate details, but he did get make and colour. Tony called in "Adam they've left via James Arrott Drive heading west in a metallic coloured SUV. There were four men in the vehicle but I can only be certain one of them got in; I didn't see if the other one got in or went elsewhere."

"Thanks Tony, stay there and stay alert" Adam answered.

Adam alerted the team with him in the waiting room and called dispatch to put out an alert for the SUV whilst Marcus walked to the 'patients room'.

Acting as if he was just checking on his ward, Marcus spoke in a low voice "Tony has just spotted one of the guys from the photos in front reception; we don't know if he's left or just his mates so stay alert." John nodded from his hospital bed but Marcus couldn't see Grace from her position in the bathroom. He really wanted to take her in his arms and beg her to go home, but he knew that was a conversation they could never have; if they wanted to make this relationship last they were going to have to trust each other. And pray to whatever god they had to keep each other safe.

And for some reason, as Marcus walked back to the 'nurses station' to alert them, he thought of Lieb and Rose and realised that with whatever fate had planned, their jobs didn't really make a shortened outcome any more possible than it did for the ordinary folk. They would just have to make very sure they lived their life to the full and never squandered an opportunity to make their time together the best it could be.

Back at the waiting area Marcus couldn't sit still so he stood by the small window and looked out; behind him his colleagues settled back into their rhythm of soft-boiled preparedness.

Driver pulled the SUV out from the parking lot, turned right at the roundabout and drove up Charleston Drive and used the GPS to wind his way through the streets until he connected with the A90 and then turned south, following the signs for Perth. Once he'd skirted Perth and was heading north toward Dunkeld again, he started to talk again: the excitement at the hospital had got his sexual urges flowing again and he wanted to get his mates on the same page. "Do you like asses because they're virgin Dog?"

"Too right, they're nice and tight and as you ram your way in you can feel them tear and you know anyone who follows behind knows they're used goods. What a fabulous way to mark your territory" he answered and then he barked a laugh. The Chemist started his maniacal chuckle and urged him on, so Dog told how he'd first found the delight in a ten year old boy "and when I pushed into him I even heard his pelvis crack. Man I was hooked."

Biter was getting in the mood too and started biting his upper arm; the tissue responding to its punishment by swelling and bruising, an activity that matched the response in his trousers.

"I've got candy, shall we go for a picnic" the Chemist enquired?

"Lets" they all agreed. And so they forgot about Import and his business and turned off the A9 north of Perth and went hunting.

One of the most popular beauty spots in Perthshire, The Hermitage is an outstanding grove of giant trees beside the waterfalls, rapids and swirling pools of the River Braan. It's a picturesque landscaped `wild tree garden` created by successive Dukes of Atholl, including one of the tallest trees in Britain – a majestic Douglas fir measured at 64.5metres (212ft). It was still growing at the side of the `black pool`, near to the bend in the river. The `black pool` is so named because as the waters calm down after thundering through the falls, their peaty content makes them look black – a strong contrast with the foaming white water higher up river. The Braan Walk follows a riverside and woodland path for 6km and it was along this walk a party of five walked. They were excited to be on an unsupervised outing mid-week and the mood was high and the banter loud and jovial.

Jason walked hand-in-hand with Cynthia whilst his twin sister Mona walked behind with her best friend Rachael and Lachlan: Rachael and Lachlan were holding hands too. Most would think Mona was an odd person out as the other were clearly two couples, but Jason and Mona were twins with all the attributes of shared feelings and Rachael and Mona were real close too so a fivesome was not awkward in the slightest. Having an extra actually helped the group develop as individuals as well as couples. And it was known to happen that Mona and Rachael shared an intimacy the guys were only allowed to enjoy from the sidelines. It all made for a fascinating social dynamic of a group of teenagers still existing in the freedoms of late childhood.

They walked and talked and played 'better lyrics' for the popular songs of the time; adding interpretations and their own words which left them all in bouts of hysterics. They had a day off from school in Perth compliments of a bout of food poisoning amongst the teachers. No parent truly believed they would spend the day in the library studying so they had been given a day of leisure; their parents jealous they couldn't do the same. They had packed a picnic and driven to the Hermitage, parked the car, climbed above the small waterfall and walked off to find somewhere private for the day.

Driver pulled the SUV into the parking lot alongside the only other vehicle and climbed out. The rest of the pack did likewise and they stood silently beside the vehicle and listened. They could hear the sound of joviality coming from a number of youngsters in the direction of the waterfall. Driver held up a hand and counted the number of voices he heard with his fingers. The Chemist, Biter and Dog did likewise. All agreed there were five. A grin broke across the faces of each man.

Driver went to the rear of the vehicle and retrieved four poles and a back pack that contained rope and camping equipment. The Chemist grabbed another pack and filled it with bottles of water which he handed to Biter to carry and then stuffed his pocket with packs of candy: he stifled his maniacal cackle but it reflected in his eyes. Driver led the way and the rest of the pack followed; except Import who was busy elsewhere.

Chapter 26

Jon was lying quietly in the bed using the time to review his training, which had included how to stay alert when you're waiting. A mirror had been strategically placed so he could view the doorway without turning his head to look: an oxygen mask obscured his face and an IV was dripping fluids into a needle that was strapped to his arm and not into his arm, soaking an all-day adult diaper hidden under the bedclothes.

Grace was sitting in the dark watching Jon and the doorway beyond. She had watched Marcus walk in about fifteen minutes ago and heard soft talking but it had been too soft to hear. However Marcus' failures to raise his voice or look her way was a clear explanation of the message she didn't see or hear; something was happening and Marcus wouldn't compromise her by making her presence obvious to anyone watching. She respected him from not making a fuss as she supposed many partners of cops would: he understood this was her job and whilst it may seem dangerous the situations were controlled, somewhat, and contingencies planned. Not like the cancer that had taken her mother at thirty-three or the exhaustion that had claimed her father three years later when he had stumbled across the road, so tired from working two jobs he didn't see the speeding vehicle too close to avoid.

Grace concentrated harder when the background noise escalated, but not anything clear to announce present danger, until she heard a shot and a man was standing in the doorway, firearm raised.

Marcus turned from the window and looked at Adam, his eyebrow raised questioningly. Adam returned the look with his own interpretation of concern. There had been a background noise of 'three nurses and an orderly' at work but now the sounds had changed. Instead of quiet banter there was a change in pitch in the voices and a muffled banging noise.

Then, in quick succession, four firearm shots rang out. They turned and ran the one hundred paces to the 'patients' room'.

Driver, the Chemist, Dog and Biter happened upon an idyllic scene: five playthings sprawled on blankets on the ground. On one blanket laid a young man with his head resting in the lap of a pretty lassie. On another blanket, a pretty lassie lying with her head in the lap of another lassie and these two were kissing: Biter felt his erection stretch his jeans.

The fifth plaything was another male and he was heading off to the bushes, undoing his jeans fly as he went. Driver motioned for Dog to intercept him. Whilst Dog went to complete his task, the other three watched and enjoyed the scene.

When Dog returned, Driver handed each a pole and showed them how to extend the pole to a full length and then the mechanism to close the loop. What they all had now was a dog pole; a strong pole with a loop at one end for catching and restraining animals. On his instruction they moved around behind their playthings using the bushes for cover. When they were in place, Driver gave the signal and they moved as one, capturing and securing the four friends stretched out on the blankets.

Initially the girls screamed and struggled, Jason swore and fought but the poles were designed to subdue and restrain large vicious dogs and they used them well. Driver had Jason and he used the pole to force him onto his knees and then he kicked him in the belly with such force Jason screamed and lay curled up on his side moaning: this shut the girls up. Cynthia and Rachael started crying, Mona just glared at them. Dog handed his pole to Biter so he had both Rachael and Mona contained and they knelt at the end of their poles holding hands, with Mona trying to console Rachael.

Dog helped Driver hog tie Jason and secure him to a tree. Then the two of them lashed all three girls to a tree of their own so they were standing in a semi-circle around the 'perfect spot' they had found for an afternoon of fun. Little had they thought the fun was someone else's' and they were the sport.

"Let's set the scene" Driver instructed "Dog, you and Biter roll that large trunk over here would you?" The large trunk was about two metres long and a metre in diameter, the remnant of a tree felling that hadn't been hauled away. After Dog and Biter, supported by much grunting and swearing, had rolled and pushed the log in to centre, Driver got them to help him anchor it to the ground using tents straps and pegs hammered into the ground. Then the Chemist handed out water and packets of candy and all the grizzling about the hard work evaporated. They stripped off their clothes and sat around admiring each other's erections and talking about the fun they were going to have.

"Tell me again Dog about the delight of sodomising a virgin anus?" Biter asked "And does it work as well on boys." Dog wasn't quiet telling of his delight in screwing from behind and the more his excitement grew the greater the despair in the young people secured in a semi-circle around them.

Driver jumped up full of enthusiasm and with a penile erection that measured twenty three centimetres and Cynthia became hysterical. "You leave us alone you perverts" Jason shouted but the pain in his gut silenced him smartly.

Mona called out to Lachlan to run and get help but the Chemist just started to cackle maniacally at her. He picked up a pole and left with Dog to retrieve Lachlan. Once secured with the pole they untied his feet, stripped him naked and forced him back to the circle where they paraded him before all the others. The group's despair grew another notch and Cynthia stopped screaming and settled into seismic sobs instead.

Lachlan's hands were bound in front of him: Dog forced him to his knees in front of the log, and the Chemist stretched his hands out in front of the log and pinned them with more tent pegs driven into the ground. The Chemist then secured each leg below the knee to the ground with rope and tent pegs. Lachlan was now hog-tied over the tree trunk; soundly pinned to the ground by all four limbs but kept upright by the mass of wood under his torso.

Next the pack paraded their erections in front of the four captives, teasing and playing eenie-meenie-miny-mo, trying to decide what order the sport should play. And as they played, they ripped the clothing from the four captives; played with their hair, sucked their nipples and thrust their erections in a parody of what was to come.

Then the Chemist turned his attention to Lachlan, splayed out before them. He knelt down by his head, caressed the skin of his back and shoulders, and then injected a substance into the vein he felt pulsing there. Lachlan screamed as the chemicals burned their way through his blood stream.

"Mine mine?" Dog begged Driver, who nodded in turn and Dog skipped over and knelt behind Lachlan.

"God no" Jason moaned.

Dog started to caress the offering before him, rubbing Lachlan's buttocks and down over his thighs. Lachlan struggled but the effort was futile as he was most securely bound.

Mona was horrified at what she was watching: so appalled but unable to tear her eyes away. She had been unaware the Chemist was standing just behind her until he spoke into her ear "The ropes won't give, my boat work made sure of that." Mona jumped at the words and looked over her left shoulder to see the Chemist's wild eyes centimetres from hers. He stepped behind her, rubbing his erection on her naked buttock and taking her nipples in his fingers he began to play. As Mona desperately tried to find a way to make him stop, Dog entered Lachlan's anus, ramming his erection hard and fast up through Lachlan's rectum. Lachlan screamed but the drugs stopped him from fainting; in fact the terror only made them work better at keeping him alert. The forest filled with his screaming.

The Chemist moved around in front of Mona and kissed her; driving their lips together with such force Mona felt her lips split and swell. She bit down but found he held her so it was her lip she bit, not his so she stopped. Over her shoulder she could see the sodomy being perpetrated on Lachlan; could see his struggle with the veins sticking out on his neck, and could feel his anguish as her own body was assaulted. And it never stopped; she was certain it went on for hours. But finally the man got off Lachlan and walked toward her. The man playing with her had moved to her nipples and was chewing and tugging on them and rubbing his hands between her thighs. He stopped as the man approached and looked at him "More?" the approaching man asked and Mona thought "Oh my god, not me now."

"Sure, I'll get a hit, but this one's mine." And the Chemist moved to his pack and took out a syringe and drew up more solution, then approached Lachlan and injected into his neck. "That should give you more" the Chemist said and moved back to Mona.

Dog called Biter over and instructed him on the finer points of sodomising another man. When he mounted Lachlan the screaming started all over again, especially when an excited Biter started tearing lumps of flesh from his back. Satiated for a while, Biter withdrew and started dancing and whooping like a sun-stroked crazed man: he and Dog even partook in a game of sword fight with their erect penises.

The Chemist shook his head then left Mona for another visit to his bag. This time he prepared two syringes, taking only the smaller one to Lachlan's neck and injecting it. Very quickly Lachlan's body lost all muscle definition and slumped over the trunk. The Chemist untied Lachlan's lifeless body and motioned for Biter and Dog to drag it away.

Then the Chemist asked Driver for his pick: Driver picked Cynthia. He draped the pole hoop over her neck and cinched it tight. Then Dog undid her legs and Driver dragged her toward the trunk. Cynthia begged and cried but they never paid any heed. Once secured, the Chemist injected her with the multiplier potion: it multiplied Cynthia's pain perceptions but also her tolerance so she hurt more, felt more but could not lose consciousness and therefore find release. The Chemist gestured Driver she was good to go. Then he wandered back to his bag and collected a tube of gel which he carried back to Mona.

When he first applied a dollop to her bruised and swollen lips, wiping the solution on the inside of her lower lip as well, she had the strange sensation he was taking care of her. But then he took her head in his hands and kissed her brutally again, and she found out the solution had another purpose as her sexual emotions ramped up and her body betrayed her. Her nipples got large and hard and the growl from between her legs almost had her begging to be next. The Chemist watched her reaction and started cackling joyously.

In front of her Cynthia was prepared as a sacrificial virgin on an altar and the knife that was to torment her was hovering in anticipation. Drivers unusually large and drug enhanced erection was rubbing itself on Cynthia's labia in anticipation. The waiting was tormenting Cynthia enormously: and then it happened. Driver rammed his enormous erection into Cynthia that she screamed with such magnitude pieces of her vocal cords tore loose and filled her mouth with blood. Her tight virginal vagina suffered forth degree tears so that Driver both raped and sodomised her simultaneously.

And as he bucked and thrust from behind her, the Chemist slipped a thumb across Mona's labial folds and felt her swoon. He kept up the teasing, watching as Mona's eyes crazed as her body betrayed her. Cackling with enjoyment he slipped his thumb between Mona's vaginal lips and fingered her until his hand was drenched in her fluids. Beside them Rachael railed at her, demanding she stop and when that didn't work, called her all the wickedness she could think of for enjoying herself at her friends expense. But Mona's body begged for more, and try as hard as she could, the words crossed her lips and escaped for all to hear.

When it was Jason's turn, Biter got to go first and he relished the new found pleasure he had at the tight male anus and when Dog followed him he tried out Biter's favourite of tearing skin from the flesh squirming underneath him. Jason died without the injection, the kick to his stomach had caused slow painful internal bleeding that the rape only exacerbated. All the while the Chemist applied sexual lotion to Mona's lips and kissed her ferociously hard breaking the small blood vessels and increasing absorption. He sucked her nipples and thumbed her clitoris and drove her into sexual frustration, never satisfaction. And all the while he cackled joyously.

With Rachael's turn the Chemist applied a halter and had Dog and Biter arrange her so she was on her back. He poured heaps of the lotion into her mouth and instructed Driver how to lift her jaw to aid entry. He poured more lotion over her labia and instructed Biter how to make her squeal so the screaming through her bronchus would create waves of the bronchial muscles to stimulate Driver. Then the Chemist returned to Mona.

As Mona watched on in horror, her beautiful sexual partner Rachael was raped from both ends; Driver driving his huge penis through her lips and deep into the trachea which allowed air entry into her lungs. From the other end worked Biter and as Rachael's body convulsed to the relentless onslaught, the Chemist used his tongue and teeth to torment Mona the same way Biter did Rachael.

Finally the sun was getting low within the trees. They untied and dragged Mona to the altar: The Chemist used his erection as a sabre, thrusting ever deeper into her. Then Dog climbed on board and sodomised her in his usual fashion, but before Biter could start his routine and whilst Mona struggled to understand what had changed, the Chemist injected her with something and her world of torment ended.

Chapter 27

As they arrived at the doorway differences became apparent very obviously. There was a body on the floor whose blood was quickly spreading and Grace was ripping the bedclothes off and shouting at Jon. Jon seemed in shock and was wide-eyed and gasping. Then he took a long deep breath and held up a weak hand and announced he was OK.

Grace shouted at Adam “there was a fourth shot - check the others” and Adam and Marcus bolted from the room. They found Joyce, Glenda and Sheila trapped behind a locked linen cupboard door: Joyce had her pistol in her hand. “I fired as a warning shot when we got locked in” she explained. “Is everyone alright?” Glenda added.

“We haven’t found Neil” Adam said.

“He went to the toilet” Sheila started as Marcus and Adam hurried down the corridor toward the gents, handguns still drawn and perceptions on maximum alert. They found Neil slumped in a corner, unconscious and barely breathing. “Go back to the locked door that separates the wards and get help” Adam asked of Marcus. “I’ll just make sure there’s no-one else.”

Marcus made his way back passed the nurses’ station and when this was clear, checked on John and Grace. “Glenda and Sheila please go to Adam and help him check for anyone else.” They nodded and moved off. “Jon are you OK?” he asked.

“Yes thanks to Grace.” Marcus nodded at Grace and she honoured him with her award-winning smile. “Neil needs help; I’m just going to unlock the door and get some” Marcus explained and then he moved off.

The alert had gone out when the kids weren’t home by 17:00. It had taken some initial convincing at the local Tayside Police to set up a search, but with the recent murders the Duty Sergeant suggested they use the GPS tracker for the cell phones. Only one had pinged but when called was never answered. The Sergeant assigned two constables to check it out, and when they had reported back the vehicle was in the carpark at the Hermitage in Dunkeld and there was no response to their calls, the Sergeant responded to the voices of concerned parents fearful of the kids being lost or injured, and agreed to send other staff with torches and tracker dogs.

The additional police arrived at 19:10 and the search had begun. It took until 19:30 before they had finished searching the lower falls area and had then climbed up and over the falls and the dogs found a scent, got excited and took off.

Driver heard one dog and then several others. "It's time to be gone" he said to the Chemist. The Chemist reluctantly withdrew from Mona's warmth, moved to his pack and withdrew the prepared injection. Then they all heard the distant calling of dogs and people, so the Chemist pushed the injection into Mona and left, following his pack away from the coming throng but in a direction to their vehicle.

When they made it to the carpark they found a single constable keeping guard over the vehicles. Driver whispered to the pack and they prepared: then moving as one they used the dog poles to secure the constable whilst the Chemist found his bulging neck vein and injected him with 20cc of morphine. The Constable dropped at their feet and they waited until the Chemist declared he was dead and they could leave.

Once in the vehicle and moving away with speed the pack started howling like crazed dogs. They discussed their afternoon of sport with Biter trumpeting the delights of virgin male sodomy. The Chemist found he was still horny from the delights of Mona.

The police group moved into a clearing with the dogs barking excitedly. Senior Constable Deena Storey quickly identified the odour pervading the glen and asked the dogs be contained. "Tyne, let's you and I walk a perimeter to see what we have here?" Deena said, then added "Can the rest of you stay where you are and take notes of everything you can see, hear and smell please."

Deena and Tyne began the perimeter sweep, firstly coming across one tree with rope lashing, then a second and a third. After about forty more paces the stench of death was predominant and they came upon the bodies of four naked, very dead youngsters. Tyne let out a visible groan: and there was a response. Deena lifted her torchlight beam and about twenty paces in front of her was the body of another young girl, trussed to a fallen log. As Deena was taking in the scene information the girl groaned again and Deena moved with lightning speed shouting orders as she went.

"Tyne, finish the perimeter sweep; Harry and Charles, take the dogs and head back to the vehicle with all haste, using the lighting markers to mark your path so the team can get here fast; call for the air ambulance, three ground vehicles and all the scene lighting gear. Also get Senior Inspector Hamish Dudley and as many others as possible out here with extreme urgency. Lucy, fish your knife from your search kit and carefully come here to me, using the lighting markers to mark your path as well."

And to Mona, trussed out in front of her, Deena said softly "Hold on there young one, we'll have you free real quick."

When Harry, Charles and the dogs got near the carpark the dogs started barking again and Harry quickly found their dead colleague near the vehicles. They used their torches to survey the area and when no immediate threat was identified they call in the instructions Deena had imparted them with and added the 'officer down moniker' as well. Then they secured the two dogs into the back of their vehicle and found a blanket to cover Donald's body. It was a long wait until all the backup arrived; firstly from the air and then by road. Harry escorted the helicopter paramedics up the lighted path to the clearing where Mona was barely holding onto life and then he returned to escort Senior Inspector Hamish Dudley to the same site: they met the paramedics coming back.

The rest of a night was a blur for the young constables: senior officers appearing before them giving them messages to run, errands to complete and the farewell of their colleague Donald, who'd graduated with Harry and Charles not eight months ago.

At one point the media had turned up and the youngsters distraught parents as well. Senior Inspector Hamish Dudley took them to a local pub that Harry had arranged to provide recluse. There he explained the death of four of the youngsters and the critical condition of one lassie. Initially Hamish wasn't sure if the parent of the survivor was before him as news of the deaths of four of the five was announced. Finally Suzanne Harrison spoke up "Jason was my son, Mona is his twin sister".

Hamish nodded and took her aside "I'm very sorry for Jason Mam: Mona is on her way to Ninewell's Hospital by air ambulance." Do you want to stay here to wait for Jason or be taken to Mona?" Suzanne looked at him in horror; how could he ask her to decide which child to be with? As if Hamish understood he added "Mona will be with medical staff for the next number of hours so there'll be little chance to see her. And there are senior detectives already at the hospital on another matter; I could ask them to stay so you can be here?" Suzanne nodded so Hamish returned her to be with her friends and support each other in their grief.

Hamish then rang Adam and told him of the incident he had walked into. "There is a single survivor: Mona Harrison is on her way in by air ambulance."

"Thanks Hamish, the air ambulance has arrived and the young girl is on her way to surgery. We'll wait around."

Episode 3

The SAT Pack

Chapter 28

Senior Constable Jon Addams approached Grace's desk at Tayside Police and when she looked up Jon looked over to Adam McAdam to ensure he was paying attention. "I have a nurse Bernadette Macdougall wants a word with you" Jon said to Grace. "She says it's to do with the SAT Pack case" he added.

"Why not Adam, he's the senior" Grace responded.

"She insisted it was you; said it was female stuff. And she wanted a private word" Jon added.

Grace looked at Adam and he nodded: Grace was his partner so he saw no reason for her not to take point on some things.

Grace and Adam stood and Grace said to Jon "Can you bring her to the interview room please Jon."

Adam moved away and quietly entered the viewing room attached to interview room two. Grace met the nurse at the door of interview two, and noticing how distressed the nurse appeared asked her if she needed water.

The nurse just nodded so Grace opened the door to the interview room and said quietly "wait in here; I'll get some water and be straight back." Again the nurse just nodded and, keeping her eyes downcast, walked into the room and sat down. Grace observed her for a moment, then closed the door and went for water.

Seated back in front of the nurse Grace started "Nurse Macdougall is it?" the nurse nodded and just as Grace wondered how she was going to get anything useful from her, the nurse added "Bernadette."

"OK Bernadette; Senior Constable tells me you asked to speak with me; what about?"

"I saw you at the hospital, speaking with Mona Harrison about the assault" Bernadette started: it was Grace's turn to nod. Bernadette continued "This is very hard for me; I've never shared this story with anyone. It's just; I think I know who one of the attackers is."

Bernadette looked imploringly at Grace and Grace just reached out and put a hand on Bernadette's forearm and nodded encouragement. "I need to tell it all so you fully understand my information, but the telling is going to be difficult; embarrassing even. It can't get out, especially back to the hospital. I couldn't work there if they knew."

"Well, so long as it's not information of a criminal undertaking that should be no problem." Grace continued to support Bernadette; the hand on her forearm gently stroking and offering comfort and encouragement. Bernadette looked at her for a long time, then with a shuddering breath she started.

"We were only nineteen, Sandy and I; student nurses at Ninewell's. It was a new time for us, away from the parents' home but like at boarding school somewhat. Being a student nurse was two very extreme spectrums; when we were in the quarters there was always a senior nurse making sure we behaved. And when we were on the wards we were always supervised. But on our days off, we had freedom; and we had our own money and we had a list of experiences we just had to try.

Sandy met a guy in a pub on Perth Road and she thought he was so sophisticated." Bernadette stopped talking: she was wringing a handkerchief and struggling with the memories. Eventually she lifted her eyes and looked at Grace; Grace could see the memories engraved in the soft tissues around Bernadette's eyes, giving her a tormented look. Grace just gave her an encouraging smile and nodded; prompting her to go on.

Bernadette took a deep breath that shuddered across her constricted chest and wheezed from her throat. "I'm not homosexual and neither is Sandy; but we did really enjoy each other's company. Then when this guy took an interest with Sandy I came along like a special option."

"I've never spoken on this for years; was trying to convince myself it was just a movie." Bernadette then got back to her story.

"He had a room over the pub and after we drank and chatted; flirted I guess, he'd invite us upstairs. We were so eager; well Sandy was; it made us feel so grown up."

"He gave Sandy a lip gloss in a little tub and would rub it onto her lips and then kiss her so passionately she often had swollen lips for days after. And it used to get her so horny but then he'd encourage the two of us to get down to it. And we would; strip naked and kiss and touch and play with each other; and he would just watch. And he would cackle."

"After a while he would strip off and lie on the bed and touch us – Sandy mainly: he'd screw her with his fingers and his mouth. She would holler her pleasure and that used to get me even hornier: I don't know what was in the lip gloss but we could go on for hours: some drug I suspect. We used to call it our pot of gold"

"How long did you meet with this man?" Grace asked.

"Four months." Bernadette explained. "It seemed we couldn't get enough. And it wasn't just touching and oral sex, he did screw us too: well Sandy mostly. Even he got to a point where he needed it all. Often times it was doggy style, with Sandy on her knees and him pumping her from behind and me on my back sucking and nibbling on her nipples."

"Sometimes when she was absolutely spent but I was still begging for more he used to screw me too. But I had to be horny as hell cos I didn't exactly like him; he scared me. It was that cackle. And that's what caught my attention at the hospital; Mona's description of that cackle."

"There's more, did you want to know it?" Grace nodded, knowing the telling was cathartic for Bernadette.

"After a few weeks of just using his lip gloss, he introduced Sandy to a liquid which he put in a shooter with gin for her. She told me it burned through her like wildfire and put her in a heaven she never believed possible. She said it heightened her sexual response and also her stamina."

"What happened to this man?" Grace asked. Bernadette became agitated again and dropped her head.

"You won't divulge this information will you?" she asked, her voice clearly displaying her agitation.

"Not the details, but maybe the edges where the puzzle meets other pieces" Grace answered truthfully. Bernadette nodded, paused and continued.

"We met with him regularly over the autumn months, August to January. The itinerary was much the same; we'd meet at the pub after shift, drink laced gin shooters, and then go upstairs and have an orgy for hours. Sometimes it would be midnight before we finally gave in to exhaustion; and the complaints from the landlord."

"Then Sandy met a guy and they got serious real quick. One minute the Chemist and the pub were our whole world, and then she was hitched up to Kevin and moving to Glasgow."

"I went round to tell him; the Chemist. He was at the pub, deep in conversation with the guy behind the bar who made the shooters. I thought he would just send me packing when there was no Sandy: she was just his type, dark hair and dark eyes. But he said something like 'finally, I get to have you and those beautiful tits all to myself."

"I guess I was flattered: I hadn't realised my resentment of Sandy getting most of the attention. Now I was to have full attention and that made me feel special. So I took him up on his offer of a night together; allowed the barman to make me shooter after shooter. And then we went upstairs."

"He undressed me and sucked and nibbled and licked me until I was begging for sexual release. And he obliged with a number of positions but I was so hyped on his chemical additives it wasn't enough. So he offered me his latest game: said he had been saving it for me. I begged for it all and he just cackled. In my memories it's creepy and somewhat insane sounding, but I know the sex was consensual in that I was waiting around for more: I never attempted to leave."

"Well the latest game included an anal massage with his gloss" Bernadette stopped and added for Grace's non-clinical benefit "the anus is very vascular, hence haemorrhoids." "Oh" Grace exclaimed.

"So the anal massage just made my eroticism even more pronounced, so when he entered me I just accepted whatever was on offer. I was kneeling over the back of the bed so he could get good access: after an age of that he stopped and rolled me on my back and we had mormon sex for a while." "Mormon sex?" Grace enquired. "On my back, him on top." Grace nodded.

"Then he got out the gloss and rubbed it on his lips and started sucking my labia and clitoris. My heart was screaming and in hindsight it's a wonder our hearts didn't crash from exhaustion."

"Anyway, he rolled me on my belly again and began to play with something that wasn't him. When I asked why he'd stopped and what he was doing he just cackled and said 'this'. Then he pushed something firm into my anus and started working me with, I guess, a dildo. And then he somehow strapped the dildo onto his person and entered me vaginally himself as well. I was engulfed and consumed and rendered asunder." Bernadette stopped and started sobbing. Grace patted her shoulder and made comforting noises.

In the viewing room Adam threw up.

After minutes of sobbing and wringing the handkerchief until it seemed there was no life left in it, Bernadette resumed her tale of horror.

"I must have eventually passed out. When I came to I was on the bed curled into a ball. The Chemist was talking to the barman, arranging transportation I guess. I could feel unbelievable pain from my navel to my knees, like I was being raped with red hot pokers. So I curled up tightly into a ball and begged for more drugs. I don't know what he injected me with but I woke up in my apartment."

"My bed was soaked with sweat and blood and urine and faeces. I'm a nurse so I knew I was in trouble: But I also knew to call for help meant being taken to the hospital where I was known and having to explain. So I rang a surgical intern I knew: I told him I was in real trouble and I needed him to discreetly bring a surgical kit and come tend to me."

"And bless him he did. I think he first wondered if it was a backyard abortion, but when he tried to stop the bleeding he realised it was far worse. He packed me and he inserted a urinary catheter and an IV and gave me antibiotics: for three days he tended to me but I got no better, only weaker, so he rang Matron and she came."

"Fortunately I was in and out of consciousness and too far gone to care. But Matron treated me with exceptional kindness: made sure the hospital admission and surgery was done with the utmost privacy. She asked me to press charges but I said no; and she accepted my decision without judgement. It's why I still work at Ninewell's."

"I told you all this because I needed to convince you of how sure I am about my accusation." Grace looked deep into Bernadette's grey misted eyes and nodded her unquestioning belief.

"The Chemist worked out of a pub on Perth Road, where it meets Glamis Road. I cannot be sure of his name as we always called him the chemist and it was such a traumatic encounter I have deliberately suppressed his memory. His partner, the barman, whom I always suspected of watching somehow, was tall with poxy skin, thin red hair and bad teeth. I think his name was Bill because Sandy and I used to say 'when the bar-bill rings, the fun begins'. Our stupid rhyme meaning when Bill the barman made our laced gin shooters it was the opening of another round."

"That's good Bernadette, this gives us a good place to start" Grace said. But Bernadette said "wait, there's more." Grace looked at her and sat again.

"He used to bite. When Matron took over my care and organised surgery she instructed the surgeon to excise the bite on my shoulder and to apply a skin graft. Matron then had the excised skin plus bite mark preserved." Bernadette reached into her bag and pulled out a specimen jar, filled with fluid and a large piece of tissue. "There's also the pathology report that details all the vital elements and the shape." She handed these to Grace.

"I paid a heavy price for indulging a sick man his fantasies: it almost killed me. The legacy is I will never have children; hell I can't even enjoy lovemaking. I need to self catheterise monthly with a special surgical instrument, squatted over a mirror, just so I can pee. No such luck for my anus and rectum; they needed to be surgically excised and I have a permanent colostomy. I'm told I should be thankful I'm alive. Maybe I'll have that conversation with Mona one day seeing she's the closest I'll ever get to finding someone who has been through my nightmare. Although probably not, seeing my decision to not report him is the most likely reason for those kids being raped and murdered. I'm not sure I'll ever forgive myself for that." Bernadette dropped her head again and resumed sobbing and murdering her handkerchief.

Grace got up and went to the door to speak quietly with Adam "Seems like we have some good leads" she said, handing over the jar of tissue and the report.

"Tend to Bernadette and I'll get started." Adam replied and turned and walked away from Grace, thankful for something active to do.

Chapter 29

Lieb dressed carefully; and missed Rose especially because she always had this stuff in control. Whenever Lieb needed to attend court or some other official business, Rose always made sure he dressed in a suit, crisp white or soft-coloured unpatterned shirt and bold dark-coloured tie. For work, it was always trousers and shirts with bolder colours, even plaids and stripes, just not garish. She used to say he needed to be dour-conservative at court, scary even, so as to bring heaviness to the information he needed to share. At work though, he needed to look professional but approachable; the staff didn't need to find him scary. Lieb chuckled without mirth at that last thought: some of the staff were still wary of him.

Today he needed his official cover, scary even: today he was visiting Ninewells Hospital to speak with Dr David McTavish, the Palliative Care Consultant at the centre of a growing storm of controversy. As a carer of people with end-stage cancer it was expected he would have death certificates as a general outcome to his caseload.

And there had been little complaint from families over the doctor's care of his patients; their loved-ones. A number of these Margaret Marshal, Executive Director of Governance had interviewed for Lieb though, did make comments about 'how quick the end had come'. To stop raising alarm from the families, Margaret had conducted the interviews at the hospital under the ruse she was undertaking typical follow-up following their recent loss; part of the hospital's bereavement service and a requirement for accreditation of the hospital, to see if there were any elements the hospital could improve upon. Lieb had been sitting in an adjoining room watching and listening on video intercom, and he was particularly aware how eager the families seemed to talk, another factor which wasn't lost on Lieb.

Lieb had introduced the investigation to the hospital Board by reporting concerns from a deceased patient's family, and he added further support to Margaret's cover, by having Dr Suzanne Avery, the hospital's Clinical Governance Board member and Dr Charles Downer the hospital's Medical Executive join him to observe the interviews.

Following on from the interviews Margaret had performed for him, Lieb shared with the two doctors his findings from post-mortem testing he had performed on three of Dr McTavish's patients.

"I obtained specimens of heart whole blood to test, which I submitted to gas chromatography – mass spectrometry. The results were mean oxycodone concentrations 0.820 mg/L - 1.800 mg/L; way above normal."

"They were cancer patients on the Liverpool Care Pathway" Dr Downer interjected.

Lieb held Dr Downers gaze for a long moment, then added "and the methamphetamine levels were 0.58 - 0.62 mg/L. Mixing Oxycodone and Crystal Meth, is sometimes called a redneck martini or Heaven. The mixture quickly produces a euphoric effect; and before the meth wears off, one develops a critical respiratory depression, then coma, and death."

"Why would an inpatient have Crystal Meth in their medication package" Lieb asked, pointedly looking at both doctors. They looked at each other and neither spoke.

"Another interesting piece of information I have that may help you explain what's been going on: Crystal Meth is a concoction, made from a variety of substances. And the low-lifes who produce it have their preferred suppliers and chemical mixes. These chemical recipes are logged so when a drug-bust or drug-related crime is perpetrated, the Tayside Police know where the Meth came from. And the Meth I found in your patients is known to the Tayside Police: it's not from a legitimate pharmacy supplier."

The two doctors before Lieb were squirming; Lieb didn't see guilt as if they were involved, but culpability written in their body-language.

"OK this is how we are going to proceed: I am going to call a detective from Tayside to bring along some uniformed officers to make a very public arrest. Whilst I make the phone call and before the Tayside contingent arrive, you are going to locate Dr David McTavish and find a plausible reason to hold him in the staff room. I also want you to announce to the staff they have this one and only opportunity to come forward and co-operate; after that I will include them in the submission of wrong-doing."

The two doctors before him simply nodded and stood.

"You have ten minutes to have Dr David McTavish and the rest of the staff meet in the staff room. Once the police arrest the doctor, you can extend my offer to the other staff; remember to tell them this is a once only now offer" Lieb emphasised.

The two doctors hurried out and Lieb placed a call to Marcus who he knew was waiting in the carpark. Lieb also knew uniformed officers were deployed in preparation of photographing any staff hurriedly leaving the premises and to stop Dr David McTavish if he tried to flee.

Lieb and Marcus carried a very sombre atmosphere when they walked through the doors into the clinical staff lounge: their intent was to shake the foundations of centuries of learned behaviour that could protect the most heinous of doctors. There would be some that would argue Dr McTavish was acting out of pity; dying patients assisted to die before they suffered, but it was against the law and couldn't be sanctioned. Allow a doctor one gram of latitude and they would take a kilo more. And it could be argued, he knew he worked outside the scope of humanity because he'd never discussed his plans with his patients; never obtained their consent, so no matter how righteous his diatribe may be, no-one could condone it.

All eyes were on Lieb and Marcus as they walked into the room: Marcus's announcement was clear and strong, no-one missed it "Dr David McTavish, I am arresting you on suspicion of three accounts of Voluntary Culpable Homicide; Constable, please cuff him."

Whilst Marcus was making the arrest Lieb was looking at the sea of faces before him: body language showed a mixture of incredulity and reservation, no obvious signs of guilt. As the Constables lead Dr McTavish from the room, Lieb nodded at Dr Charles Downer who cleared his throat and announced "Dr Lieb Canavan is the Procurator Fiscal: he has been investigating this matter. He offers a once only opportunity for you to speak up; and no, before you ask, it won't be anonymously. If you have any information you need to stay right where you are; Dr Canavan will interview you and Dr Avery and myself will be present as well as Detective Campbell who will be taking statements. This is the only opportunity to speak; and thinking you can hide from these serious allegations is senseless, like Dr McTavish you will be found out." As Dr Downer concluded his nervous diatribe the shuffling of feet was the only sound.

As previously queued by Lieb, Margaret Marshall quietly spoke "Dr Downer, I feel I should speak with Dr Canavan." Dr Downer grimaced obviously and then nodded. Surprisingly two younger doctors followed Margaret's lead: Lieb had thought he would get stonewalled, especially from the medical profession.

"OK everyone, back to work" Charles Downer said. "I expect everyone to remain tight-lipped about what has happened here; both in the hospital and in the public arena, and at home. If I link anyone with gossip or heaven forbid, newspaper fodder, the disciplinary process will be swift and harsh. Am I understood?"

There was quiet mutterings as they filed out.

"Marcus, do you have constables who can separately supervise our doctors whilst we start by interviewing...?" Lieb looked at Margaret, continuing the ruse about not knowing who she was.

"Margaret Marshal, Executive Director of Governance."

"Margaret" Lieb concluded. Marcus nodded and spoke to the officers standing behind him, then to Dr Downer who spoke of two offices that could be used to house the doctors until it was their turn to speak with Lieb. With the arrangements in place Marcus turned to Lieb "give me a couple of minutes and I'll just have John escort Dr McTavish back to the department and book him: he can wait in the holding cell until we're finished here. The doctor will want a lawyer anyway and that takes time."

"I have documents in my office I'd like to share with you" Margaret shared before Marcus could leave. Lieb looked at her for clarification. "My office is in the executive wing, just down the corridor from the Boardroom."

"OK" Marcus said, "I'm sure someone can wait and show me to the Boardroom?" Marcus enquired.

"I'll wait here for you" Suzanne Avery offered: and everyone moved off to their required destinations.

Chapter 30

Detectives Adam McAdam and Grace Scott were pouring over the information they'd been gathering from 07:00: they needed a warrant.

Computer searching had revealed a pub on Perth Road where it meets Glamis Road; it was called the Left Luggage Inn, and the alcohol license was issued to a William Gacey. These two pieces of information fitted with the information the nurse had provided them. Adam and Grace did not want to visit him and tip off 'The Chemist' prematurely so they had continued to dig.

They searched for arrest warrants and duty calls to the pub for the period ten to fifteen years previously: fortunately a special grant had seen them entered onto the information database. This search had highlighted twenty two noise complaints and one very intriguing entry about a concerned citizen who had enquired if there had been a murder or maybe an abduction the previous evening: the citizen was certain the noises he heard around midnight could not have been consensual. The bartender William Gacey and a resident Gerald Ross were interviewed: William had agreed with the police that Gerald had been a bit wild the night before and Gerald had sheepishly added he had a new girl and they were enjoying young love. He gave them the name of a nurse at the local hospital and agreed for them to check his room: they found no sign of a crime in his room, although they had commented the room smelt like a whorehouse. They had also rung the nurse and confirmed she was still alive and didn't want to press any charges, so they left the investigation there.

The other tantalising information had come from the Fiscals office: Lieb's deputy Martin Ashton had provided forensic evidence from the bitten skin nurse Bernadette Macdougall had provided, and that had made a hit on the database: Gerald Ross.

And the final tantalising piece of information they had gathered was another address for William Gacey, which was also listed as the address for a Henry Brown, whose name had come up when they searched initially for sexual predators.

Henry Brown was questioned over a sexual assault where biting had occurred; all the forensic evidence had been collected but before the case went to trial the young woman was killed in a hit-and-run. William's tax return and Henry's unemployment allowance were sent to the same address in Dundee.

At 11:10 the warrant for the address arrived and Adam and Grace gathered their troops: Detective Scott McDermid, Senior Constable Jon Addams and Constables Shiela McMurtry, Deena Storey and Neil Johnstone. Quietly confident of their information and in due consideration of the cases so far, all officers donned protective vests, checked their firearms and communicators and left with a determined air.

They didn't stop at the Lost Luggage Inn although the search warrant for this premise was also in hand; they wanted The Chemist and Henry Brown if they were at the address. If Henry was alone they were hoping he'd squeal on his buddies.

It took just eight minutes to reach the address off Glamis Road; a little dead-end street that overlooked the Balgay Cemetery. The housing was a mixture of single and double-story terrace houses in a u-shape: dirty cream coloured with brown slate roofs, but the yards were well maintained. Number sixty was single storey, an end property tucked off to the right side; with a low fence bordering it and more terrace housing starting and running southward.

Adam spoke quietly and briefly to the team: "Grace and I will knock, Scott can you take Sheila and Neil and cover the back, Jon can you cover the street and our backs with Deena?" They all nodded their understanding and moved into position.

"Grace, stay behind me and cover the door will you whilst I knock?" Adam's tone indicated this was not a request so Grace just nodded. The front door was set back from the front of the property, so Grace positioned herself to offer a response for Adam and at the same time protect herself from an attack at the door. Adam knocked and announced he was Tayside Police with a warrant.

Jon was standing in a parking space fifty metres from the door Adam and Grace were approaching, and in a position he could see the front window and also Deena who was standing further back behind him, where she could watch the street approach.

A tree stopped him from seeing Biter's approach from outside the house, in the vacant area between number sixty and the southern neighbours. What he did see, and hear, was the retort of a firearm and the cry from Grace. In slow motion Jon saw Grace take three hits in rapid-fire; saw the force of the hits spin Grace and make her fall, her blood spraying from her trauma.

Jon had not seen Biter's approach around the side of the house; likewise Biter never saw Jon. In one swift decisive movement Jon stepped forward clearing the shrubbery from his vision, took aim and fired three shots: the first hit Biter in the chest, the second blew his neck apart and the third scalped the falling dead man.

In the next decisive movement Jon used his communicator to announce "Officer down, officer down – Oh my god it's Grace" and he started to run.

Grace was watching the front door intently, listening for everything and after Adam knocked and announced their presence and the warrant there was the distinct sound of a chair being pushed back and other activity. Grace stood prepared, firearm in hand when a loud noise and instant anguish tore into her right hip, followed instantly by pain in her lower chest and agony in her upper right arm. Mercifully she lost consciousness.

Adam was watching the door and listening to the subtle sounds emanating from within: all his senses on overload. When the roar of firearms discharge exploded around him he fired five times through the closed door, the ballistics tearing chunks of wood as they skittered away inside. Then Adam looked to Grace and saw her on the ground behind him and a shout of anguish tore from his throat.

"Go Adam, I've got her and help is on the way. Go!" Jon shouted at him.

Adam turned and fled into the house through the shattered front door, chasing the sounds of retreating feet. Deena had run to the house in response to Jon's actions and now she followed Adam into the house: both were thankful for their training and the distraction.

Deena caught up with Adam in the hallway where he'd stopped and dropped to one knee, inspecting blood spatter and a blood trail leading towards the back. Per their training they continued deeper into the house, checking for adversaries along the way. As they reached the kitchen they heard the sounds of motorbikes fire up and shouting and shots fired coming from the rear of the property.

Adam's communicator crackled alive and Scott's voice filled the air "two have escaped on bikes into the cemetery and one is dead here at my feet."

"Does the dead one have any wounds that you can't attribute to your shots?" Adam asked.

"Maybe, he's quite a mess, but there were three of us shooting so the wounds could be from any one of us. Why do you ask?"

"I'm pretty sure I managed to wound one through the door" Adam replied.

"Sorry, can't say. How's Grace?"

"Not good. Can I leave you this site so I can go with her to the hospital?"

"Sure Adam. We'll wrap this up and I'll join you there."

"Thanks Scott."

Adam hurried back to the front of the house and knelt beside Grace. The paramedics had arrived and were frantically trying to control the bleeding. "We need to move fast, only an OR can stop this bleeding. Can you give us an escort?"

Adam looked at Jon who said "I'll drive escort, you travel with Grace."

"Thank you." Adam was too choked up to add more.

As if sensing his thoughts Jon added "I'll get onto Marcus so he can meet us at the emergency department." Adam just nodded.

The paramedics Gina and George secured Grace into the back of the ambulance and left with dignified haste. Even with the ambulance blues and two's and a police escort, the four minutes to the hospital seemed an eternity. But eventually they were there and the scene became surreal as Adam relinquished command and let the healthcare process take control.

Instructions were called and answered, activities rushed precisely, questions asked were too personal for anyone to answer so they stopped asking and Grace was rolled away to theatre. And then for Adam there lowered a fog where he struggled to comprehend, where images and sounds became out-of-focus, and where his thought processes were clogged and dull.

"Adam, tell me what happened?" This time Marcus shook him to emphasise his questioning, and Adam's fog lifted.

"Grace was behind me so I could protect her. We had all points covered but one of them came from nowhere and fired. I'm so sorry; I tried to keep her out of harm's way."

"Did you get them?" This question came from behind Marcus, and Adam looked to see Lieb Canavan standing in the doorway; his hands were clenched and his body language was exceedingly tense.

"Jon shot dead the man who shot Grace. Scott, Sheila and Neil shot dead another and I wounded a third."

"Are they bringing the wounded guy here?" Lieb asked.

"No, he and one other got away."

"Well you'd better go find them and finish the job." Lieb instructed. Adam looked at Marcus.

"Yes Adam, go. I'll keep vigil for Grace and call you if there's any change" Marcus added.

Adam nodded and walked over to Jon; they shared a quiet conversation and then left.

Chapter 31

"Theatre's ready so let's move. We aren't making headway here" emergency physician Alex Johns barked. Unlike his colleagues who respected all their patients as if it was one of their family, for Alex it really could be: his partner Lionel was a cop with Tayside Police. Alex always silently dreaded the day the lost soul in front of him was Lionel.

In the emergency theatre two surgeons were scrubbing: Mr Michael King and Mr James Macdonald. Theatre nurse Holly Parker had already scrubbed and was in the theatre room setting out instruments and completing surgical counts. As the surgeons stood accepting sterile gown and gloves from the scout nurse, the doors burst open and Grace was wheeled in and shifted onto the theatre table. Dr Angus McIver expertly intubated and started a cocktail of anaesthetic drugs, carefully monitoring Grace's vital signs.

Michael and James looked at the xrays taken in the emergency department and agreed the chest wound was priority one.

"Stephen can you arrange Grace onto her left side and break the table for a thoractomy please" Michael asked. Stephen and the scout nurse Liz made the positional adjustments the surgeons had requested. When the table was 'broken' Grace's hips and shoulders were lowered and her lower chest area raised. This not only allowed easier access to the damage to Graces lower chest, gravity made the lungs fall upward toward the shoulders and the internal organs fall toward the pelvis; effectively moving them out of the way.

Michael and James moved one each side of the table, taking sterile sheets from nurse Holly, opening and spreading them across Grace's still form to make a sterile working area with an gap in the sheets providing a strategically placed opening. It was here the surgeons started. Working in tandem and with the precision of an exceptionally skilled and practiced team, Michael and James opened the wound at the base of Grace's ribcage. Whilst it was unfortunate the vest had not fully protected this area, it certainly had made a difference.

The vest had failed as the first shot had hit Grace at the top of the right pelvis, spinning her and causing her to fall. In the split second after, the second shot's trajectory caught Grace mid-liver and travelled toward her shoulder under the vest, tearing the pleura, then the lower lobe of the right lung and stopping by shattering two ribs. Grace now had a haemopneuomothorax, meaning the bullet tract had allowed Grace's chest cavity to fill with air and blood and thus collapse the lung and make breathing on that side impossible.

"Wedge resection of the lung with stapling?" Michael asked and James concurred. And in just twelve minutes the two surgeons had removed the shredded lower section of the lung and deftly stapled the wounds closed, including the protective pleural lining. James then pushed a sharpened metal stake through Grace's rib cage from the outside and into the hole left where Grace's lung tissue had been removed. Nurse Liz then connected the external end of the tube to a bottle and used the suction device to create a vacuum in the tube. The effect was to suck the blood and air out of the chest cavity and allow Grace's lung room to work again.

"That's had a positive effect" Angus commented.

Next Michael and James examined the liver: there was a ten centimetre tear across but not through the body of the organ. And fortuitously a large blood clot had formed and slowed the bleeding from this organ.

"Holly, can we have ten mil of fibrin glue prepared please" James asked.

Nurse Liz whose role in the theatre was to fetch and assist in the non-sterile procedures hurried to the fridge to collect the glue. When she returned she expertly opened the outside container so Holly, who was working the sterile procedures, could take the sterile inside container and not compromise her sterile outfit which could potentially harm the patient with a post operative infection. This tandem team work in theatre had proven life-saving ever since Joseph Lister had pioneered antiseptic surgery in the 19th century.

Using a small suction tube and gentle strokes, James removed the large blood clot from the body of the liver. And before uncontrolled bleeding could re-establish, Michael applied the special glue and watched to ensure the bleeding stopped and the laceration was held in place. Satisfied he and James explored the other surrounding organs and, finding no other trauma; they asked Stephen to return the theatre table to its flat shape.

When Grace was flat and turned onto her back, Michael and James folded back the sterile sheet now soaked in Grace's blood, to expose the trauma to her hip. Holly handed them another sterile sheet, and like they had previously, Michael and James made a sterile work area over the first bullet hole.

As the scalpel split the abdominal muscles and exposed the trauma, blood quickly filled the abdominal cavity. In a frantic fifteen minutes Michael and James worked to find the bleeding sites and control them; and Angus worked feverishly to stabilise Grace's vital signs as alarms on the anaesthetic machine announced a dangerous drop in blood pressure and harmful heart rhythms.

Stephen rushed out to the blood fridge to collect four more units and Liz opened additional theatre swabs, double-counting the number with Holly and recording the information on her count sheet. Even though the pace was frenetic and the urgency real, a mistake such as leaving a swab or needle in the operative wound could result in the patients demise after surviving the initial trauma. No-one could accept that.

Once the bleeding was controlled, Michael and James assessed the damage. The bullet had impacted into the bone at the top of Grace's right pelvis shattering both the bone and the bullet. The shattered bullet had then fireworked into her pelvic organs, tearing muscle, nerves and blood vessels. It had been the damage to the Internal Illiac Artery that had been the source of the significant blood loss. Michael and James had clamped off undamaged ends but this major artery fed blood to Grace's right hip and buttock, internal and external pelvic organs and could not be left disconnected for long.

"Let's use a bypass graft to replace the destroyed artery" Michael decided and James simply nodded his agreement. To Liz, Michael requested "Can you fetch a 10cm, 6 internal standard Gor-Tex graft please. Holly can you prepare an atraumatic 5/8th needle with Polyamide suture please."

When Liz and Holly had prepared the graft items, Michael and James spent time resecting the shredded artery and carefully installing the artificial graft and then James used a magnifying eyepiece to ensure the artery had no further breaks.

"Looks good, you can remove the clamps" James said to Michael, and then he watched as the blood flow re-established itself through the graft. "Excellent, next job" James concluded.

Michael and James had now been working for two hours and they were only half way through the list of injuries Grace needed fixing. "Is she good for more?" Michael asked Alex.

"She's stable, keep going" Alex replied.

And so Michael and James continued; for an hour they sutured torn muscles and nerves and blood vessels; and where repair was impossible, they tied off. As they worked Michael dictated to Liz so she could keep a dossier on the damage and the end result of the surgery, including the loss of Grace's right ovary, which was removed full of bullet shrapnel and bone.

"What shall we do with the pelvic bone pieces" James enquired?

"She's been lucky there's no dislocation of the sacroiliac joint, but her pelvis is unstable and I should imagine will be extremely painful when we wake her up. And that pain will restrict her breathing which will compromise her chest healing" Michael answered James, using the opportunity to think out loud and listen to his own assessment.

"Well, we have to get the orthopaedic toolkit out to pin her humerus fracture" James left the statement open in support of Michael's out loud musings.

"Yes. Yes" Michael said. Then to Liz, "You heard the man, can we have the toolbox and three 2mm TPLO plates with countersunk screws for the pelvis. We'll have to confirm when we open the upper arm but whilst you're collecting plates and screws can you also grab a collection of larger plates and rods so we can push on?

"Will do" and Liz hurried off to get the orthopaedic equipment and the plates and screws the surgeons would use to fix Grace's fractured pelvis and upper arm.

The orthopaedic tools looked similar to a carpenter's, with drills and saws and screwdrivers, chisels and rasps and Michael and James used them in very similar manner to a carpenter, to drill holes and fix them into bones, locking the disconnected pieces together again.

Another hour later they were shifting Grace to the intensive care unit. Liz had asked Stephen to alert Marcus before he came to help move Grace from the OR, so he was waiting anxiously in the ICU family room with Lieb when Grace was wheeled passed. The sight of her pale and still and wired for monitoring was too much for him and he began to shake.

"Sit before you fall down" Lieb instructed him. "We spoke of this; how scary it would be to see Grace straight out of surgery. But they won't let you in to see her if they think you can't handle it" Lieb added. "So sit and calm your breathing." Marcus just nodded and followed Lieb's instructions.

To Marcus it was another eternity before surgeon Mr Michael King came to sit in front of him. Michael pulled up another chair and sat directly in front of Marcus; their knees touching, and their heads close as if they were sharing a secret. Michael spoke quietly but loud enough so Lieb could hear, as Michael was very aware who Lieb was.

"OK, Grace is stable, but she's got some very significant injuries and she's lost a lot of blood. Firstly, the second bullet cut across her liver, then travelled into her chest shredding the lower part of her lung and collapsing the rest. We removed the lower part of her lung and stapled the wound closed, and we've inserted a chest tube under vacuum to drain the blood out and let her lung work again. Do you understand so far?" Marcus nodded and left his eyes firmly fixed on Michael's to make sure Michael was telling him everything.

Michael nodded and continued, unphased by Marcus' scrutiny "The liver was cut but not all the way through so we sealed the cut with special biological glue." Marcus thought about this and then nodded he was ready for Michael to continue.

"Now her pelvic area is more of a mess. The pelvic bone itself is shattered and the bullet then fragmented and tore its way into Grace's organs. It took some doing but we managed to control the bleeding and then start to repair. We've had to remove a shredded section of a major artery, but we've successfully installed a specialised graft and that looks good now. Other nerves and muscles we either repaired or tied off. We had to remove Grace's right ovary" Marcus' eyes widened and he lifted his head to look at Lieb but Michael was already explaining to him. "The bullet shrapnel was embedded in it along with bone shards."

"Will that have long term consequences for Grace" Marcus enquired?

"No, not likely if her other one is healthy. Now as her pelvic bone took the full impact of the first bullet it was badly fractured and literally in pieces, so we've use special fixation plates and screws to hold it all in place. And we've had to do the same with the right Humerus; the long bone of Grace's upper right arm."

Michael stopped and breathed softly, watching Marcus for signs of understanding: Marcus sat nodding and chewing his lip. "Can I see her?"

"Just a short visit for now; But first you need to understand what's going on in there. There's the chest tube in Grace's chest draining blood; there's electrical leads monitoring her vital signs; she has a urinary catheter so we can assess if there's been damage to her kidney or urinary system; and she's being ventilated so we can help her body cope with the trauma and the shock it causes. The blood transfusions have stopped for now but Grace is very unwell and things can change quickly. Some things we can address by altering her medications or the machines helping her; and there are times we need to change dressings, or drainage bags etc and that can appear unnatural. You can visit for three minutes now; you can come back in three hours for ten minutes more; but all the time you must be aware the healthcare team's needs change and if they need you to leave, you must let them do their job. Do you understand all that?"

Marcus nodded, so Michael stood and placed a hand on Marcus' shoulder "Then come visit Grace and give her a reason to get well."

Marcus stood and looked at Lieb "I'll be right here." And then Marcus swallowed hard and followed Michael into the bowels of the ICU.

Chapter 32

Driver, aka William Gacey, and the Chemist slowed their motorcycles on the edge of the cemetery and looked back for signs of pursuit; Driver was panicked with eyes like a marmoset's and the searching tenseness of a meerkat. When he finally zeroed in on the Chemist he saw him tearing at his shirt "Give me a hand will you?" the Chemist barked at him. Driver walked his bike over alongside the Chemist's and helped him disconnect the strip of shirt he had torn off the bottom.

"You're bleeding" said Driver, looking at a significant flow from the Chemists upper right leg.

"Yes genius" the Chemist replied as he lifted his leg and passed the cloth underneath. "Come help me tie this tight so I don't bleed to death." The Chemist's withering looked sparked Driver into action but also shook loose his tongue.

"Dog's dead! And probably Biter too! And you've been shot and they've probably got Import, and"

"Stop blabbering will you. Pull it tighter" the Chemist barked. "I haven't been shot; I got hit by a piece of wood from the front door when that cop started shooting through it."

"Now pay attention" the Chemist continued. "You need to ride quietly and directly to the pub; through that off-road trail we take. Are you paying attention?" Driver nodded his affirmation.

"Get quietly to the pub and quietly inside, locking up behind you. Pick up the mail and go behind the bar to turn stuff on just like you do every day. Then go up to the apartment: if anyone sees you act like you've just got up and you're starting your day. Got it?" Driver nodded.

"Once in the apartment, turn the TV on and go down the secret stairs and unlock the basement hideout. I'll be about ten minutes behind you so don't dawdle. Right?" again Driver nodded so the Chemist revved his bike. "Go, I'll lead them away but if they know about the house they will know about the pub and they will be visiting soon."

"What should I do?" Driver asked, his voice rising in octaves as the knowledge of what just went down overwhelmed him again.

"What I just said and no more. Once I'm in the basement I'll tell you more. Now go" the Chemist barked, and roared away from Driver on his small off-road bike.

Driver rode away as well, but in a more direct and less visible manner. He could hear the Chemist riding and altering his speed and the echoes bouncing off buildings then being muffled by woodland made it seem there were two bikes heading northward.

William got to the pub and parked his bike in the shed, locking it away. He quietly let himself in through the service entrance and walked quickly to the front door where he picked up mail and then walked behind the bar and turned on the pumps and some lights. His whole concentration was focussed on the Chemists instructions, so when he got to the landing in front of his apartment at the top of the stairs and a voice spoke, he almost ran.

"Morning: just setting up for another day?"

William started shaking.

"Sorry Bill didn't mean to startle you."

William turned to see a tenant standing just outside the shared bathroom "morning didn't see you there. Yeh just turned the pumps on" William managed to answer.

"Have a great day then" the tenant answered and turned and walked away along the corridor. William stood there a moment longer: he found himself shaking uncontrollably and a wave of nausea erupted within him and threatened to knock him to his knees. But the fear of the Chemist was stronger so he shuffled to the apartment and let himself in.

He followed the Chemists instructions, using the tasks to focus and keep moving forward. Once he'd entered the apartment he locked the door, put the mail down and turned on the TV. Then he moved into his bedroom and opened the doors to a large wooden armoire fixed to the wall. He moved the coats and other items hanging there to one side and then fingered a lock cleverly hidden in the internal structure and a door swung out from the back of the cupboard. He stepped carefully through the cupboard onto a landing at the top of a set of steep stairs. He switched on a light so he could see the landing below and hurried down.

When they had built this secret hideaway and access they had made every effort to ensure the light from the stairs could not be seen in the bedroom and the noise of movement down the stairs could not be heard. This section of the old pub had been perfect as the wall had been common with the old delivery chutes so no-one could identify unusually shortened rooms and the basement was old storage that hadn't been used in decades so no-one knew it was there. You entered the basement room from the outside via the rear alley which only provided access to the pub, into a storage room used for all the pubs stock. The state of the art security system here was not out of place, as security of a business was reasonable by anyone's standards. But it provided more than lights and video surveillance of the pubs storage area and visitors, it also provided video surveillance for the pack in the hideout.

William had just turned on lights and unlocked the door when he heard movement in the storage room. Panic overwhelmed him as he imagined the cops were poking around out there, so when the door opened he yelped.

"Shut up and give me a hand will you?" the Chemist barked. William moved forward and lifted the Chemists arm over his shoulder and helped him move inside to a chair.

"Go check I've not been followed and make sure there's no blood trail to the door." William nodded and scurried off. Moments later he returned and announced "It's all good."

"OK can you get me a dish of hot water, my kits and the locked box from the cupboard and a fresh shirt please? Oh, and throw a clean doona on one of the beds." As William hurried off to collect the required items the Chemist took stock of their preparations. They had eagerly agreed to help him construct this hideout in case the police got close and they needed to lie low.

The area they were in now was comfortably furnished although a little cramped for five for more than a few days. There was a large sitting room with a number of sofas and a small TV with a Sky box so they could stay entertained. There was also a table and five chairs if they wished to sit down for a meal together. Off to one side was a small fully stocked kitchen, the other side housed a bathroom and a bedroom with two single beds. In a cupboard in the bedroom they had placed two sets of clothes each plus travel gear and bedding.

And then there was the access to William's apartment upstairs which they could use if they needed alternative egress.

William returned with the items the Chemist had requested and helped him strip off his blood soaked jeans. "I'm OK here; you've got to prepare for the cops."

"What? I can't" William blubbered.

"Of course you can; this is what you need to do and say. Ready?" William nodded his acquiescence too frightened to speak in case his voice failed him.

"Go to the TV cabinet drawer and get a blunt; quickly now." William hurried over and took a blunt from the cigar box stored in a special drawer in the TV cabinet.

"Here, swallow this" the Chemist instructed, handing William a small blue pill.

"What is it?"

"Happy times my man. Quickly now before we run out of time."

William swallowed the small pill and dashed to the kitchen to wash it down with a cup of water.

"OK pay attention as that pill fills you with calm and happiness. I want you to go upstairs and turn on your shower. Then I want you to smoke that blunt OK?" William nodded.

"Once it's all smoked I want you to shower, make a cup of tea and then go downstairs to the bar and work like it's any other day. OK?" William nodded again.

"When the cops show up, and they will, they will have a search warrant; that's cool OK? You've got nothing to hide except you smoked a blunt for breakfast. It's good for hangovers OK?" William kept nodding as he listened to the Chemist and the little blue pill worked its magic and unwound the knots in his stomach.

"When they ask about last night you tell them you worked til the pub closed at midnight, then tidied up and went to bed about one thirty, two o'clock. Not long been up today OK?"

"When they ask about the house, tell them you let a friend stay there: you get some mail delivered there you don't want to come to the pub: you call over every couple of weeks to get your mail and check the place is OK. Have you got all that?"

"Yep" William replied. That pretty blue pill had him chilled right out.

"OK, get out of here. Make sure you turn off the light and secure the armoire. I'll be OK for a good while, so don't come down here until much later."

William took his blunt and hurried off to follow the Chemist's instructions. He'd learned the hard way many years ago what happened when one didn't do what the Chemist wanted, how he wanted and when he wanted. He may not be the brightest bloke in the pub, but William was smart enough to learn from his mistakes.

After William left, the Chemist groaned as if the pain he was feeling came from his needing to deal with William, not from the wildfire roaring in his right thigh. He washed his hands thoroughly in the soapy water, and then sorted through the two large kit bags William had placed on the table, along with the small locked box. He opened the locked box first and took out a glass ampoule, needle and syringe; snapped the ampoule across the neck, connected the needle to the syringe and used it to draw all the liquid content from the ampoule: it was 10cc of morphine. He held the syringe with the needle pointing toward the ceiling and flicked the syringe to ensure all the air found its way to the top of the syringe, then he pushed the plunger until all the air was emptied. He tore open an alcohol swab and cleaned an area on his thigh, away from the gash that was the source of the wildfire: then he plunged the needle deep into the muscle and injected half the morphine. The instant dulling of his pain only made it bearable: that was ok, he needed his whits for the job ahead and once he was finished, he'd take the rest.

Whilst the morphine got to work taking the edge off his pain, the Chemist drew the contents of another larger ampoule and injected this deep into the muscle of his thigh. This one was Penicillin. Knowing the next job was going to hurt like hell, regardless of the morphine, the Chemist kept working. He removed the needle from the Penicillin syringe and discarded it, and then he took a dish and two solutions from his kit bag and laid them alongside the syringe.

Next he took out a small package, opened it and laid out a suture needle with sterile thread attached. Finally he took out dressings and bandages and placed these all in easy reach. He placed the large plastic dish on the floor under his leg and stretched his leg out, placing his foot on a second chair.

He breathed deep a number of times, steeling his nerves for the task in front of him. Then he mixed equal portions of solution from both bottles into the small dish: hydrogen peroxide and sterile water. He used the scissors to cut the tourniquet away and discard it: blood started to ooze out but not in the sheer flood that it had been initially.

He used the Penicillin syringe to draw up 10 ml of the solution and squirted the solution into the gaping wound: it took all his resolve not to faint or cry out. The solution fizzed and foamed and washed blood and debris from the wound; pouring into the dish on the floor. He repeated the process four times until all the solution was used and the wound looked clean: it was raw and deep and angry but he was happy there was no more damage than muscle and skin.

Next the Chemist used the suture and needle to stitch the wound closed, digging deep to ensure the muscle as well as the skin was closed enough to knit together. He would argue with himself later which hurt most: the peroxide wash would win out, but the stitching gave it a run for its money.

Once the wound was closed, he wrapped a large dressing over it and held it in place with a large crepe bandage. Then he treated himself to the rest of the morphine: intravenous into his arm. Before it gave him the oblivion he sought, he hobbled to the bedroom and stretched out on the cot, dragged the doona over him and then gave in to the drugged stupor and slept.

Upstairs William got to his tasks with fervour, following every instruction the Chemist had given him. He dragged the fumes from his blunt in such a hurry his head swam and nausea threatened to empty the contents of his stomach. He put the unfinished blunt on a small saucer and climbed into the shower that had been running for ten minutes or more. After he'd scrubbed himself clean, towelled dry and dressed in clean clothes, he took another couple of drags on the blunt and made a cup of tea. He also grabbed a couple of muesli bars and headed downstairs to continue his ruse.

As he entered the bar area Helen came from the kitchen and placed a plate of food on the bar for a regular patron: it was Harold who had spoken to, and spooked William earlier.

"Morning boss" Helen spoke to William. He nodded in reply, and started to look through the items in the bar, making a note of what needed restocking.

On his second trip return with glasses, two cops walked through the door. William stopped and drank his tea as they approached the bar.

"William Gacy?"

"That's me" William replied.

"Senior Inspector Adam McAdam and Detective Scott McDermid" Adam introduced them.

"Do you own the property at 60 Birnam Place?" Adam continued.

"Yeh, was my Grandpappy's" William answered.

"And what do you know of a Mr Henry Brown?" Adam continued.

"He's the guy who lives there" William answered, warily looking over his teacup.

"Is that all you know about him?" Adam asked.

"What more do you want? What's this all about?"

"Where were you between 11:00 and 12:00 today Mr Gacy?" Scott asked, speaking for the first time.

"He was here" Harold piped in. "I know that cos I heard him workin' down here when I went for my shower and forty minutes later when I came out of the bathroom he was just making his way back to his apartment."

Adam looked at Scott and then started another line of questioning with William "why are you so nervous about us being here William?"

"I just finish smoking a bunt for breakfast and two cops appear and start asking me a whole bunch of personal information" William countered.

"So you know nothing about the shootings at your house about an hour ago?" Scott added to the conversation. "Shootings that ended in two of your tenants dead, and a colleague of ours in hospital fighting for her life?"

"Who's dead?" William asked.

Adam ignored the question and tried to further rattle William by asking "what happened to your friend Gerald Ross? Does he still live here?"

What rattled William was the cops knowing all their names and he gulped down his tea in a manner that had him coughing it back from his lungs.

"Was Gerald also living at the house then William? Is he one that got shot and killed or is he the one who shot our friend and got away? Did he come here William? Have you got him hidden away somewhere and that's really why you're so nervous?" Scott barked at William.

"No" was all William managed to say.

"No?" Scott continued; "No what? No he isn't the one that's dead or no he isn't hiding here?"

"Do you know where Gerald Ross is?" Adam asked.

"He didn't tell me what to say to that question" William said mainly to himself and his teacup, but Adam heard him.

"If you haven't seen him William, and you aren't hiding him William, then how could he tell you what to say?"

"I don't know what you mean: he isn't here" William countered.

"We'll see about that" Scott responded. "We have a search warrant and we'll find him."

Adam handed over the warrant and asked William "When Gerald stayed here which was his room?"

"It's my room."

"Well, let's start there shall we?"

And for the next hour Adam and Scott, Jon Addams, Shiela McMurtry, Deena Storey and Neil Johnstone along with a team from Lieb's office methodically searched the Lost Luggage Inn.

In William's apartment they discovered the remains of the bunt and the pungent odour confirmed for them it had been smoked very recently. They didn't find the entrance in the armoire, nor the entrance from the store room in the cellar: but they did find Gerald's motor bike and one of the Tech confirmed it had blood on it and took samples to compare it with samples from the Birnam Place.

They also found blood on a box in the storeroom from which they took samples, but they found no further evidence to explain where Gerald Ross was hiding, so they withdrew.

The unsuccessful search deflated them and they left in a sullen mood: Jon stayed to watch the storeroom and back alley with a promise from Adam he would be relieved soon.

Chapter 33

It was another day of needing to dress with care for Lieb; "I'm going to need to put stuff in for dry-cleaning or I will have to make official visits in my weekend cargos, and they're probably dirty too" Lieb muttered to himself as he dressed.

He reviewed his casenotes over coffee and microwaved croissants: the drug signatures they'd discovered in the SAT Pack cases (Lieb still couldn't think of them as Roses' killers) had a flavour of the military about them; well at least the modafinil. Mac had reached out to the local military for their help; discreetly of course. Late yesterday afternoon the call had come from Macs office that Lieb needed to meet with Mac and senior military personnel at 08:00 this morning. Lieb checked his watch, slurped the last of his coffee, collected the file and headed for the car. Once he'd dumped his satchel containing the file and his personal articles on the front seat, he then headed back inside to grab the laundry bag.

Finally he was behind the wheel and scooting down the A92 toward Dundee and the Tayside Police headquarters, imagining how he'd hear the information that would put all this nastiness behind him. He pulled into a parking bay kept for official visitors and headed upstairs to Macs office.

The Scottish military was actually the British Armed Forces after the Act of Union in 1707. And the Colonel Mac introduced Lieb to, came from the 225 (Scottish) Support Medical Regiment (Glenrothes) Territorial Army.

They all shook hands during the round of introductions and sat to the side of Mac's desk, on bench sofas. Mac, Adam and Lieb looked expectantly at Colonel Angus McPherson so he took the lead and opened the discussion.

"We searched for a former TA staffer with the profile you gave us: looked at every dishonourable discharge for the last ten years. Sorry that took so long but the computer has limited information and the records are stored in Glasgow; so we needed to inspect the computer lists, identify possible suspects and have a team look at their records for more intel. After that produced no results and I rang you Lieb and we had that further discussion about the modafinil I went back and asked my superiors to confirm we weren't using it. But I didn't stop there: I'd asked our computer tech to search for all other discharges with a stores role and that produced three results. I had those files sent to me from Glasgow and I have one suspect that became more intriguing the deeper I dug: Sergeant Gerald Ross was in the 225 Medical Regiment, here in Dundee."

Angus McPherson noticed the reaction from Adam, as did Lieb and Mac.

"That name mean something to you Adam" Mac asked?

"A Gerald Ross was the person identified as the sexual deviant in the investigation ten years ago at the Left Luggage Inn. We interviewed William Gacey at the pub yesterday about his whereabouts but he was unhelpful. A search warrant was executed and although we found a motorbike with blood we didn't find an injured fugitive."

"I'll ring the lab and see if we can get some answers on the blood from the bike; see if it ties to the scene at the house. Would you have fingerprints or DNA on Gerald Ross" Lieb asked the Colonel?

"Of course, but we'd need a court order to release them. Sergeant Ross wasn't dishonourably discharged; he has rights about his military file being kept secure without just cause."

Mac noticed Lieb's irritation and interjected "Colonel, why don't you tell us what flagged the Gerald Ross' file for you?"

Angus nodded and continued his report. "Sergeant Ross was in charge of supplies. There had been a couple of investigations over stock discrepancies, none of which involved drugs although they were in his remit; the 225 is a medical supply unit. The third investigation revealed Sergeant Ross had a medical condition, chronic insomnia and it was postulated this chronic fatigue was the likely culprit in his failure to maintain accurate records; so he was medically discharged. Unsubstantiated rumour was he took drugs and spent long hours in sexual orgies and that was why he was so tired. Other unsubstantiated rumours were he did keep accurate records; that he deliberately botched count numbers to hide an illicit supply racket on the side and made a fortune. I repeat, both these rumours are unsubstantiated; but they seem to fit the profile you were looking for."

"Let me make a phone call" Lieb stood and moved over to the window behind Mac's desk.

"Colleen" Lieb spoke to his DNA expert "Do you have any news on the blood taken from the motorbike at the Lost Luggage Inn?"

"Yes Lieb, we have confirmed the sample on the bike and the sample taken from inside the house at Birnam Place are from the same person" she responded.

"Anything else to date" Lieb asked?

"Byron has found a hit on the fingerprints; all three of the deceased had prints in the system. Plus a fourth and fifth set found at the house..." Colleen made sure Lieb was paying attention "one is William Gacey's and the other we got a hit from the military database; a Gerald Ross."

"If I could get you a sample of Gerald Ross' DNA could that help your DNA analysis" Lieb asked?

"Absolutely, a comparison is much quicker than a new profile" Colleen replied.

"Leave it with me" Lieb signed off. And he returned to the sofa conversation.

"Well, we have proof Gerald Ross was at the house. And we have proof whoever bled in the hallway of the house rode a motorbike to the Lost Luggage Inn. A comparable DNA sample would make a faster confirmation that person was Gerald Ross" Lieb explained.

"My hands are tied" the Colonel explained.

"I'll get a warrant for the DNA" Mac stood up, ending the meeting.

"Wait" the Colonel said, rising. He fished a small sealed package from inside his uniform jacket. "It will be quicker if I give this to you now; just please don't open it until the warrant is signed" he added, handing the package to Lieb.

Lieb nodded and took the package, noting its biological signage alerting the handler they had organic samples in their possession.

"OK, let's rock n roll people" Mac spoke with authority, spurring the men into action.

Whilst Mac was heading to see a judge for a warrant, Lieb was taking the biological sample to Colleen in the DNA lab and Adam was escorting the Colonel from the building, thanking him for his efforts and assuring him Lieb would wait for the warrant before processing the DNA samples; Marcus was driving north to Arbroath harbour.

Chapter 34

It had been seventy hours since Grace had been shot and although her chest tube had been removed and she was breathing on her own, her doctor was concerned her hip was causing so much pain; uncontrolled pain, that it was impeding her recovery.

Dr Cassandra Lim was a pain specialist called in for advice and she had recommended a herbal tea; a special blend that needed certain ingredients and the only place the good doctor would trust was in Arbroath. She was so convincing Marcus left immediately for the twenty minute trip north. Cassandra had called forward to place the order so 'Marcus would not have to be away for too long'. As soon as she was assured Marcus was out of the picture, for about an hour, Cassandra started her consultation with Grace.

"Now Grace, Marcus isn't here to fuss, so let's try again shall we to control your pain?" Grace just nodded.

"I haven't just sent him on a wild goose chase, what he comes back with will produce a tea more effective than Valium and without the horrid side-effects. Sleeping will help you heal faster than anything, but we need to make you comfortable to enable you to achieve deep sleep." Cassandra spoke in a soft voice, making Grace concentrate to hear her and the sing-song quality of her voice calmed Grace. And while she talked, Cassandra was unwrapping the bedding from Grace to expose her shattered hip.

"OK Grace, remember I need you to close your eyes and just concentrate on my voice. I'm going to put three acupuncture needles in your hip, in key positions to allow your muscles to release. And before I take them out I am going to put some small warmed cups over those sites as well. Cupping creates a vacuum which draws the old blood out of the area, making room for fresh, oxygenated, nutrient-rich blood to replenish the tissues and accelerate the healing process."

"The acupuncture will immediately reduce your pain score and the cupping will help the healing and reduce the number of times your pain score will reach the unbearable. Just remember, bone pain from a fracture is painful enough, you have the unenviable additions of pain from surgery, pressure pain from the oedema and old blood in the soft tissues and muscle spasm from the pelvic muscles trying to hold your pelvis in place when that place has been disrupted."

"So the acupuncture will help the muscle spasms and the cupping will reduce the oedema and the pills will help with the pelvic fracture, so take them as prescribed. The tea is for yourself and Marcus, it will help you both calm down and cope. Then you'll both sleep and we'll keep up the treatments and turn the upward spiral of the pain downwards. It will all be alright."

Cassandra's practiced hands worked, completing the acupuncture and cupping tasks she'd described to Grace. And as she worked she talked, lulling Grace into a relaxed fugue, so when she finished her forty minute treatment, Grace was relaxed and asleep. Cassandra covered her with a specially warmed bear-hugger wrap: it was designed to rewarm a patient who had been uncovered in theatre or someone suffering from mild hypothermia. In this case, it was to offer the subliminal comforts of a warm and comfortable bed; perfect for inducing deep and healing sleep.

Cassandra left the single room Grace was housed in and placed a special sign in the slot alerting the staff the patient was under her care and was not to be disturbed. The special sign was a laminated picture of a sleeping bear and all staff, non-clinical staff included, was aware to never violate the sleeping bear sign.

Cassandra also called into the nurse's station to complete Grace's medical record entry and alert the staff the sleeping bear was in place; she also alerted them to Marcus' imminent arrival and that they should page her when that happened.

Chapter 35

Marcus made the turnoff into Arbroath and wound his way round the harbour streets til he found the herbalist store on the corner of Commerce and High street. He turned into High Street and followed the signs to a parking site 200metres further along, parked and walked back.

He was surprised when he opened the door; he'd been expecting a dark, musty looking store with mounds of products stacked haphazardly on make-do shelving. What he saw was a bright clean environment much like a regular pharmacy but with interesting and inviting smells, not the pungent odour of disinfectant and apothecary.

He made his way to the counter, moving around six other customers who were browsing for their intended goods, where he found he would need to wait for service. The calm the curiosity had engendered when he'd first entered the store now fled from him, as thoughts of Grace allowed entry to panic once more. He wondered if his police badge would allow him to jump queue.

The sole attendant was an older Asian man and he was deep in explanation to the two women he was counselling about the correct preparation of their purchases. Marcus could see two other customers waiting in line behind them, purchases in hand and questions on their face. Marcus raised his arm to attract the attendant and spoke up "I've come to collect a package."

The attendant raised his head and the two women he was addressing stopped their dialogue long enough to cast disparaging looks his way. Marcus lowered his arm and shuffled his feet, caught between his upbringing of social etiquette and the urgency he felt to get back to Grace.

The attendant concluded his explanatory conversation with the two women, placed their items in a large brown bag and rang their purchases through the till. As the next customer approached him and before she could engage him in conversation, the attendant looked at Marcus and called over his shoulder "Henry, can you come to the counter please?"

A younger version of the attendant appeared through a gap in the shelving lining the wall behind the counter: Henry looked at the customers gathered in front of him and addressed the older Asian man "What would you like me to do Uncle?"

"That gentleman over there is after a pre-order; I placed it in the collection box under the counter" the man responded.

Henry nodded and moved along the counter where he reached under and withdrew a cane basket that housed a number of prepared parcels, all wrapped up in brown paper bags. As he was sorting through them he called back to his uncle "The Chemist hasn't been in to collect his order."

"No" the uncle replied, wrapping up the young woman's order as he spoke, and taking her plastic banking card from her. Whilst she entered her banking details into the receiver to conclude her purchase, the older Asian man continued the conversation with Henry "he's probably finally passed out from exhaustion. I told him his body would pay him back for the excessive aphrodisia; sex is not supposed to be a marathon."

Marcus wasn't paying full attention, but the gist of the conversation seemed important so he rewound the conversation in his head, drawing the fragments of conversation from his memory and piecing it together as his detective training had taught him. The older Asian man was concluding his conversation with Henry and preparing to talk with the next customer in his line "He'll be in for a health tonic next" when Marcus reached into his inside pocket, retrieved his police ID. Raising it to where the older Asian man could see it he spoke up "Please tell me more about this chemist."

The older Asian man looked at Henry, looked at Marcus' ID and badge and shrugged his shoulders. Henry took up the response, saying to Marcus "He's a regular customer. He came up with a pharmacy combination that he claims provides hours of sexual stamina and male hardness. He's been experimenting with different aphrodisiac compounds for years, for both men and women. He claims he has weekends of orgies" and then Henry shrugged his shoulders to add his doubts without voicing them.

"You don't believe him?"

"Who's to tell; we only have his word on it."

"Haven't you tried his herbal combination yourself?" Marcus asked Henry in a way to goad him into bragging of his using the preparation.

Henry looked imploringly at his Uncle, wanting him to believe he would not break an unwritten code. The older Asian man spoke to both of them to end the fantasy "He couldn't: The Chemist brings his own special ingredient I mix with certain herbs for him and make into tablets."

Henry watched Marcus to try and read the conclusions he'd make and whether the line of conversation could be dropped. Marcus was nodding as he thought about his next best move, so Henry pulled the other packages from the basket and asked "Is the one for Doctor Cassandra the one you're picking up?"

Marcus nodded again, distracted: he was thinking "we could stake out the place and hope 'The Chemist' finally came for his parcel; but he could be dead, or injured so that wouldn't pan out. If he used his badge to confiscate the parcel Lieb's team may be able to break down the contents, confirm the modafinil was the extra ingredient and track where the ingredients come from.

Henry was asking for payment so Marcus passed over his bank card, punched the codes and PIN into the receiver and then said, holding his ID for weight to his request "I'll take The Chemist's package too."

Henry looked at his uncle and the older Asian man said "I don't see how we can do that."

"Its official police business: I believe this is evidence used in a number of sexual attacks and murder. And if you want me to call for back up and a warrant I can have twenty police officers and lab technicians here in twenty minutes to go through everything in the store?" Marcus let his words hang as an ominous storm cloud over the counter: for thirteen seconds, it hung there until the older Asian man said "You need to pay for them." Marcus nodded and handed back his bank plastic.

"Can I have the recipe you use as well please?"

The older Asian man moved through the gap in the shelving into the rear work area and came back with a typed piece of paper kept clean in a zip-lock bag.

"Thank You" Marcus said accepting the second parcel and the zip-lock bag. He turned and hurried out the door, pulling his phone from his pocket and punching in Lieb's number.

Lieb was back in the lab handing the biological package to Colleen and assuring her the warrant was signed when Marcus' call came in. He was so agitated that Lieb's first thoughts were of Grace and they were dark ones. But finally he pieced together enough of Marcus' information to ascertain it was other case information.

"Marcus, stop and breathe for a moment man. Now let's start again. Is Grace OK?"

"Yes, she was in a lot of pain from her shattered hip so they called in a pain specialist."

"Cassandra Lim by any chance?"

"Yes actually, how'd you know that?"

"Her reputation is legendary. Grace is in good hands" Lieb said. "So where are you now?"

"She sent me to Arbroath to get some herbs" Marcus explained in a more structured sentence this time.

"And while you were there?" Lieb prompted.

"And whilst I was there I discovered 'The Chemist' hadn't been in for his regular delivery; of aphrodisiac pills that 'provides hours of sexual stamina and male hardness' for 'weekends of orgies'" Marcus read from his notes.

"Sound like you've found our supplier?" Lieb asked expectantly.

"Only half way unfortunately; the herbalist said 'The Chemist' supplied an ingredient himself. I was hoping you could confirm that was modafinil; that would give us enough to haul the herbalist in for questioning and a warrant to search the place for more info, like a contact name and address."

"Sure, can you bring the parcel here?"

"I really need to get back to Grace; Dr Lim is waiting for the parcel."

"OK I'll make arrangements to get it collected."

"Can't you come to the hospital? Check out Grace's treatment and offer some advice? She's really in a heap of pain" Marcus' stress let his anguish poor from his mouth again.

"I'm working on another break through, but I'll come over later to visit Grace". And before Marcus could start blurting his distress again Lieb added "She's in excellent hands Marcus; there's nothing I can add. Let Cassandra work her magic."

Lieb could hear Marcus nodding. "I'll get someone to come collect the parcel and I'll be over to visit later."

"OK" was all Marcus said before ending the call.

Lieb was only twenty paces closer to his office however when Marcus called back. "She's sleeping, so I'll come to you first. See you in thirty."

"Bring coffee and Subways OK?" Lieb said to Marcus.

"Sure, see you in forty then" and Marcus ended another call.

Chapter 36

Gerald Ross, AKA 'The Chemist' came to in a single bed, soaked in sweat and in a heap of pain. He struggled to recall where he was and why he was in so much pain and the fog in his head cleared and his memory came into focus. He groaned again and rolled with some difficulty onto his side to look at the clock: it read 2:20. Damn these infernal 12 hour clocks; just because it was dark didn't mean it was the middle of the night because he was underground without any ambient light. He couldn't be sure if he'd slept one hour, thirteen hours or twenty five.

He struggled to sit up and his leg reminded him of its trauma and the treatment he'd metered out. It had to be more than an hour he decided as he was definitely feverish: what he didn't understand was why William hadn't come down once the pub closed for the night. Maybe he had slept twenty five hours and William was behind the bar again; or maybe William had gone and got himself arrested.

Gerald gritted his teeth and stood: his ripped right leg could hold his weight to at least get him to the toilet and back into the kitchen for fluids and more drugs. So he switched on the bedside light and shuffled his way to the toilet. By the time he was washing his hands he was sweating profusely and shaking with fever chills, so he splashed water over his head and shoulders then towelled dry.

Then he shuffled into the small kitchen and drank a beer stein of water. The fever chills intensified when the cold water hit his stomach; the shaking threatening to knock him off his feet. He clutched the side of the kitchen bench and struggled to control his rigors.

When the need to sit down before he fell down overcame his reluctance to move, he shuffled over to the table and sat where he had been previously. William had definitely not been here because the discarded dressing wrappers remained on the table and the bowl with captured wound debris still sat on the floor. Gerald looked at them with disgust, then added to them by breaking out more syringes and needles and injecting himself with Penicillin and 5cc of morphine; intramuscularly this time.

Five minutes later the effects of the two drugs had controlled the pain and rigors to a point where Gerald could move with more purpose, so he headed back to the kitchen and boiled water in the kettle and poured it over an instant soup. Gerald took this back to the sofa with a box of crackers, turned the TV on and sat back to watch reruns on TV and get some sustenance inside him.

Outside the Lost Luggage Inn; in the alley behind where the storage entry was, Constable Neil Johnstone was checking in with dispatch. At midnight he'd taken over from Constable Glenda Goodrich, who had been on since she had relieved Jon Addams at 18:00. The rules were they were to check in every half hour unless they had something to report.

"Margaret hang on a minute" Neil said into his communicator.

"What is it Neil" Margaret enquired?

"Light, from inside the storage area; flickering light; I'm going to check it out."

"Shall I send back-up?"

"Not yet, give me three minutes; in silence please, just in case there is someone there."

Neil moved quietly into the storage area and stopped inside the second row of stored crates so the outside light would not impede his vision. He saw it again and recognised it for what it was: a TV.

Outside again he used his communicator to contact dispatch "Margaret, send Senior Inspector McAdam and lots of back-up; tell SIM his hunch was right. And tell them to come quietly."

"Will do; stay safe until they arrive" Margaret spoke quietly back. Then she placed the calls.

It seemed and age but suddenly Neil could make out the arrival of three squad cars plus two detectives unmarked vehicles. Senior Inspector Adam McAdam and Detectives Scott McDermid and Joyce Mainwaring approached him and Adam took the lead "What have you got?"

"Somewhere in there a TV is on" Neil explained, and turned to lead the three detectives into the store room, to the spot he had visited three times in the last thirteen minutes: he'd wanted to assure himself he was seeing what he believed he was.

The three detectives and Neil withdrew to the alley and spoke in hushed but excited tones.

"There has to be a secret room back there somewhere" Scott started.

"Or a collection of what appears to be storage boxes that's actually a hideout" Joyce interjected.

Adam nodded at both suggestions "Whatever, we don't want to be banging around in there and alert him / them to our presence: Suggestions?"

"Jon Addams mapped out the storage area in the daylight so we could check it out in the dark without making noise. What if I use a single torch and move to key points and try to pinpoint the exact location of the light?"

"Show me this map" Adam instructed.

They moved out onto the street and used their torches to inspect the map and agree key vantage points Neil could use.

"What if the entrance is not from the storage room but from the pub itself? Joyce asked.

"Good point, what do you suggest" Adam asked?

"Let me go wake William Gacey" Scott suggested, "Bring him down here and ask him again about the missing Gerald Ross."

"OK, but let's also leave two officers on each of the two other exits and let's get more patrols in here to watch the streets."

So with Scott and Joyce incessantly ringing the door bell until William Gacey came to find out what the fuss was about, Neil was carefully making his way around the storeroom until he could locate the source of the flashing light: "it came from under the back wall" he reported to Adam.

Adam turned on William Gacey "How do I get into that hole Gerald Ross has crawled into?"

William started shaking, Senior Inspector Adam McAdam was intense but William knew what would happen if The Chemist found out he'd ratted him out. "don't ask man; he'd kill me if I said anything."

"Get him out of here" Adam barked.

"Call in Urban Search and Rescue; tell them to bring in listening devices and heavy duty cutting equipment; we've got a rat to flush out."

Fifteen minutes later a crew from Specialist Rescue stood in front of Adam Neil and Joyce and talked about options. Neil had taken Senior Officer Frank McKay to the site where he had determined as the source of the TV light. Frank had carried a listening device with him and confirmed there was a TV on behind the wall.

"Trouble is detective, to get in cutting equipment we'd need to shift a lot of those stores and that would be noisy. Let's look for another way in."

Adam nodded and asked Neil to accompany Frank on the inspection: they returned ten minutes later to report that "no other external approach was possible".

"Damn" Adam exclaimed. "We've already executed a search warrant and not found any secret doors. Plus we've had a search of the building plans stored at the municipal offices and that shed no light. We have to go in and get the rat out and we have to assume that there's another exit. So if we go in noisy he could get away."

Joyce looked at her watch and spoke "It's four forty five now. If we have all possible exits covered as a precaution, why not spend the ninety minutes til it's light, quietly removing the boxes?"

Adam glared at her, so Joyce continued; "Let's form up a chain and pass the required cases along the chain until we clear the path fire & rescue need?"

"It's as good an idea as any" Frank added.

Neil eased in "Adam, we all know how badly you want this guy for shooting Grace; surely the objective here is to get him, not let him get away?"

Adam stood glaring at Neil, then Joyce, his fists clenching and unclenching until he finally nodded "you're right, success is key here. Let's do it. Frank can you monitor the noise behind the wall and let me know the moment something changes?"

"Will do" Frank answered and moved away to instruct his team.

And for the next one hundred minutes Adam and all the police not on security detail passed carton after carton along the human chain under the direction of Frank's officer. Finally Frank was assured the pathway cleared was sufficient to allow access to the rear wall.

"OK what's the plan?" Frank asked Adam. "You realise whatever we do it will be noisy?"

"We should use that to our advantage; make so much noise the rat hasn't got time to think, let alone run" Neil injected.

"We should also be aware he's likely armed and dangerous" Adam added. "So let's break down the wall, turn on those scene lights frank brought and throw in some flash-bang grenades to add to his confusion. Joyce, can you go let the perimeter security teams know we start in five minutes?"

"Sure" and Joyce left to pass the word.

"Neil, can you get the tactical entry team ready?"

"On it" he answered, swung on his heel and purposefully strode away.

"Let's get the lighting set up" Frank said and walked Adam toward his team and the equipment.

Inside the secret hideout Gerald awoke to a noise and decided it came from the TV. He had fallen asleep in front of the TV but the pain was back as was his rigors, so he limped back to the toilet for a pee, then back to the kitchen for more water, and then to the table where he collected his drugs and paraphernalia, finishing his journey back on the sofa.

Once settled he drew up and injected another shot of Penicillin and 5cc more morphine, both into the muscle of his good leg; his right thigh was swollen, tense and too painful to touch, let alone inject into.

He lay his head back on the sofa and willed the drugs to ease his torment.

Suddenly hell broke loose with a shattering boom that demolished the wall into the storeroom. Bricks flew and fell in an avalanche that covered the area all the way to the table.

Then as Gerald staggered to his feet to hurry to the exit at the rear that led up to the armoire, a flash-bang grenade exploded barely two meters to his right. The flash momentarily activated all the photoreceptor cells in his eyes, blinding him for five seconds; the concussive blast of the detonation caused temporary loss of hearing, and disturbed the fluid balance in his ears, causing him to fall down.

Before he had time to recover Adam had located and cuffed him. Neil took great delight in telling Marcus later of the maniacal Senior Inspector Adam McAdam appearing from the smoke, hauling a snivelling Gerald Ross with him.

Chapter 37

As promised, Lieb was at Ninewell's hospital: he'd visited with Grace but now he was in the waiting room getting Marcus a cup of tea. Marcus was pacing, agitated as Grace had woken from her sleep and the nurses were washing her and changing dressings. Everyone insisted Grace's pain was better managed but Marcus found that hard to believe. As soon as he'd entered her room she'd started to sob: "it was breaking his heart" he'd confided to Lieb.

Lieb brought the tea to Marcus and handed it to him "I'm a pratt aren't I; a major dumbass" Marcus suddenly sat down with his tea held in two hands.

"Sorry" Lieb countered "You lost me there good man."

"Here I am blubbering on about my distress over Grace's injuries and pain, and you're only months after Rose was killed. God man, why didn't you bitch-slap me or something?

"Argh" Lieb answered and sat across from Marcus.

"I was so wrapped up in Grace I was never there for you; how can I ever apologise" Marcus asked?

Lieb was quiet for a moment, lost in thought, very aware Marcus' eyes were watching him.

"I remember you hammering at the door every hour for three days; even sleeping in your car one night." Marcus just nodded, glumly staring into his tea.

"And then at the funeral, you stopped in front of me and demanded I share my pain: I didn't do that."

"But you did promise to one day" Marcus finally spoke.

"Yes. So let me now." Lieb dragged in a ragged breath and tried to calm his yammering heart. Marcus raised his head to look at Lieb, and for a moment was going to stop him baring his pain but instinctively knew that was the wrong thing to do.

Lieb dragged in, held and then exhaled another deep breath, then started "you know the despicable traumas Rose endured?"

Marcus nodded.

"Do you know Rose was pregnant?"

Marcus started to explain he had been told that but Lieb held up his hand.

"I didn't. The autopsy showed the victim was five weeks pregnant but I didn't know it was Rose then. We had talked about it; Rose had even tried to discuss it before she left for her sister's but I killed the conversation."

"So she knew" Marcus enquired?

"I really don't know."

"I'm real sorry man; to lose Rose and a baby."

It was Lieb's turn to try and see courage at the bottom of his cup of tea. Marcus sat studying him; sensing there was something more. When Lieb didn't start speaking again, he chanced his hand and asked "what else?"

"It wasn't mine" Lieb answered ever so softly.

"What?" Marcus answered, unsure he'd heard right.

"It wasn't mine: couldn't have been mine."

"How can you be so sure? What could possibly make you think that?" Marcus was dumbfounded by the words Lieb was sharing.

"Because I had testicular mumps when I was fifteen; made me sterile. Doctor confirmed only that week my little sperms have no tails; dead in the water: Seminal fluid actually." Lieb explained.

"Did Rose know?"

"Nope, never got a chance to tell her. I chickened out when she brought up the topic at dinner that night before she was leaving for her sister's."

Marcus just looked at Lieb and his detective training again started pulling together conversations, comments and angst and he started to truly appreciate the gravity of the misery Lieb found himself in. Before he could find words to soothe Lieb's troubled soul, Marcus' phone started to ring. He stood and moved to the window to answer it whilst Lieb sat and stared into the depths of his tea.

Lieb never heard the phone conversation but from the snippets he did hear he knew someone was ringing for an update on Grace. Marcus never glossed over the gravity of Grace's condition but also never shared the gory details. Eventually Marcus rejoined Lieb.

"That was Arthur, my eldest brother that lives in Perth, Western Australia" Marcus explained. "I had sent them, as well as George and Elena in Glasgow, a text when Grace was shot, and then brief updates over the last days so they can know what's going on."

"It's a good time to have family" Lieb answered.

"It was the darndest conversation with my older brother though: he was telling me about lollipops." Lieb looked suitably perplexed.

"It seems the local children's hospital has a radio called lollipops. Research says laughter really is the best medicine so they play this radio program to sick kiddies so they sing and laugh and don't feel so bad."

"Sounds like Mary Poppins" Lieb chuckled "so what does the lollipop thing mean?"

"Loads of lovin' in place of pain; or something like that" Marcus elaborated.

"Well, actually the science is sound" Lieb explained. "In my junior medical years I had a gynae registrar that used to tell women with pelvic pain to go out and have lots of sex: Said the hormones produced from successive orgasms relieved the pain of pelvic congestion."

"Yeah right! Grace is in a hospital bed and her pelvis is shattered. Even if I could convince the nursing staff to let us be, I'm sure Grace would find the strength to throttle me if I tried."

Lieb sat nodding at Marcus' words then said "Well, whenever we had pregnant couples who were suffering without intimate relations we used to suggest an alternative coupling position."

Marcus glared at Lieb like he had two heads, but Lieb pushed on "Grace is already on her back, knees raised right?" Marcus nodded.

"Well, you lay on your side so those bent knees are over your pelvis."

"She would still scream if I poked my penis anywhere near her."

"Then don't. Make love to her. In that position you can reach a nipple with either fingers or lips: you can kiss her neck: and you can reach her labia and clitoris with the other hand. Just make love to her" Lieb insisted.

"Here, in a hospital bed?"

"I'll guard the door; and I'll put up one of Cassandra's bears."

Marcus just sat there, his mouth somewhat agape: he wanted to say something but he couldn't think what to. He shook his head and finally said in a soft voice so only Lieb would ever hear "when I visited just before they tossed me out to do her dressings and such, she said she wanted me to take her home and make wild passionate love to her."

"Well, not wild and passionate, but love yes; what have you got to lose" Lieb asked?

Marcus sat and sipped his tea in silence: after five minutes thus a nurse approached and said Grace was resting and he could visit again.

Marcus stood up and headed for Grace's room; Lieb followed a ways behind.

When Marcus reached Grace's bedside she said she was comfortable but well over this hospital gig "Can't you take me home? I'm sure I'd be more comfortable in my own bed."

Marcus kissed her and bent down and kissed her neck; she moaned softly "will you lie beside me and hold me?"

"Sure; give me just a moment."

Marcus walked to the door, opened it and spoke to Lieb "guard the door with your life."

Lieb just nodded and leaned on the door jamb, his back to the wall.

Marcus closed the door and stuffed a chair under the handle for extra security. Then he closed the curtain, in case that nurse had xray eyes, walked around the window side of Grace's bed and stripped off his clothes. Before he lost his nerve he slipped in beside Grace who indulged in a few short giggles.

Marcus stroked Grace's face and then bent over to smother her face with small lingering kisses. He carried this tenderness down her neck and feeling the responsiveness from her; he reached over and supplemented the kisses with gentle tugs on her nipple.

Grace moaned and snuggled closer; encouraged Marcus carefully raised her legs and slid himself underneath so her legs rested over his pelvis, then went back to his kissing and caressing, raising himself up on an elbow and leaning over to suck and nibble on Grace's nipple.

Marcus felt the excitement start at the top of Grace and ripple downward; when it reached her pelvis snuggled against his, his penis jumped as if electrified and an erection grew. Grace continued to moan and respond to his touches so Marcus shifted his hand between her legs; gently stroking and teasing her labia. Then it became musical, with Grace responding to his touches and his erection responding to her, growing so that the head of his penis pushed aside her labial lips and snuggled just inside her.

Marcus tugged rhythmically on Graces clitoris and Grace started panting; ripples of ecstasy running down her body and crashing into Marcus' erection. The crescendo of pleasure finally peaked and both Grace and Marcus enjoyed that dynamic kaleidoscope of gratification together.

Marcus shifted his hand and reached across Grace's body, holding her in his embrace as gently as he could; until finally Grace's breathing deepened and she started to snore softly.

As carefully as he could, Marcus extricated himself from under Grace, and stood by the bed watching her. It may have been his imagination but he felt certain some of the tenseness she displayed previously had dissipated. He bent over and gently kissed her on the mouth.

Then he went to the bathroom, washed and dressed and walked to the door. He breathed deep and smiled to himself, removed the chair and opened the door.

Lieb stood leaning on the far wall and he looked up when he heard the door open. Reading Marcus' demeanour he asked "lollipop?"

Marcus grinned and answered "lollipop."

Chapter 38

Natalie was excited when Robbie collected her from college; it was exciting to have a boyfriend with a car, especially one that would pick her up and make all those lovely overtures like waiting by the car and smiling and kissing her when she appeared. All the girls in her class were so jealous and they hung on every word as she detailed how Robbie treated her last night or on the weekend. She did enjoy the attention; at school she was shy and steered herself away from interactions with the boys.

She was giggly when she climbed into the front seat and Robbie pulled her over and indulged in a long passionate kiss; he liked the attention he got from the other girls too.

"I've got a picnic supper prepared so let's go find a quiet place where I don't have to share you with anyone."

"Cool" was all Natalie answered but she gifted it with a large puppy dog smile.

Robbie indicated and pulled away from the curb. He drove through Dundee traffic and then headed south on the A90 until he found the turnoff to Kinnoull Hill, then he turned right and followed the vehicle tracks. It was Friday afternoon and curfew with Natalie's parents was 10 o'clock tonight.

Kinnoull Hill and the surrounding woodlands was the Dundee side of Perth: a pretty woodland park with lots of walking trails and the Hill itself is 200 metres high, affording magnificent views of the Tay Estuary.

Robbie drove through mixed woodland of Scots pine, larch, oak, birch and Norway spruce until he found a secluded spot; a spot where they were not likely to be disturbed. They jumped out of the car and spread a blanket on the ground in the late afternoon sunshine; Natalie stripped off her shoes and tights and loosened her belt and untucked her blouse whilst Robbie collected alcopops from the cooler. Stretched out together they talked about their day and sipped at their alcopop; Natalie told Robbie about the gossip from the college and the mistakes their ditsy shorthand instructor made. And they laughed. Robbie told Natalie about his day at the council animal refuge; the animals that came in and the antics they got up to. Natalie oohed at the sad tales and laughed at the funny ones.

The evening grew more obvious as shadows lengthened and their conversation faltered. Robbie kissed Natalie passionately and when that was reciprocated he slipped his hand into her blouse and plucked at her nipple.

Natalie sat up and undid her belt and threw it over by the car where she would pick it up later. She also unclipped her bra and slipped the shoulder straps out through the sleeves of her blouse and tugged the rest of it out. She tossed this the way of the belt. Robbie's eyes lit up.

Then Natalie put her arms around Robbie's neck and resumed their passionate kissing: Robbie returned his hand up Natalie's blouse and fondled her now unencumbered breast.

Just when passions appeared ready to overwhelm them, Natalie eased back and took Robbie's hand in hers.

"We've got all evening, so let's save some: how about some food?"

Robbie groaned and tried to hide his disappointment. Like any young man in the thralls of a hormonal firestorm, his body was shouting for deliverance; but he knew this was Natalie's first time as it was his and he accepted that it had to be consensual for both of them. So he got the picnic basket and more alcopops.

They spend the next while enjoying the cold chicken, cheese and crackers, cherry tomatoes and pork pies Robbie had prepared, and talking about items that came to mind: nothing of any substance or with any deep meaning.

Finally Natalie wiped her hands on a napkin and lay down beside Robbie, snuggling in and inviting his advances. Robbie's hormones kicked into full throttle again and the passionate exploring of each other continued in earnest.

First he got her skirt off so Natalie was just in panties and her blouse: she got him willingly out of his shirt. They kissed, then he carried his kisses down her neck and she responded with moaning and back arching, so he opened her blouse and licked her nipples, then he nibbled.

Natalie grabbed handfuls of his hair and hung on for the ride.

They heard something and stopped: it was quiet so they continued.

"No wait, there's something there; maybe a wild animal" Natalie said?

Robbie prayed he hadn't heard her so he continued nibbling her nipples and he slid his leg up into her crotch where Natalie's raging hormones latched on and she gyrated on his leg.

Then Robbie got nervous and suggested "Let's move into the car for some privacy?"

Natalie nodded and offered her hand: Robbie pulled her into his embrace and kissed her passionately again.

She pulled on the door handle to the rear of the car and the two of them tumbled in.

Robbie stopped to remove his jeans and give his erection room to blossom: Natalie slipped off her panties.

There wasn't enough room to fully close the door: and there wasn't enough time as the hormonal forces overcame them. Penis into vagina happened as if the forces of the universe guided the way.

Their love-making that first time was fast and furious: and wonderful and clumsy and memorable. Afterwards they lay in each others embrace hugging and kissing and speaking tender words to each other.

And they dozed off.

It was darker when they came too: Robbie checked the clock and it was 8:15 pm. He grabbed another couple of alcopops and they drank them enjoying each other's nudity.

Robbie sprinkled some alcopop onto Natalie's nipple and sucked it off again.

"Aww, what about the other one; it feels left out" Natalie teased. So Robbie sprinkled the other one and licked that clean as well.

That lead to the fires of passion rekindling and the rollercoaster started again; with fast escalating passion dashing down as Robbie shifted his focus from Natalie's nipples to her neck. Then he tried something different and pushed his head between her legs and licked the wet labia he found there.

Natalie squealed with exquisite yearning until Robbie lifted up and slid his erection home for another round.

Suddenly things happened differently and in rapid succession: Robbie kicked the door wide open and the cold rushed in; Robbie's lovemaking rhythm changed to an apoplectic seizure; and something stung Natalie's foot with such vicious intent she too had a seizure and lost consciousness.

"Secure them well" Mona instructed and watched as her two compatriots bound Robbie and Natalie.

They then went around to the other side of the car and opened the other door; dragging first Robbie and then Natalie out, careful with their heads but not their legs. Neither were conscious to be appreciative.

When Natalie awoke it was dark and cold, yet there was a full moon so she could see: and what she saw was the lambswool rugs under her and her hands bound and secured to the branch of a tree overhead.

She looked around for Robbie and used the noises to locate him and three woman; about a hundred metres away in a small clearing. The women had secured Robbie around a tree trunk that had fallen and been stripped of any branches. He was bound in such a way his legs, arms and torso could not move: in a semi-kneeling position bound and held by the tree trunk.

Robbie's instincts told him her was being watched so he looked around until his eyes stopped on Natalie's. Both were gagged so they used the emotion in their gazes to share how scared and confused they both were.

Two of the women returned to Natalie and sat with her, watching the third woman continue with a task. As they watched they crooned softly to Natalie, stroking her hair: Natalie stopped paying attention to them and watched to see what was happening to Robbie.

The third woman, Natalie called Bob for she had a short bobbed hairstyle, threw a cover over Robbie's back and Natalie momentarily thought she was making him comfortable; keeping him warm.

But then she smeared a fatty looking substance over his bare buttocks; and grabbed his genitals that were now hanging limply across the tree trunk. She wiped her hands on the cover she'd thrown on Robbie's back, reached down to a small bag resting on the ground, took out a jar, and whistled softly.

Suddenly three massive dogs appeared from out the woods and milled around her; she fed them something from the container and then took a handful over to Robbie and put some on the cover on his back.

Finished she joined the two women, who Natalie called Barbie because she was tall and blonde; and Squirrel who had a long curly mane. Bob reached up and tugged on the rope that connected Natalie to the tree forcing her into a kneeling position. Then she knelt in front of Natalie and crooned softly "it's OK pet; that filthy man will no longer degrade you with his foul male urges. We'll love you as only a woman can."

And then she undid the gag from Natalie's mouth and smeared some ointment from a jar over her lips and then kissed her passionately. She held Natalie's head gently but firmly and kissed her longingly and deeply. Initially she was taken aback, but the kiss was passionate and not threatening; and she found her body was excitedly responding to the interaction.

Natalie then found Squirrel was caressing her buttocks and sliding her hands between Natalie's thighs; teasing her labia with her thumbs.

And Barbie was sucking and nibbling on her nipples, whilst Bob had moved to kissing her neck.

But there was a noise: a choking terrified smothered scream as if one animal was killing another. Natalie opened her eyes and looked across Bob's shoulder: one of the dogs had mounted Robbie and was fully engaged in interspecies sexual intercourse.

Robbie's eyes were terrified and his neck muscles were bulging as he tried to scream out his pain and terror. But the gag held firm and the torment continued.

Natalie's eyes were locked on Robbie's but her body was succumbing and responding to the pleasures she was encountering.

As the second dog mounted Robbie and pushed his erect canine penis into the only orifice available, Bob lay under Natalie and pushed her head between Natalie's legs. Bob's tongue sucked and licked Natalie's clitoris and then pushed between the labia and rhythmically thrust into her vagina. Barbie's breast snuggled and caressed Natalie's breasts as she began to kiss Natalie's lips deep and passionately.

Natalie's mind snapped: whilst she watched the third dog rape Robbie and then all three take another round; her own body swam in sexual exultation. She tried; desperately tried, to take her eyes from Robbie and the assault he was being subjected to. And she tried to not succumb to the exquisite sexual bliss she was encountering; but it was so good. Over and over again the three women found ways to make her body dance and sing.

Over and over again the dogs had their way with Robbie.

Finally Natalie lost consciousness.

When she came to all was quiet. Natalie found her hands were unbound and she was curled up naked on the thick lambswool blankets, snuggled up to Bob, Barbie and Squirrel. Their soft snores and murmurings told Natalie they were asleep.

She listened carefully and could hear nothing from Robbie: but she heard the dogs, grunting and huffing away close by. Panic rose as memories of Robbie's assault returned and she knew she had to escape. Carefully she rose and fled, naked into the early dawn light.

Chapter 39

Senior Inspector Hamish Dudley came into Tayside Police Station early Saturday morning to be confronted with the sounds of distressed mothers, accusing fathers and cajoling junior police staff.

He grabbed a coffee and a muesli bar and headed to the passage where he could attract the attention of the senior-most police officer on duty and get a report before the parents saw him.

Hamish managed to alert Sergeant Justin Anderson to his presence, who excused himself and headed for the detective.

"What do we have?"

"Couple of teenagers didn't come home last night. A seventeen-year-old Natalie Pinkum, whose mother is the hysterical one waving hands and shouting accusingly at those two" he said, using his finger to point out individuals as he explained.

"The father of Natalie is the fella sat there with his head in his hands. Wifey has convinced him their sweet little angel has been raped and murdered 'like those other poor souls'. I did try to explain to her we had shot and killed three of those monsters and the other two were in custody." Justin shrugged to show how hopeless that tactic had been, then he continued "the missing lad is Robert Duncan McTavish, Robbie to his mum. Apparently, Natalie and Robbie have been an item for a year and it seems they're pretty committed: Natalie's mother believes her little girl is too young to be settled on one man, but Robbie's parents feel telling them no will only push them closer together. You know the story" Justin concluded.

"Actually, no I don't: single myself."

"OK, call Detective Gloria Hanson and let her know we have a case and I'll pick her up in fifteen. And call the dog squad and let them know we need their services" Hamish instructed. Then he sighed deeply and approached the parents.

"Mrs and Mr Pinkum I'm Senior Inspector Hamish Dudley; can I get you go with the officer to conference room two; you'll be more comfortable there and I'll be along in a moment."

Alice Pinkum stopped midsentence, and with her finger loaded and stabbing vitriol held ominously pointed at Robert Duncan senior, she looked almost comical. She was about to round on Hamish when her husband Charlie shushed her and led her away.

"Mrs and Mr McTavish, Senior Inspector Hamish Dudley; May I ask you a couple of questions?"

Carol and Robert looked at each other and nodded.

"Tell me about Robbie" Hamish started.

Robert took the lead and answered "he's a good boy; great actually. He's never been in trouble; finished High School and is apprenticed at the Council Animal Shelter in animal husbandry. He wants to become a park ranger."

Carol nodded through the commentary agreeing with the assumptions.

"So, tell me about Natalie" Hamish continued.

Carol took up the story "she's a sweet girl; they celebrated their one year anniversary a couple of weeks ago. They dote on each other; always together; never any fights" Carol drifted away in small sobbing hiccups.

"And you don't feel they have run off together?"

"No" Robert said whilst Carol shook her head. Then Carol answered in a soft voice punctuated with sobs "Robbie packed a picnic basket; but he knew Natalie's curfew was 10pm."

"OK, let me speak with the Pinkums and then we'll take the dogs out to search. The officers tell me they have a ping off Robbie's phone near Kinoull Hill, so we'll start there."

"Can we come?"

"No, we'll send you home with an officer." Hamish held up his hand to ward off the objections. "We need you to be there in case Robbie turns up or contacts you. Please" Hamish added.

And then to arrest any further argument on the matter, he called an officer over to take the McTavish's home.

When Hamish walked into speak with the Pinkum's Alice started questioning him as he walked through the door: what had the McTavish's said, when were the police going to look for Natalie...Hamish held up his hand as he had done with Carol and Robert McTavish.

"Please, sit down a moment Mrs Pinkum": Alice flopped into a chair.

"Now, tell me about Natalie" Hamish asked.

"She's young and thinks she's in love" Alice answered.

"Do you not approve of her liaison with Robbie?"

"Oh he's nice enough, but they're both too young. They need to learn to live a bit" Alice added.

"Mr Pinkum – Charlie, what do you think" Hamish asked?

"We were that young when we met; love happens that way at times."

"Yes, it does. So, there were no fights between them" Hamish asked?

Both Alice and Charlie shook their heads.

"I have to ask, was Natalie sexually active?"

"How dare you suggest our little girl deserves trouble because she's loose" Alice started. Hamish used his hand again to halt the tirade "I needed to ask. Now we've had a ping off Robbie's cell phone so we have a place to go look. And they're bringing the dogs along to help. I need you to go home with an officer in case Natalie turns up or phones."

Much to Hamish's relief they just nodded and left with the officer who had come into the room with Hamish.

Chapter 40

Outside at the cars Hamish explained their plan: collect Gloria on the way south to Kinoull Hill, Sergeant Jeffry Hill who had just come on duty along with technician Daniel Carlisle, would lead the convoy out and use the tracking equipment to locate Robbie's cell phone, and then they would discuss options when they had investigated the scene.

Gloria was waiting kerbside, coffee in a thermal mug and chomping toast when Hamish pulled up. "So what's the story?" she asked when she was seated next to Hamish. He filled her in whilst he drove south.

Twenty minutes later as they approached Kinfauns castle, Jeffry Hill slowed and turned right, then left down an unsealed road. This unsealed road ran alongside the A90 they had been on and they stayed on it for a kilometre or so when Jeffry indicated and turned right again. Off to their left Gloria could see the tower on top of Kinoull Hill.

This second unsealed road finally ended in a wooded area so Jeffry stopped the vehicle and climbed out. Hamish pulled his vehicle in alongside and they also got out. And then the three accompanying vehicles housing additional police officers and three dogs joined them.

"Ok lads and lassies, we don't know what if any circumstances there are. So keep your yabber down and look for items of interest and the noises of two youngsters that have stayed out passed curfew."

"Lead the way Daniel and Jeff" Hamish instructed.

And they headed off: initially following tyre tracks that showed on the grass that had been crushed when it was driven over.

After a number of false stops and starts caused by poor signals amongst the trees, Jeffry and Daniel found the car. Gloria called Robbie and Natalie's names but the only response was birds shouting their displeasure at being disturbed. Carefully they moved forward to examine the scene.

It was obvious from a distance the rear door was open, but when they moved closer they could see signs of drag marks.

"Take photos please Daniel, lots of them" Hamish instructed.

Whilst Daniel moved to the other side of the vehicle, Gloria examined the interior of the car.

"Smells faintly of sex in here" she said to Hamish.

"That fits with what we have here: lots of photos then bag this stuff please" Hamish instructed.

"Joseph there's good scent on these items of clothes" Hamish said holding up a pair of panties in a gloved hand. Joseph took the item and let the dogs smell deep. When it was obvious they had a scent, he allowed them to find where it went.

"OK everyone, let's stay alert" Hamish directed and they moved out in search formation behind the baying dogs.

The dogs led them down a trail for a-ways then south and upward toward the Hill that dominated the skyline.

For fifteen minutes, the dogs sniffed and barked and urged their human charges to hurry. Suddenly they broke free of the trees they had been pushing through onto the edge of a clearing. And on the other side of the clearing, about three hundred metres away the naked figure of a young woman stumbled across their vision.

When Natalie had fled from the dogs she was sure they were chasing her. Added to the terror were her shredded emotions, with nightmarish images of Robbie and dogs flashing through memories. That she was naked never registered.

She ran and paid no heed to the branches that caught and tore her flesh and banged large bruises into her limbs and forehead. It was the patch of sharp stones that cut her feet that slowed her down: but her ragged breaths registered as closing dogs so she ran on.

Suddenly Natalie saw them, the dogs. They were brutal and excited and very close; just across the clearing from her. She dug deep and found extra energy to turn and run some more. Getting away so she wouldn't end up like her Robbie was all she thought. She ran until her lungs burned, her ripped and swollen feet slipped on the blood they produced: she ran until she could escape, until she flew away.

Gloria called Natalie's name but the excited yapping of the dogs was hard to call over. She watched momentarily until she saw Natalie turn and run further away, and then she broke into a sprint as well. Hamish and the dogs and their handlers were close behind.

All of them ran and watched and registered in horror as Natalie fell from their sights. They slowed and ambled to the edge of a 200-metre cliff and looked over and down. To a man they looked mortified, unbelieving at what had just taken place.

Jeffry started swearing; Daniel dropped to his knees and sobbed; Hamish and Gloria just stared at each other, lost for words.

Roger turned on Matthew who was holding his dog Greta firmly by the lead "I told you your ugly face was enough to scare off the devil hisself."

"It was your wild mountain man looks was the cause" Matthew retaliated.

"Stop right there you two. Respect the dead for Christ's sake will you" Hamish bawled them into silence. Then he looked at Gloria "You got any idea what we just witnessed?"

"Maybe she was on drugs? Maybe she's scared of dogs?" Gloria shrugged helplessly.

"OK, we still have Robbie to find. Roger, Matthew and Malcolm, please take your dogs over to where we saw Natalie emerge from the woods and see if they can pick up the scent" Hamish instructed.

"Gloria, can you take Daniel back to the car and make your way down to Natalie please?" Hamish took another look just to make sure she hadn't moved: she was positioned just as she'd fallen.

"Call the Fiscals office on your way and get them to meet you. Daniel, can you help Gloria with that" Hamish enquired? Daniel just nodded.

"Officer Michaels" Hamish addressed a distressed looking young female officer; "Can you please stay here and keep vigil over Natalie until Gloria and the Fiscal arrive? And then can you make it back to the vehicles?"

"Yes sir" she replied.

"OK the rest of you; let's see if we can find Robbie."

"Mona, wake up" Squirrel shook Bobs shoulder gently "she's gone."

Mona woke and looked around; dawn had broken and the light was strengthening. "OK let's dress and get out of here" she said.

"What about him" Barbie asked?

"Leave him for the worms: that's all any man would do if it was one of us." The venom in Mona's tone was not lost on her friends. They helped her collect the lambswool rugs and rope and walk north to where they'd left their vehicle.

Chapter 41

Senior Inspector Hamish Dudley and Detective Gloria Hanson sat in the office of the Procurator Fiscal's office: Lieb Canavan had called them in to discuss the autopsy findings of Robbie McTavish and Natalie Pinkum.

Hamish and Gloria were cleared in the investigation initiated following Natalie's unusual death. The investigation exoneration had not however, convinced Natalie's parents they were not responsible. Hamish and Gloria were both hoping Lieb could offer them some solace in the matter.

"Well, I'm sure you're very aware Hamish, the cause of death for young Robbie" Lieb began. He then looked into Gloria's haunted eyes and added "be thankful you never had to witness the sight that befell your colleagues." Gloria nodded.

"The instigator of that prolonged and brutal rape on Robbie was three dogs: Bullmastiffs confirmed by DNA and there was plenty of that. They inflicted horrendous injury but the cause of death was heart failure due to prolonged distress" Lieb explained.

"Natalie's cause of death was multiple compound fractures, internal organ trauma and blood loss due to her fall."

Hamish and Gloria looked at each other; their pained expressions obvious to Lieb who interrupted their moment of shared anguish by saying "before you decide to shoot each other, how about you take a deep breath and learn the rest of my information: including the name of the perpetrator?"

Lieb continued "Both young people had evidence of tasering on a foot each, so it appears they were rendered unconscious and abducted. Robbie was covered in a substance that's used by vets to illicit sexual urgency in breeding stock: it would be how the dogs were enticed to partake in the act. That plus some canine Viagra I would suggest."

Lieb let this information sink in and then started again "And Natalie was also raped. But there was no semen or trauma, just lots of saliva."

Hamish started to ask for an explanation but Lieb held up a hand to stop him.

"And there was plenty of evidence of a sexual stimulating agent that we've seen before; from 'The Chemist."

"But he's rotting in prison along with his mate and we shot the others" Hamish objected.

"Someone's got his recipe or found his stash? That's your role to unravel" Lieb concluded.

"You said you knew who the perpetrator was" Gloria finally chimed in.

"Yes, there were three distinct samples of saliva from Natalie's mouth, nipples and genitals: one of the samples matched in the database - Mona Harrison."

Hamish and Gloria looked at each other and then both looked at Lieb: they knew the name but couldn't place where or why.

"She was the survivor in the pack rape of those youngsters at The Hermitage" he explained.

Chapter 42

Lieb watched as Hamish and Gloria exited his office and walked toward the front of the office; Marianne spoke to them in comforting tones as they approached reception. They both managed to acknowledge her but continued their conversation out into the carpark Back at the office they updated Mac and Adam on the findings all four shared a look of deep concern. They may have closed the SAT pack down, but it seemed the nightmare wasn't yet over; not by a long shot.

Grace wriggled, looking for comfort. Marcus had her settled in a large comfy sofa, by the fireside and in a circle of comforting sunshine. Ophelia was curled at her feet, leaning on her good leg and purring deep, willing her life-force to help mend the newest member of their pride. Fuzzbutt was sitting on the window-sill, enjoying the sun and trying to imitate a cat 'who didn't give a darn' but her regularly opening eyes and subtle scrutiny blew her cover.

Marcus was in the kitchen arranging hot chocolate: the phone had rung and he was muttering quietly into the receiver. Grace heard him hang up saying "OK I'll let her know" and she wondered again at just how astounding is was, that regardless of things, even big things, the world just kept on turning.

To be continued

www.ingramcontent.com/pod-product-compliance
Ingram Content Group UK Ltd.
Pitfield, Milton Keynes, MK11 3LW, UK
UKHW050414240426
12048UKWH00020B/1502

9 781643 674001